Don Marq

C000085465

Danny's Own Story

Don Marquis

Danny's Own Story

1st Edition | ISBN: 978-3-75242-024-1

Place of Publication: Frankfurt am Main, Germany

Year of Publication: 2020

Outlook Verlag GmbH, Germany.

Reproduction of the original.

DANNY'S OWN STORY

By Don Marquis

CHAPTER I

How I come not to have a last name is a question that has always had more or less aggervation mixed up with it. I might of had one jest as well as not if Old Hank Walters hadn't been so all-fired, infernal bull-headed about things in gineral, and his wife Elmira a blame sight worse, and both of em ready to row at a minute's notice and stick to it forevermore.

Hank, he was considerable of a lusher. One Saturday night, when he come home from the village in his usual fix, he stumbled over a basket that was setting on his front steps. Then he got up and drawed back his foot unsteady to kick it plumb into kingdom come. Jest then he hearn Elmira opening the door behind him, and he turned his head sudden. But the kick was already started into the air, and when he turns he can't stop it. And so Hank gets twisted and falls down and steps on himself. That basket lets out a yowl.

"It's kittens," says Hank, still setting down and staring at that there basket. All of which, you understand, I am a-telling you from hearsay, as the lawyers always asts you in court.

Elmira, she sings out:

"Kittens, nothing! It's a baby!"

And she opens the basket and looks in and it was me.

"Hennerey Walters," she says—picking me up, and shaking me at him like I was a crime, "Hennerey Walters, where did you get this here baby?" She always calls him Hennerey when she is getting ready to give him fits.

Hank, he scratches his head, for he's kind o' confuddled, and thinks mebby he really has brought this basket with him. He tries to think of all the places he has been that night. But he can't think of any place but Bill Nolan's saloon. So he says:

"Elmira, honest, I ain't had but one drink all day." And then he kind o' rouses up a little bit, and gets surprised and says:

"That a *baby* you got there, Elmira?" And then he says, dignified: "So fur as that's consarned, Elmira, where did *you* get that there baby?"

She looks at him, and she sees he don't really know where I come from.

Old Hank mostly was truthful when lickered up, fur that matter, and she knowed it, fur he couldn't think up no lies excepting a gineral denial when intoxicated up to the gills.

Elmira looks into the basket. They was one of them long rubber tubes stringing out of a bottle that was in it, and I had been sucking that bottle when interrupted. And they wasn't nothing else in that basket but a big thick shawl which had been wrapped all around me, and Elmira often wore it to meeting afterward. She goes inside and she looks at the bottle and me by the light, and Old Hank, he comes stumbling in afterward and sets down in a chair and waits to get Hail Columbia for coming home in that shape, so's he can row back agin, like they done every Saturday night.

Blowed in the glass of the bottle was the name: "Daniel, Dunne and Company." Anybody but them two old ignoramuses could of told right off that that didn't have nothing to do with me, but was jest the company that made them kind of bottles. But she reads it out loud three or four times, and then she says:

"His name is Daniel Dunne," she says.

"And Company," says Hank, feeling right quarrelsome.

"*Company* hain't no name," says she.

"*Why* hain't it, I'd like to know?" says Hank. "I knowed a man oncet whose name was Farmer, and if a farmer's a name why ain't a company a name too?"

"His name is Daniel Dunne," says Elmira, quietlike, but not dodging a row, neither.

"*And company*," says Hank, getting onto his feet, like he always done when he seen trouble coming. When Old Hank was full of licker he knowed jest the ways to aggervate her the worst.

She might of banged him one the same as usual, and got her own eye blacked also, the same as usual; but jest then I lets out another big yowl, and she give me some milk.

I guess the only reason they ever kep' me at first was so they could quarrel about my name. They'd lived together a good many years and quarrelled about everything else under the sun, and was running out of subjects. A new subject kind o' briskened things up fur a while.

But finally they went too far with it one time. I was about two years old then and he was still calling me Company and her calling me Dunne. This time he hits her a lick that lays her out and likes to kill her, and it gets him scared. But she gets around agin after a while, and they both see it has went too fur that time, and so they makes up.

"Elmira, I give in," says Hank. "His name is Dunne."

"No," says she, tender-like, "you was right, Hank. His name is Company."
So they pretty near got into another row over that. But they finally made it up
between em I didn't have no last name, and they'd jest call me Danny. Which
they both done faithful ever after, as agreed.

Old Hank, he was a blacksmith, and he used to lamm me considerable, him
and his wife not having any kids of their own to lick. He lammed me when he
was drunk, and he whaled me when he was sober. I never helt it up agin him
much, neither, not fur a good many years, because he got me used to it young,
and I hadn't never knowed nothing else. Hank's wife, Elmira, she used to lick
him jest about as often as he licked her, and boss him jest as much. So he fell
back on me. A man has jest naturally got to have something to cuss around
and boss, so's to keep himself from finding out he don't amount to nothing.
Leastways, most men is like that. And Hank, he didn't amount to much; and
he kind o' knowed it, way down deep in his inmost gizzards, and it were a
comfort to him to have me around.

But they was one thing he never sot no store by, and I got along now to
where I hold that up agin him more'n all the lickings he ever done. That was
book learning. He never had none himself, and he was sot agin it, and he
never made me get none, and if I'd ever asted him for any he'd of whaled me
fur that. Hank's wife, Elmira, had married beneath her, and everybody in our
town had come to see it, and used to sympathize with her about it when Hank
wasn't around. She'd tell em, yes, it was so. Back in Elmira, New York, from
which her father and mother come to our part of Illinoise in the early days,
her father had kep' a hotel, and they was stylish kind o' folks. When she was
born her mother was homesick fur all that style and fur York State ways, and
so she named her Elmira.

But when she married Hank, he had considerable land. His father had left it
to him, but it was all swamp land, and so Hank's father, he hunted more'n he
farmed, and Hank and his brothers done the same when he was a boy. But
Hank, he learnt a little blacksmithing when he was growing up, cause he liked
to tinker around and to show how stout he was. Then, when he married
Elmira Appleton, he had to go to work practising that perfession reg'lar,
because he never learnt nothing about farming. He'd sell fifteen or twenty
acres, every now and then, and they'd be high times till he'd spent it up, and
mebby Elmira would get some new clothes.

But when I was found on the door step, the land was all gone, and Hank
was practising reg'lar, when not busy cussing out the fellers that had bought
the land. Fur some smart fellers had come along, and bought up all that

swamp land and dreened it, and now it was worth seventy or eighty dollars an acre. Hank, he figgered some one had cheated him. Which the Walterses could of dreened theirn too, only they'd ruther hunt ducks and have fish frys than to dig ditches. All of which I hearn Elmira talking over with the neighbours more'n once when I was growing up, and they all says: "How sad it is you have came to this, Elmira!" And then she'd kind o' spunk up and say, thanks to glory, she'd kep' her pride.

Well, they was worse places to live in than that there little town, even if they wasn't no railroad within eight miles, and only three hundred soles in the hull copperation. Which Hank's shop and our house set in the edge of the woods jest outside the copperation line, so's the city marshal didn't have no authority to arrest him after he crossed it.

They was one thing in that house I always admired when I was a kid. And that was a big cistern. Most people has their cisterns outside their house, and they is a tin pipe takes all the rain water off the roof and scoots it into them. Ourn worked the same, but our cistern was right in under our kitchen floor, and they was a trap door with leather hinges opened into it right by the kitchen stove. But that wasn't why I was so proud of it. It was because that cistern was jest plumb full of fish—bullheads and red horse and sunfish and other kinds.

Hank's father had built that cistern. And one time he brung home some live fish in a bucket and dumped em in there. And they growed. And they multiplied in there and refurnished the earth. So that cistern had got to be a fambly custom, which was kep' up in that fambly for a habit. It was a great comfort to Hank, fur all them Walterses was great fish eaters, though it never went to brains. We fed em now and then, and throwed back in the little ones till they was growed, and kep' the dead ones picked out soon's we smelled anything wrong, and it never hurt the water none; and when I was a kid I wouldn't of took anything fur living in a house like that.

Oncet, when I was a kid about six years old, Hank come home from the bar-room. He got to chasing Elmira's cat cause he says it was making faces at him. The cistern door was open, and Hank fell in. Elmira was over to town, and I was scared. She had always told me not to fool around there none when I was a little kid, fur if I fell in there I'd be a corpse quicker'n scatt.

So when Hank fell in, and I hearn him splash, being only a little feller, and awful scared because Elmira had always made it so strong, I hadn't no sort of unbelief but what Hank was a corpse already. So I slams the trap door shut over that there cistern without looking in, fur I hearn Hank flopping around down in there. I hadn't never hearn a corpse flop before, and didn't know but what it might be somehow injurious to me, and I wasn't going to take no chances.

So I went out and played in the front yard, and waited fur Elmira. But I couldn't seem to get my mind settled on playing I was a horse, nor nothing. I kep' thinking mebby Hank's corpse is going to come flopping out of that cistern and whale me some unusual way. I hadn't never been licked by a corpse, and didn't rightly know jest what one is, anyhow, being young and comparitive innocent. So I sneaks back in and sets all the flatirons in the house on top of the cistern lid. I hearn some flopping and splashing and spluttering, like Hank's corpse is trying to jump up and is falling back into the water, and I hearn Hank's voice, and got scareder yet. And when Elmira come along down the road, she seen me by the gate a-crying, and she asts me why.

"Hank is a corpse," says I, blubbering.

"A corpse!" says Elmira, dropping her coffee which she was carrying home from the gineral store and post-office. "Danny, what do you mean?"

I seen I was to blame somehow, and I wisht then I hadn't said nothing about Hank being a corpse. And I made up my mind I wouldn't say nothing more. So when she grabs holt of me and asts me agin what did I mean I blubbered harder, jest the way a kid will, and says nothing else. I wisht I hadn't set them flatirons on that door, fur it come to me all at oncet that even if Hank *has* turned into a corpse I ain't got any right to keep him in that cistern.

Jest then Old Mis' Rogers, which is one of our neighbours, comes by, while Elmira is shaking me and yelling out what did I mean and how did it happen and had I saw it and where was Hank's corpse?

And Mis' Rogers she says, "What's Danny been doing now, Elmira?" me being always up to something.

Elmira she turned around and seen her, and she gives a whoop and then hollers out: "Hank is dead!" and throws her apern over her head and sets right down in the path and boo-hoos like a baby. And I bellers louder.

Mis' Rogers, she never waited to ast nothing more. She seen she had a piece of news, and she's bound to be the first to spread it, like they is always a lot of women wants to be in them country towns. She run right acrost the road to where the Alexanderses lived. Mis' Alexander, she seen her coming and unhooked the screen door, and Mis' Rogers she hollers out before she reached the porch:

"Hank Walters is dead."

And then she went footing it up the street. They was a black plume on her bunnet which nodded the same as on a hearse, and she was into and out of seven front yards in five minutes.

6

Mis' Alexander, she runs acrost the street to where we was, and she kneels down and puts her arm around Elmira, which was still rocking back and forth in the path, and she says:

"How do you know he's dead, Elmira? I seen him not more'n an hour ago."

"Danny seen it all," says Elmira.

Mis' Alexander turned to me, and wants to know what happened and how it happened and where it happened. But I don't want to say nothing about that cistern. So I busts out bellering fresher'n ever, and I says:

"He was drunk, and he come home drunk, and he done it then, and that's how he cone it," I says.

"And you seen him?" she says. I nodded.

"Where is he?" says she and Elmira, both to oncet.

But I was scared to say nothing about that there cistern, so I jest bawled some more.

"Was it in the blacksmith shop?" says Mis' Alexander. I nodded my head agin and let it go at that.

"Is he in there now?" asts Mis' Alexander. I nodded agin. I hadn't meant to give out no untrue stories. But a kid will always tell a lie, not meaning to tell one, if you sort of invite him with questions like that, and get him scared the way you're acting. Besides, I says to myself, "so long as Hank has turned into a corpse and that makes him dead, what's the difference whether he's in the blacksmith shop or not?" Fur I hadn't had any plain idea, being such a little kid, that a corpse meant to be dead, and wasn't sure what being dead was like, neither, except they had funerals over you then. I knowed being a corpse must be some sort of a big disadvantage from the way Elmira always says keep away from that cistern door or I'll be one. But if they was going to be a funeral in our house, I'd feel kind o' important, too. They didn't have em every day in our town, and we hadn't never had one of our own.

So Mis' Alexander, she led Elmira into the house, both a-crying, and Mis' Alexander trying to comfort her, and me a tagging along behind holding onto Elmira's skirts and sniffling into them. And in a few minutes all them women Mis' Rogers has told come filing into that room, one at a time, looking sad. Only Old Mis' Primrose, she was awful late getting there because she stopped to put on her bunnet she always wore to funerals with the black Paris lace on it her cousin Arminty White had sent her from Chicago.

When they found out Hank had come home with licker in him and done it himself, they was all excited, and they all crowds around and asts me how,

7

except two as is holding onto Elmira's hands which sets moaning in a chair. And they all asts me questions as to what I seen him do, which if they hadn't I wouldn't have told em the lies I did. But they egged me on to it.

Says one woman: "Danny, you seen him do it in the blacksmith shop?"

I nodded.

"But how did he get in?" sings out another woman. "The door was locked on the outside with a padlock jest now when I come by. He couldn't of killed himself in there and locked the door on the outside."

I didn't see how he could of done that myself, so I begun to bawl agin and said nothing at all.

"He must of crawled through that little side window," says another one. "It was open when I come by, if the door *was* locked. Did you see him crawl through the little side window, Danny?"

I nodded. They wasn't nothing else fur me to do.

"But *you* hain't tall enough to look through that there window," says another one to me. "How could you see into that shop, Danny?"

I didn't know, so I didn't say nothing at all; I jest sniffled.

"They is a store box right in under that window," says another one. "Danny must have clumb onto that store box and looked in after he seen Hank come down the road and crawl through the window. Did you scramble onto the store box and look in, Danny?"

I jest nodded agin.

"And what was it you seen him do? How did he kill himself?" they all asts to oncet.

I didn't know. So I jest bellers and boo-hoos some more. Things was getting past anything I could see the way out of.

"He might of hung himself to one of the iron rings in the jists above the forge," says another woman. "He clumb onto the forge to tie the rope to one of them rings, and he tied the other end around his neck, and then he stepped off'n the forge. Was that how he done it, Danny?"

I nodded. And then I bellered louder than ever. I knowed Hank was down in that there cistern, a corpse and a mighty wet corpse, all this time; but they kind o' got me to thinking mebby he was hanging out in the shop by the forge, too. And I guessed I'd better stick to the shop story, not wanting to say nothing about that cistern no sooner'n I could help it.

Pretty soon one woman says, kind o' shivery:

"I don't want to have the job of opening the door of that blacksmith shop the first one!"

And they all kind o' shivered then, and looked at Elmira. They says to let some of the men open it. And Mis' Alexander, she says she'll run home and tell her husband right off.

And all the time Elmira is moaning in that chair. One woman says Elmira orter have a cup o' tea, which she'll lay off her bunnet and go to the kitchen and make it fur her. But Elmira says no, she can't a-bear to think of tea, with poor Hennerey a-hanging out there in the shop. But she was kind o' enjoying all that fuss being made over her, too. And all the other women says:

"Poor thing!" But all the same they was mad she said she didn't want any tea, for they all wanted some and didn't feel free without she took it too. Which she said she would after they'd coaxed a while and made her see her duty.

So they all goes out to the kitchen, bringing along some of the best room chairs, Elmira coming too, and me tagging along behind. And the first thing they noticed was them flatirons on top of the cistern door. Mis' Primrose, she says that looks funny. But another woman speaks up and says Danny must of been playing with them while Elmira was over town. She says, "Was you playing they was horses, Danny?"

I was feeling considerable like a liar by this time, but I says I was playing horses with them, fur I couldn't see no use in hurrying things up. I was bound to get a lamming purty soon anyhow. When I was a kid I could always bet on that. So they picks up the flatirons, and as they picks em up they come a splashing noise in the cistern. I thinks to myself, Hank's corpse'll be out of there in a minute. One woman, she says:

"Goodness gracious sakes alive! What's that, Elmira?"

Elmira says that cistern is mighty full of fish, and they is some great big ones in there, and it must be some of them a-flopping around. Which if they hadn't of been all worked up and talking all to oncet and all thinking of Hank's body hanging out there in the blacksmith shop they might of suspicioned something. For that flopping kep' up steady, and a lot of splashing too. I mebby orter mentioned sooner it had been a dry summer and they was only three or four feet of water in our cistern, and Hank wasn't in scarcely up to his big hairy chest. So when Elmira says the cistern is full of fish, that woman opens the trap door and looks in. Hank thinks it's Elmira come to get him out. He allows he'll keep quiet in there and make believe he

9

is drowned and give her a good scare and make her sorry fur him. But when the cistern door is opened, he hears a lot of clacking tongues all of a sudden like they was a hen convention on. He allows she has told some of the neighbours, and he'll scare them too. So Hank, he laid low. And the woman as looks in sees nothing, for it's as dark down there as the insides of the whale what swallered Noah. But she leaves the door open and goes on a-making tea, and they ain't skeercly a sound from that cistern, only little, ripply noises like it might have been fish.

Pretty soon a woman says:

"It has drawed, Elmira; won't you have a cup?" Elmira she kicked some more, but she took hern. And each woman took hern. And one woman, a-sipping of hern, she says:

"The departed had his good pints, Elmira."

Which was the best thing had been said of Hank in that town fur years and years.

Old Mis' Primrose, she always prided herself on being honest, no matter what come, and she ups and says:

"I don't believe in no hippercritics at a time like this, no more'n no other time. The departed wasn't no good, and the hull town knowed it; and Elmira orter feel like it's good riddance of bad rubbish and them is my sentiments and the sentiments of rightfulness."

All the other women sings out:

"W'y, *Mis' Primrose*! I never!" And they seemed awful shocked. But down in underneath more of em agreed than let on. Elmira she wiped her eyes and she said:

"Hennerey and me has had our troubles. They ain't any use in denying that, Mis' Primrose. It has often been give and take between us and betwixt us. And the hull town knows he has lifted his hand agin me more'n oncet. But I always stood up to Hennerey, and I fit him back, free and fair and open. I give him as good as he sent on this here earth, and I ain't the one to carry no annermosities beyond the grave. I forgive Hank all the orneriness he done me, and they was a lot of it, as is becoming unto a church member, which he never was."

And all the women but Mis' Primrose, they says:

"Elmira Appleton, you *have* got a Christian sperrit!" Which done her a heap of good, and she cried considerable harder, leaking out tears as fast as she poured tea in. Each one on em tries to find out something good to say about Hank, only they wasn't much they could say. And Hank in that there cistern a-listening to every word of it.

Mis' Rogers, she says:

"Afore he took to drinking like a fish, Hank Walters was as likely looking a young feller as I ever see."

Mis' White, she says:

"Well, Hank he never was a stingy man, nohow. Often and often White has told me about seeing Hank, after he'd sold a piece of land, treating the hull town down in Nolan's bar-room jest as come-easy, go-easy as if it wasn't money he orter paid his honest debts with."

They set there that-a-way telling of what good pints they could think of fur ten minutes, and Hank a-hearing it and getting madder and madder all the time. The gineral opinion was that Hank wasn't no good and was better done fur, and no matter what they said them feelings kep' sticking out through the words.

By and by Tom Alexander come busting into the house, and his wife, Mis' Alexander, was with him.

"What's the matter with all you folks," he says. "They ain't nobody hanging in that there blacksmith shop. I broke the door down and went in, and it was empty."

Then they was a pretty howdy-do, and they all sings out:

"Where's the corpse?"

And some thinks mebby some one has cut it down and took it away, and all gabbles to onct. But for a minute no one thinks mebby little Danny has been egged on to tell lies. Little Danny ain't saying a word. But Elmira she grabs me and shakes me and she says:

"You little liar, you, what do you mean by that tale you told?"

I thinks that lamming is about due now. But whilst all eyes is turned on me and Elmira, they comes a voice from that cistern. It is Hank's voice, and he sings out:

"Tom Alexander, is that you?"

Some of the women scream, for some thinks it is Hank's ghost. But one woman says what would a ghost be doing in a cistern?

Tom Alexander, he laughs and he says:

"What in blazes you want to jump in there fur, Hank?"

11

"You dern ijut!" says Hank, "you quit mocking me and get a ladder, and when I get out'n here I'll learn you to ast what did I want to jump in here fur!"

"You never seen the day you could do it," says Tom Alexander, meaning the day he could lick him. "And if you feel that way about it you can stay there fur all of me. I guess a little water won't hurt you none." And he left the house.

"Elmira," sings out Hank, mad and bossy, "you go get me a ladder!"

But Elmira, her temper riz up too, all of a sudden.

"Don't you dare order me around like I was the dirt under your feet, Hennerey Walters," she says.

At that Hank fairly roared, he was so mad. He says:

"Elmira, when I get out'n here I'll give you what you won't fergit in a hurry. I hearn you a-forgiving me and a-weeping over me, and I won't be forgive nor weeped over by no one! You go and get that ladder."

But Elmira only answers:

"You wasn't sober when you fell into there, Hennerey Walters. And now you can jest stay in there till you get a better temper on you!" And all the women says: "That's right, Elmira; spunk up to him!"

"All of a sudden, a live fish come a-whirling out of that hole
. . . and it lands kerplump into Mis' Rogers's lap"

They was considerable splashing around in the water fur a couple of minutes. And then, all of a sudden, a live fish come a-whirling out of that hole, which he had ketched it with his hands. It was a big bullhead, and its whiskers around its mouth was stiffened into spikes, and it lands kerplump into Mis' Rogers's lap, a-wiggling, and it kind o' horns her on the hands, and she is that surprised she faints. Mis' Primrose, she gets up and pushes that fish back into the cistern with her foot from the floor where it had fell, and she says right decided:

"Elmira Walters, that was Elmira Appleton, if you let Hank out'n that cistern before he has signed the pledge and promised to jine the church you're a bigger fool 'n I take you to be. A woman has got to make a stand!" With that she marches out'n our house.

Then all the women sings out:

"Send fur Brother Cartwright! Send fur Brother Cartwright!"

And they sent me scooting acrost town to get him quick. Which he was the preacher of the Baptist church and lived next to it. And I hadn't got no lamming yet!

CHAPTER II

I never stopped to tell but two, three folks on the way to Brother Cartwright's, but they must of spread it quick. 'Cause when I got back home with him it seemed like the hull town was there. It was along about dusk by this time, and it was a prayer-meeting night at the church. Mr. Cartwright told his wife to tell the folks what come to the prayer-meeting he'd be back before long, and to wait fur him. Which she really told them where he had went, and what fur. Mr. Cartwright marches right into the kitchen. All the chairs in our house was into the kitchen, and the women was a-talking and a-laughing, and they had sent over to Alexanderses for their chairs and to Rogerses for theirn. Every oncet in a while they would be a awful bust of language come up from that hole where that unreginerate old sinner was cooped up in.

I have travelled around considerable since them days, and I have mixed up along of many kinds of people in many different places, and some of 'em was cussers to admire. But I never hearn such cussing before or since as old Hank done that night. He busted his own records and riz higher'n his own water marks for previous times. I wasn't nothing but a little kid then, and skeercly fitten fur to admire the full beauty of it. They was deep down cusses, that come from the heart. Looking back at it after all these years, I can believe what Brother Cartwright said himself that night, that it wasn't natcheral cussing and some higher power, like a demon or a evil sperrit, must of entered into Hank's human carkis and give that turrible eloquence to his remarks. It busted out every few minutes, and the women would put their fingers into their ears till a spell was over. And it was personal, too. Hank, he would listen until he hearn a woman's voice that he knowed, and then he would let loose on her fambly, going backwards to her grandfathers and downwards to her children's children. If her father had once stolen a hog, or her husband done any disgrace that got found out on him, Hank would put it all into his gineral remarks, with trimmings onto it.

Brother Cartwright, he steps up to the hole in the floor when he first comes in and he says, gentle-like and soothing, like a undertaker when he tells you where to set at a home funeral:

"Brother Walters."

"Brother!" Hank yells out, "don't ye brother me, you sniffling, psalm-singing, yaller-faced, pigeon-toed hippercrit, you! Get me a ladder, gol dern you, and I'll come out'n here and learn you to brother me, I will." Only that wasn't nothing to what Hank really said to that preacher; no more like it than a little yaller, fluffy canary is like a buzzard.

"Brother Walters," says the preacher, ca'am but firm, "we have all decided that you ain't going to come out of that cistern till you sign the pledge."

And Hank tells him what he thinks of pledges and him and church doings, and it wasn't purty. And he says if he was as deep in eternal fire as what he now is in rain-water, and every fish that nibbles at his toes was a preacher with a red-hot pitchfork a-jabbing at him, they could jab till the hull hereafter turned into snow afore he'd ever sign nothing a man like Mr. Cartwright give him to sign. Hank was stubborner than any mule he ever nailed shoes onto, and proud of being that stubborn. That town was a awful religious town, and Hank he knowed he was called the most onreligious man in it, and he was proud of that too; and if any one called him a heathen it jest plumb tickled him all over.

"Brother Walters," says that preacher, "we are going to pray for you."

And they done it. They brought all them chairs close up around that cistern, in a ring, and they all kneeled down there, with their heads on 'em, and they prayed fur Hank's salvation. They done it up in style, too, one at a time, and the others singing out, "Amen!" every now and then, and they shed tears down onto Hank. The front yard was crowded with men, all a-laughing and a-talking and chawing and spitting tobacco and betting how long Hank would hold out. Old Si Emery, that was the city marshal, and always wore a big nickel-plated star, was out there with 'em. Si was in a sweat, 'cause Bill Nolan, that run the bar-room, and some more of Hank's friends, or as near friends as he had, was out in the road. They says to Si he must arrest that preacher, fur Hank is being gradual murdered in that there water, and he'll die if he's helt there too long, and it will be a crime. Only they didn't come into the yard to say it amongst us religious folks. But Si, he says he dassent arrest no one because it is outside the town copperation; but he's considerable worried too about what his duty orter be.

Pretty soon the gang that Mrs. Cartwright has rounded up at the prayer-meeting comes stringing along in. They had all brung their hymn books with them, and they sung. The hull town was there then, and they all sung, and they sung revival hymns over Hank. And Hank he would jest cuss and cuss. Every time he busted out into another cussing spell they would start another hymn. Finally the men out in the front yard got warmed up too, and begun to sing, all but Bill Nolan's crowd, and they give Hank up for lost and went away disgusted.

The first thing you knowed they was a reg'lar revival meeting there, and that preacher was preaching a reg'lar revival sermon. I been to more'n one camp meeting, but fur jest natcherally taking holt of the hull human race by the slack of its pants and dangling of it over hell-fire, I never hearn nothing could come up to that there sermon. Two or three old backsliders in the crowd come right up and repented all over agin on the spot. The hull kit and biling of 'em got the power good and hard, like they does at camp meetings and revivals. But Hank, he only cussed. He was obstinate, Hank was, and his pride and dander had riz up. Finally he says:

"You're taking a ornery, low-down advantage o' me, you are. Let me out'n this here cistern and I'll show you who'll stick it out longest on dry land, dern your religious hides!"

Some of the folks there hadn't had no suppers, so after all the other sinners but Hank had either got converted or else sneaked away, some of the women says why not make a kind of love feast out of it, and bring some vittles, like they does to church sociables. Because it seems likely Satan is going to wrastle all night long, like he done with the angel Jacob, and they ought to be prepared. So they done it. They went and they come back with vittles and they made up hot coffee and they feasted that preacher and theirselves and Elmira and me, all right in Hank's hearing.

And Hank was getting hungry himself. And he was cold in that water. And the fish was nibbling at him. And he was getting cussed out and weak and soaked full of despair. And they wasn't no way fur him to set down and rest. And he was scared of getting a cramp in his legs, and sinking down with his head under water and being drownded. He said afterward he'd of done the last with pleasure if they was any way of suing that crowd fur murder. So along about ten o'clock he sings out:

"I give in, gosh dern ye! I give in. Let me out and I'll sign your pesky pledge!"

Brother Cartwright was fur getting a ladder and letting him climb out right away. But Elmira, she says:

"Don't you do it, Brother Cartwright; don't you do it. You don't know Hank Walters like I does. If he oncet gets out o' there before he's signed that pledge, he won't never sign it."

So they fixed it up that Brother Cartwright was to write out a pledge on the inside leaf of the Bible, and tie the Bible onto a string, and a lead pencil onto another string, and let the strings down to Hank, and he was to make his mark, fur he couldn't write, and they was to be pulled up agin. Hank, he says all right, and they done it. But jest as Hank was making his mark on the leaf of the book, that preacher done what I has always thought was a mean trick. He was lying on the floor with his head and shoulders into that hole as fur as he could, holding a lantern way down into it, so as Hank could see. And jest as Hank made that mark he spoke some words over him, and then he says:

"Now, Henry Walters, I have baptized you, and you are a member of the church."

You'd a thought Hank would of broke out cussing agin at being took unexpected that-a-way, fur he hadn't really agreed to nothing but signing the pledge. But nary a cuss. He jest says: "Now, you get that ladder."

They got it, and he clumb up into the kitchen, dripping and shivering.

"You went and baptized me in that water?" he asts the preacher. The preacher says he has.

"Then," says Hank, "you done a low-down trick on me. You knowed I has made my brags I never jined no church nor never would jine. You knowed I was proud of that. You knowed that it was my glory to tell of it, and that I set a heap of store by it in every way. And now you've went and took it away from me! You never fought it out fair and square, neither, man playing to outlast man, like you done with this here pledge, but you sneaked it in on me when I wasn't looking."

They was a lot of men in that crowd that thought the preacher had went too far, and sympathized with Hank. The way he done about that hurt Brother Cartwright in our town, and they was a split in the church, because some said it wasn't reg'lar and wasn't binding. He lost his job after a while and become an evangelist. Which it don't make no difference what one of them does, nohow.

But Hank, he always thought he had been baptized reg'lar. And he never was the same afterward. He had made his life-long brags, and his pride was broke in that there one pertic'ler spot. And he sorrered and grieved over it a good 'eal, and got grouchier and grouchier and meaner and meaner, and lickered oftener, if anything. Signing the pledge couldn't hold Hank. He was worse in every way after that night in the cistern, and took to lamming me harder and harder.

———————————

CHAPTER III

Well, all the lammings Hank laid on never done me any good. It seemed like I was jest natcherally cut out to have no success in life, and no amount of whaling could change it, though Hank, he was faithful. Before I was twelve years old the hull town had seen it, and they wasn't nothing else expected of me except not to be any good.

That had its handy sides to it, too. They was lots of kids there that had to go to school, but Hank, he never would of let me done that if I had ast him, and I never asted. And they was lots of kids considerably bothered all the time with their parents and relations. They made 'em go to Sunday School, and wash up reg'lar all over on Saturday nights, and put on shoes and stockings part of the time, even in the summer, and some of 'em had to ast to go in swimming, and the hull thing was a continuous trouble and privation to 'em. But they wasn't nothing perdicted of me, and I done like it was perdicted. Everybody 'lowed from the start that Hank would of made trash out'n me, even if I hadn't showed all the signs of being trash anyhow. And if they was devilment anywhere about that town they all says, "Danny, he done it." And like as not I has. So I gets to be what you might call an outcast. All the kids whose folks ain't trash, their mothers tells 'em not to run with me no more. Which they done it all the more fur that reason, on the sly, and it makes me more important with them.

But when I gets a little bigger, all that makes me feel kind o' bad sometimes. It ain't so handy then. Fur folks gets to saying, when I would come around:

"Danny, what do *you* want?"

And if I says, "Nothing," they would say:

"Well, then, you get out o' here!"

Which they needn't of been suspicioning nothing like they pertended they did, fur I never stole nothing more'n worter millions and mush millions and such truck, and mebby now and then a chicken us kids use to roast in the woods on Sundays, and jest as like as not it was one of Hank's hens then, which I figgered I'd earnt it.

Fur Hank, he had streaks when he'd work me considerable hard. He never give me any money fur it. He loafed a lot too, and when he'd loaf I'd loaf. But I did pick up right smart of handiness with tools around that there shop of his'n, and if he'd ever of used me right I might of turned into a purty fair blacksmith. But it wasn't no use trying to work fur Hank. When I was about fifteen, times is right bad around the house fur a spell, and Elmira is working purty hard, and I thinks to myself:

"Well, these folks has kind o' brung you up, and you ain't never done more'n Hank made you do. Mebby you orter stick to work a little more when they's a job in the shop, even if Hank don't."

Which I tried it fur about two or three years, doing as much work around the shop as Hank done and mebby more. But it wasn't no use. One day when I'm about eighteen, I seen awful plain I'll have to light out from there. They was a circus come to town that day. I says to Hank:

"Hank, they is a circus this afternoon and agin to-night."

"So I has hearn," says Hank.

"Are you going to it?" says I.

"I mout," says Hank, "and then agin I moutn't. I don't see as it's no consarns of yourn, nohow." I knowed he was going, though. Hank, he never missed a circus.

"Well," I says, "they wasn't no harm to ast, was they?"

"Well, you've asted, ain't you?" says Hank.

"Well, then," says I, "I'd like to go to that there circus myself."

"They ain't no use in me saying fur you not to go," says Hank, "fur you would go anyhow. You always does go off when you is needed."

"But I ain't got no money," I says, "and I was going to ast you could you spare me half a dollar?"

"Great Jehosephat!" says Hank, "but ain't you getting stuck up! What's the matter of you crawling in under the tent like you always done? First thing I know you'll be wanting a pair of these here yaller shoes and a stove-pipe hat."

"No," says I, "I ain't no dude, Hank, and you know it. But they is always things about a circus to spend money on besides jest the circus herself. They is the side show, fur instance, and they is the grand concert afterward. I calkelated I'd take 'em all in this year—the hull dern thing, jest fur oncet."

Hank, he looks at me like I'd asted fur a house 'n' lot, or a million dollars, or something like that. But he don't say nothing. He jest snorts.

"Hank," I says, "I been doing right smart work around the shop fur two, three years now. If you wasn't loafing so much you'd a noticed it more. And I ain't never ast fur a cent of pay fur it, nor—"

"You ain't wuth no pay," says Hank. "You ain't wuth nothing but to eat vittles and wear out clothes."

"Well," I says, "I figger I earn my vittles and a good 'eal more. And as fur as clothes goes, I never had none but what Elmira made out'n yourn."

"Who brung you up?" asts Hank.

"You done it," says I, "and by your own say-so you done a dern poor job at it."

"You go to that there circus," says Hank, a-flaring up, "and I'll lambaste you up to a inch of your life. So fur as handing out money fur you to sling it to the dogs, I ain't no bank, and if I was I ain't no ijut. But you jest let me hear of you even going nigh that circus lot and all the lammings you has ever got, rolled into one, won't be a measly little sarcumstance to what you *will* get. They ain't no leather-faced young upstart with weepin'-willow hail going to throw up to me how I brung him up. That's gratitood fur you, that is!" says Hank. "If it hadn't of been fur me giving you a home when I found you first, where would you of been now?"

"Well," I says, "I might of been a good 'eal better off. If you hadn't of took me in the Alexanderses would of, and then I wouldn't of been kep' out of school and growed up a ignoramus like you is."

"I never had no trouble keeping you away from school, I notice," says Hank, with a snort. "This is the first I ever hearn of you wanting to go there."

Which was true in one way, and a lie in another. I hadn't never wanted to go till lately, but he'd of lammed me if I had of wanted to. He always said he would. And now I was too big and knowed it.

Well, Hank, he never give me no money, so I watches my chancet that afternoon and slips in under the tent the same as always. And I lays low under them green benches and wiggled through when I seen a good chancet. The first person I seen was Hank. Of course he seen me, and he shook his fist at me in a promising kind of way, and they wasn't no trouble figgering out what he meant. Fur a while I didn't enjoy that circus to no extent. Fur I was thinking that if Hank tries to lick me fur it I'll fight him back this time, which I hadn't never fit him back much yet fur fear he'd pick up something iron around the shop and jest natcherally lay me cold with it.

I got home before Hank did. It was nigh sundown, and I was waiting in the door of the shop fur Elmira to holler vittles is ready, and Hank come along. He didn't waste no time. He steps inside the shop and he takes down a strap and he says:

"You come here and take off your shirt."

But I jest moves away. Hank, he runs in on me, and he swings his strap. I threwed up my arm, and it cut me acrost the knuckles. I run in on him, and he dropped the strap and fetched me an openhanded smack plumb on the mouth that jarred my head back and like to of busted it loose. Then I got right mad, and I run in on him agin, and this time I got to him, and wrastled with him.

Well, sir, I never was so surprised in all my life before. Fur I hadn't had holt on him more'n a minute before I seen I'm stronger than Hank is. I threwed him, and he hit the ground with considerable of a jar, and then I put my knee in the pit of his stomach and churned it a couple. And I thinks to myself what a fool I must of been fur better'n a year, because I might of done this any time. I got him by the ears and I slammed his head into the gravel a few times, him a-reaching fur my throat, and a-pounding me with his fists, but me a-taking the licks and keeping holt. And I had a mighty contented time fur a few minutes there on top of Hank, chuckling to myself, and batting him one every now and then fur luck, and trying to make him holler it's enough. But Hank is stubborn and he won't holler. And purty soon I thinks, what am I going to do? Fur Hank will be so mad when I let him up he'll jest natcherally kill me, without I kill him. And I was scared, because I don't want neither one of them things to happen. Whilst I was thinking it over, and getting scareder and scareder, and banging Hank's head harder and harder, some one grabs me from behind.

They was two of them, and one gets my collar and one gets the seat of my pants, and they drug me off'n him. Hank, he gets up, and then he sets down sudden on a horse block and wipes his face on his sleeve, which they was considerable blood come onto the sleeve.

I looks around to see who has had holt of me, and it is two men. One of them looks about seven feet tall, on account of a big plug hat and a long white linen duster, and has a beautiful red beard. In the road they is a big stout road wagon, with a canopy top over it, pulled by two hosses, and on the wagon box they is a strip of canvas. Which I couldn't read then what was wrote on the canvas, but I learnt later it said, in big print:

SIWASH INDIAN SAGRAW. NATURE'S UNIVERSAL MEDICINAL SPECIFIC. DISCOVERED BY DR. HARTLEY L. KIRBY AMONG THE ABORIGINES OF OREGON.

On account of being so busy, neither Hank nor me had hearn the wagon come along the road and stop. The big man in the plug hat, he says, or they was words to that effect, jest as serious:

"Why are you mauling the aged gent?"

"Well," says I, "he needed it considerable."

"But," says he, still more solemn, "the good book says to honour thy father and thy mother."

"Well," I says, "mebby it does and mebby it don't. But *he* ain't my father, nohow. And he ain't been getting no more'n his come-uppings."

"Vengeance is mine, saith the Lord," the big man remarks, very serious. Hank, he riz up then, and he says:

"Mister, be you a preacher? 'Cause if you be, the sooner you have druv on, the better fur ye. I got a grudge agin all preachers."

That feller, he jest looks Hank over ca'am and easy and slow before he answers, and he wrinkles up his face like he never seen anything like Hank before. Then he fetches a kind o' aggervating smile, and he says:

"Beneath a shady chestnut tree The village blacksmith stands. The smith, a pleasant soul is he With warts upon his hands—"

He stares at Hank hard and solemn and serious while he is saying that poetry at him. Hank fidgets and turns his eyes away. But the feller touches him on the breast with his finger, and makes him look at him.

"My honest friend," says the feller, "I am *not* a preacher. Not right now, anyhow. No! My mission is spreading the glad tidings of good health. Look at me," and he swells his chest up, and keeps a-holt of Hank's eyes with his'n. "You behold before you the discoverer, manufacturer, and proprietor of Siwash Indian Sagraw, nature's own remedy for Bright's Disease, rheumatism, liver and kidney trouble, catarrh, consumption, bronchitis, ringworm, erysipelas, lung fever, typhoid, croup, dandruff, stomach trouble, dyspepsia—" And they was a lot more of 'em.

"Well," says Hank, sort o' backing up as the big man come nearer and nearer to him, jest natcherally bully-ragging him with them eyes, "I got none of them there complaints."

The doctor he kind o' snarls, and he brings his hand down hard on Hank's shoulder, and he says:

"There are more things betwixt Dan and Beersheba than was ever dreamt of in thy sagacity, Romeo!" Or they was words to that effect, fur that doctor was jest plumb full of Scripter quotations. And he sings out sudden, giving Hank a shove that nearly pushes him over: "Man alive!" he yells, "you *don't know* what disease you may have! Many's the strong man I've seen rejoicing in his strength at the dawn of day cut down like the grass in the field before sunset," he says.

Hank, he's trying to look the other way, but that doctor won't let his eyes wiggle away from his'n. He says very sharp:

"Stick out your tongue!"

"'Man alive! you *don't know* what disease you may have!
. . . Stick out your tongue!'"

Hank, he sticks her out.

The doctor, he takes some glasses out'n his pocket and puts 'em on, and he fetches a long look at her. Then he opens his mouth like he was going to say something, and shuts it agin like his feelings won't let him. He puts his arm across Hank's shoulder affectionate and sad, and then he turns his head away like they was some one dead in the fambly. Finally, he says:

"I thought so. I saw it. I saw it in your eyes when I first drove up. I hope," he says, very mournful, "I haven't come too late!"

Hank, he turns pale. I was getting sorry fur Hank myself. I seen now why I licked him so easy. Any one could of told from that doctor's actions Hank was as good as a dead man already. But Hank, he makes a big effort, and he says:

"Shucks! I'm sixty-eight years old, doctor, and I hain't never had a sick day in my life." But he was awful uneasy too.

The doctor, he says to the feller with him: "Looey, bring me one of the sample size."

Looey brung it, the doctor never taking his eyes off'n Hank. He handed it to Hank, and he says:

"A whiskey glass full three times a day, my friend, and there is a good chance for even you. I give it to you, without money and without price."

"But what have I got?" asts Hank.

"You have spinal meningitis," says the doctor, never batting an eye.

"Will this here cure me?" says Hank.

"It'll cure *anything*," says the doctor.

Hank he says, "Shucks," agin, but he took the bottle and pulled the cork out and smelt it, right thoughtful. And what them fellers had stopped at our place fur was to have the shoe of the nigh hoss's off hind foot nailed on, which it was most ready to drop off. Hank, he done it fur a regulation, dollar-size bottle and they druv on into the village.

Right after supper I goes down town. They was in front of Smith's Palace Hotel. They was jest starting up when I got there. Well, sir, that doctor was a sight. He didn't have his duster onto him, but his stove-pipe hat was, and one of them long Prince Alferd coats nearly to his knees, and shiny shoes, but his vest was cut out holler fur to show his biled shirt, and it was the pinkest shirt I ever see, and in the middle of that they was a diamond as big as Uncle Pat Hickey's wen, what was one of the town sights. No, sir; they never was a man with more genuine fashionableness sticking out all over him than Doctor Kirby. He jest fairly wallered in it.

I hadn't paid no pertic'ler attention to the other feller with him when they stopped at our place, excepting to notice he was kind of slim and blackhaired and funny complected. But I seen now I orter of looked closeter. Fur I'll be dad-binged if he weren't an Injun! There he set, under that there gasoline lamp the wagon was all lit up with, with moccasins on, and beads and shells all over him, and the gaudiest turkey tail of feathers rainbowing down from his head you ever see, and a blanket around him that was gaudier than the feathers. And he shined and rattled every time he moved.

That wagon was a hull opry house to itself. It was rolled out in front of Smith's Palace Hotel without the hosses. The front part was filled with bottles of medicine. The doctor, he begun business by taking out a long brass horn and tooting on it. They was about a dozen come, but they was mostly boys. Then him and the Injun picked up some banjoes and sung a comic song out loud and clear. And they was another dozen or so come. And they sung another song, and Pop Wilkins, he closed up the post-office and come over and the other two veterans of the Grand Army of the Republicans that always plays checkers in there nights come along with him. But it wasn't much of a crowd, and the doctor he looked sort o' worried. I had a good place, right near the hind wheel of the wagon where he rested his foot occasional, and I seen what he was thinking. So I says to him:

"Doctor Kirby, I guess the crowd is all gone to the circus agin to-night." And all them fellers there seen I knowed him.

"I guess so, Rube," he says to me. And they all laughed 'cause he called me Rube, and I felt kind of took down.

Then he lit in to tell about that Injun medicine. First off he told how he come to find out about it. It was the father of the Injun what was with him had showed him, he said. And it was in the days of his youthfulness, when he was wild, and a cowboy on the plains of Oregon. Well, one night he says, they was an awful fight on the plains of Oregon, wherever them is, and he got plugged full of bullet holes. And his hoss run away with him and he was carried off, and the hoss was going at a dead run, and the blood was running down onto the ground. And the wolves smelt the blood and took out after him, yipping and yowling something frightful to hear, and the hoss he kicked out behind and killed the head wolf and the others stopped to eat him up, and while they was eating him the hoss gained a quarter of a mile. But they et him up and they was gaining agin, fur the smell of human blood was on the plains of Oregon, he says, and the sight of his mother's face when she ast him never to be a cowboy come to him in the moonlight, and he knowed that somehow all would yet be well, and then he must of fainted and he knowed no more till he woke up in a tent on the plains of Oregon. And they was an old Injun bending over him and a beautiful Injun maiden was feeling of his pulse, and they says to him:

"Pale face, take hope, fur we will doctor you with Siwash Injun Sagraw, which is nature's own cure fur all diseases."

They done it. And he got well. It had been a secret among them there Injuns fur thousands and thousands of years. Any Injun that give away the secret was killed and rubbed off the rolls of the tribe and buried in disgrace upon the plains of Oregon. And the doctor was made a blood brother of the chief, and learnt the secret of that medicine. Finally he got the chief to see as it wasn't Christian to hold back that there medicine from the world no longer, and the chief, his heart was softened, and he says to go.

"Go, my brother," he says, "and give to the pale faces the medicine that has been kept secret fur thousands and thousands of years among the Siwash Injuns on the plains of Oregon."

And he went. It wasn't that he wanted to make no money out of that there medicine. He could of made all the money he wanted being a doctor in the reg'lar way. But what he wanted was to spread the glad tidings of good health all over this fair land of ourn, he says.

Well, sir, he was a talker, that there doctor was, and he knowed more religious sayings and poetry along with it, than any feller I ever hearn. He goes on and he tells how awful sick people can manage to get and never know it, and no one else never suspicion it, and live along fur years and years that-a-way, and all the time in danger of death. He says it makes him weep when he sees them poor diluted fools going around and thinking they is well men, talking and laughing and marrying and giving in to marriage right on the edge of the grave. He sees dozens of 'em in every town he comes to. But they can't fool him, he says. He can tell at a glance who's got Bright's Disease in their kidneys and who ain't. His own father, he says, was deathly sick fur years and years and never knowed it, and the knowledge come on him sudden like, and he died. That was before Siwash Injun Sagraw was ever found out about. Doctor Kirby broke down and cried right there in the wagon when he thought of how his father might of been saved if he was only alive now that that medicine was put up into bottle form, six fur a five-dollar bill so long as he was in town, and after that two dollars fur each bottle at the drug store.

He unrolled a big chart and the Injun helt it by that there gasoline lamp, so all could see, turning the pages now and then. It was a map of a man's inside organs and digestive ornaments and things. They was red and blue, like each organ's own disease had turned it, and some of 'em was yaller. And they was a long string of diseases printed in black hanging down from each organ's picture. I never knowed before they was so many diseases nor yet so many things to have 'em in.

Well, I was feeling purty good when that show started. But the doc, he kep' looking right at me every now and then when he talked, and I couldn't keep my eyes off'n him.

"Does your heart beat fast when you exercise?" he asts the crowd. "Is your tongue coated after meals? Do your eyes leak when your nose is stopped up? Do you perspire under your arm pits? Do you ever have a ringing in your ears? Does your stomach hurt you after meals? Does your back ever ache? Do you ever have pains in your legs? Do your eyes blur when you look at the sun? Are your teeth coated? Does your hair come out when you comb it? Is your breath short when you walk up stairs? Do your feet swell in warm weather? Are there white spots on your finger nails? Do you draw your breath part of the time through one nostril and part of the time through the other? Do you ever have nightmare? Did your nose bleed easily when you were growing up? Does your skin fester when scratched? Are your eyes gummy in the mornings? Then," he says, "if you have any or all of these symptoms, your blood is bad, and your liver is wasting away."

Well, sir, I seen I was in a bad way, fur at one time or another I had had most of them there signs and warnings, and hadn't heeded 'em, and I had some of 'em yet. I begun to feel kind o' sick, and looking at them organs and diseases didn't help me none, either. The doctor, he lit out on another string of symptoms, and I had them, too. Seems to me I had purty nigh everything but fits. Kidney complaint and consumption both had a holt on me. It was about a even bet which would get me first. I kind o' got to wondering which. I figgered from what he said that I'd had consumption the *longest* while, but my kind of kidney trouble was an awful SLY kind, and it was lible to jump in without no warning a-tall and jest natcherally wipe me out *quick*. So I sort o' bet on the kidney trouble. But I seen I was a goner, and I forgive Hank all his orneriness, fur a feller don't want to die holding grudges.

Taking it the hull way through, that was about the best medicine show I ever seen. But they didn't sell much. All the people what had any money was to the circus agin that night. So they sung some more songs and closed early and went into the hotel.

CHAPTER IV

Well, the next morning I'm feeling considerable better, and think mebby I'm going to live after all. I got up earlier'n Hank did, and slipped out without him seeing me, and didn't go nigh the shop a-tall. Fur now I've licked Hank oncet I figger he won't rest till he has wiped that disgrace out, and he won't care a dern what he picks up to do it with, nuther.

They was a crick about a hundred yards from our house, in the woods, and I went over there and laid down and watched it run by. I laid awful still, thinking I wisht I was away from that town. Purty soon a squirrel comes down and sets on a log and watches me. I throwed an acorn at him, and he scooted up a tree quicker'n scatt. And then I wisht I hadn't scared him away, fur it looked like he knowed I was in trouble. Purty soon I takes a swim, and comes out and lays there some more, spitting into the water and thinking what shall I do now, and watching birds and things moving around, and ants working harder'n ever I would agin unless I got better pray fur it, and these here tumble bugs kicking their loads along hind end to.

After a while it is getting along toward noon, and I'm feeling hungry. But I don't want to have no more trouble with Hank, and I jest lays there. I hearn two men coming through the underbrush. I riz up on my elbow to look, and one of them was Doctor Kirby and the other was Looey, only Looey wasn't an Injun this morning.

They sets down on the roots of a big tree a little ways off, with their backs toward me, and they ain't seen me. So nacherally I listened to what they was jawing about. They was both kind o' mad at the hull world, and at our town in pertic'ler, and some at each other, too. The doctor, he says:

"I haven't had such rotten luck since I played the bloodhound in a Tom Show—Were you ever an 'Uncle Tom's Cabin' artist, Looey?—and a justice of the peace over in Iowa fined me five dollars for being on the street without a muzzle. Said it was a city ordinance. Talk about the gentle Rube being an easy mark! If these country towns don't get the wandering minstrel's money one way they will another!"

"It's your own fault," says Looey, kind o' sour.

"I can't see it," says Doctor Kirby. "How did I know that all these apple-knockers had been filled up with Sykes's Magic Remedy only two weeks ago? I may have been a spiritualistic medium in my time now and then," he says, "and a mind reader, too, but I'm no prophet."

"I ain't talking about the business, Doc, and you know it," says Looey. "We'd be all right and have our horses and wagon now if you'd only stuck to business and not got us into that poker game. Talk about suckers! Doc, for a man that has skinned as many of 'em as you have, you're the worst sucker yourself I ever saw."

The doctor, he cusses the poker game and country towns and medicine shows and the hull creation and says he is so disgusted with life he guesses he'll go and be a preacher or a bearded lady in a sideshow. But Looey, he don't cheer up none. He says:

"All right, Doc, but it's no use talking. You can *talk* all right. We all know that. The question is how are we going to get our horses and wagon away from these Rubes?"

I listens some more, and I seen them fellers was really into bad trouble. Doctor Kirby, he had got into a poker game at Smith's Palace Hotel the night before, right after the show. He had won from Jake Smith, which run it, and from the others. But shucks! it never made no difference what you won in that crowd. They had done Doctor Kirby and Looey like they always done a drummer or a stranger that come along to that town and was fool enough to play poker with them. They wasn't a chancet fur an outsider. If the drummer lost, they would take his money and that would be all they was to it. But if the drummer got to winning good, some one would slip out'n the hotel and tell Si Emery, which was the city marshal. And Si would get Ralph Scott, that worked fur Jake Smith in his livery stable, and pin a star onto Ralph, too. And they would be arrested fur gambling, only them that lived in our town would get away. Which Si and Ralph was always scared every time they done it. Then the drummer, or whoever it was, would be took to the calaboose, and spend all night there.

In the morning they would be took before Squire Matthews, that was justice of the peace. They would be fined a big fine, and he would get all the drummer had won and all he had brung to town with him besides. Squire Matthews and Jake Smith and Windy Goodell and Mart Watson, which the two last was lawyers, was always playing that there game on drummers that was fool enough to play poker. Hank, he says he bet they divided it up afterward, though it was supposed them fines went to the town. Well, they played a purty closte game of poker in our little town. It was jest like the doctor says to Looey:

"By George," he says, "it is a well-nigh perfect thing. If you lose you lose, and if you win you lose."

Well, the doctor, he had started out winning the night before. And Si Emery and Ralph Scott had arrested them. And that morning, while I had been laying by the crick and the rest of the town was seeing the fun, they had been took afore Squire Matthews and fined one hundred and twenty-five dollars apiece. The doctor, he tells Squire Matthews it is an outrage, and it ain't legal if tried in a bigger court, and they ain't that much money in the world so fur as he knows, and he won't pay it. But, the squire, he says the time has come to teach them travelling fakirs as is always running around the country with shows and electric belts and things that they got to stop dreening that town of hard-earned money, and he has decided to make an example of 'em. The only two lawyers in town is Windy and Mart, which has been in the poker game theirselves, the same as always. The doctor says the hull thing is a put-up job, and he can't get the money, and he wouldn't if he could, and he'll lay in that town calaboose and rot the rest of his life and eat the town poor before he'll stand it. And the squire says he'll jest take their hosses and wagon fur c'latteral till they make up the rest of the two hundred and fifty dollars. And the hosses and wagon was now in the livery stable next to Smith's Palace Hotel, which Jake run that too.

Well, I thinks to myself, it *is* a dern shame, and I felt sorry fur them two fellers. Fur our town was jest as good as stealing that property. And I felt kind o' shamed of belonging to such a town, too. And I thinks to myself, I'd like to help 'em out of that scrape. And then I seen how I could do it, and not get took up fur it, neither. So, without thinking, all of a sudden I jumps up and says:

"Say, Doctor Kirby, I got a scheme!"

They jumps up too, and they looks at me startled. Then the doctor kind o' laughs and says:

"Why, it's the young blacksmith!"

Looey, he says, looking at me hard and suspicious:

"What kind of a scheme are you talking about?"

"Why," says I, "to get that outfit of yourn."

"You've been listening to us," says Looey. Looey was one of them quiet-looking fellers that never laughed much nor talked much. Looey, he never made fun of nobody, which the doctor was always doing, and I wouldn't of cared to make fun of Looey much, either.

"Yes," I says, "I been laying here fur quite a spell, and quite natcheral I listened to you, as any one else would of done. And mebby I can get that team and wagon of yourn without it costing you a cent."

Well, they didn't know what to say. They asts me how, but I says to leave it all to me. "Walk right along down this here crick," I says, "till you get to where it comes out'n the woods and runs acrost the road in under an iron bridge. That's about a half a mile east. Jest after the road crosses the bridge it forks. Take the right fork and walk another half a mile and you'll see a little yaller-painted schoolhouse setting lonesome on a sand hill. They ain't no school in it now. You wait there fur me," I says, "fur a couple of hours. After that if I ain't there you'll know I can't make it. But I think I'll make it."

They looks at each other and they looks at me, and then they go off a little piece and talk low, and then the doctor says to me:

"Rube," he says, "I don't know how you can work anything on us that hasn't been worked already. We've got nothing more we can lose. You go to it, Rube." And they started off.

So I went over town. Jake Smith was setting on the piazza in front of his hotel, chawing and spitting tobacco, with his feet agin the railing like he always done, and one of his eyes squinched up and his hat over the other one.

"Jake," I says, "where's that there doctor?"

Jake, he spit careful afore he answered, and he pulled his long, scraggly moustache careful, and he squinched his eyes at me. Jake was a careful man in everything he done.

"I dunno, Danny," he says. "Why?"

"Well," I says, "Hank sent me over to get that wagon and them hosses of theirn and finish that job."

"That there wagon," says Jake, "is in my barn, with Si Emery watching her, and she has got to stay there till the law lets her loose." I figgered to myself Jake could use that team and wagon in his business, and was going to buy her cheap offn the town, what share of her he didn't figger he owned already.

"Why, Jake," I says, "I hope they ain't been no trouble of no kind that has drug the law into your barn!"

"Well, Danny," he says, "they *has* been a little trouble. But it's about over, now, I guess. And that there outfit belongs to the town now."

"You don't say so!" says I, surprised-like. "When I seen them men last night it looked to me like they was too fine dressed to be honest."

"I don't think they be, Danny," says Jake, confidential. "In my opinion they is mighty bad customers. But they has got on the wrong side of the law now, and I guess they won't stay around here much longer."

"Well," says I, "Hank will be glad."

"Fur what?" asts Jake.

"Well," says I, "because he got his pay in advance fur that job and now he don't have to finish it. They come along to our place about sundown

33

yesterday, and we nailed a shoe on one hoss. They was a couple of other hoofs needed fixing, and the tire on one of the hind wheels was beginning to rattle loose."

I had noticed that loose tire when I was standing by the hind wheel the night before, and it come in handy now. So I goes on:

"Hank, he allowed he'd fix the hull thing fur six bottles of that Injun medicine. Elmira has been ailing lately, and he wanted it fur her. So they handed Hank out six bottles then and there."

"Huh!" says Jake. "So the job is all paid fur, is it?"

"Yes," says I, "and I was expecting to do it myself. But now I guess I'll go fishing instead. They ain't no other job in the shop."

"I'll be dinged if you've got time to fish," says Jake. "I'm expecting mebby to buy that rig off the town myself when the law lets loose of it. So if the fixing is paid fur, I want everything fixed."

"Jake," says I, kind of worried like, "I don't want to do it without that doctor says to go ahead."

"They ain't his'n no longer," says Jake.

"I dunno," says I, "as you got any right to make me do it, Jake. It don't look to me like it's no harm to beat a couple of fellers like them out of their medicine. And I *did* want to go fishing this afternoon."

But Jake was that careful and stingy he'd try to skin a hoss twicet if it died. He's bound to get that job done, now.

"Danny," he says, "you gotto do that work. It ain't *honest* not to. What a young feller like you jest starting out into life wants to remember is to always be honest. Then," says Jake, squinching up his eyes, "people trusts you and you get a good chancet to make money. Look at this here hotel and livery stable, Danny. Twenty years ago I didn't have no more'n you've got, Danny. But I always went by them mottoes—hard work and being honest. You *gotto* nail them shoes on, Danny, and fix that wheel."

"Well, all right, Jake," says I, "if you feel that way about it. Jest give me a chaw of tobacco and come around and help me hitch 'em up."

Si Emery was there asleep on a pile of straw guarding that property. But Ralph Scott wasn't around. Si didn't wake up till we had hitched 'em up. He says he will ride around to the shop with me. But Jake says:

"It's all right, Si. I'll go over myself and fetch 'em back purty soon." Which Si was wore out with being up so late the night before, and goes back to sleep agin right off.

Well, sir, they wasn't nothing went wrong. I drove slow through the village and past our shop. Hank come to the door of it as I went past. But I hit them hosses a lick, and they broke into a right smart trot. Elmira, she come onto the porch and I waved my hand at her. She put her hand up to her forehead to shut out the sun and jest stared. She didn't know I was waving her farewell. Hank, he yelled something at me, but I never hearn what. I licked them hosses into a gallop and went around the turn of the road. And that's the last I ever seen or hearn of Hank or Elmira or that there little town.

CHAPTER V

I slowed down when I got to the schoolhouse, and both them fellers piled in.

"I guess I better turn north fur about a mile and then turn west, Doctor Kirby," I says, "so as to make a kind of a circle around that town."

"Why, so, Rube?" he asts me.

"Well," I says, "we left it going east, and they'll foller us east; so don't we want to be going west while they're follering east?"

Looey, he agreed with me. But he said it wouldn't be much use, fur we would likely be ketched up with and took back and hung or something, anyhow. Looey could get the lowest in his sperrits sometimes of any man I ever seen.

"Don't be afraid of that," says the doctor. "They are not going to follow us. *They* know they didn't get this property by due process of law. *They* aren't going to take the case into a county court where it will all come out about the way they robbed a couple of travelling men with a fake trial."

"I guess you know more about the law'n I do," I says. "I kind o' thought mebby we stole them hosses."

"Well," he says, "we got 'em, anyhow. And if they try to arrest us without a warrant there'll be the deuce to pay. But they aren't going to make any more trouble. I know these country crooks. They've got no stomach for trouble outside their own township."

Which made me feel considerable better, fur I never been of the opinion that going agin the law done any one no good.

They looks around in that wagon, and all their stuff was there—Jake Smith and the squire having kep' it all together careful to make things seem more legal, I suppose—and the doctor was plumb tickled, and Looey felt as cheerful as he ever felt about anything. So the doctor says they has everything they needs but some ready money, and he'll get that sure, fur he never seen the time he couldn't.

"But, Looey," he says, "I'm done with country hotels from now on. They've got the last cent they ever will from me—at least in the summer time."

"How you going to work it?" Looey asts him, like he hasn't no hopes it will work right.

"Camp out," says the doctor. "I've been thinking it all over." Then he turns to me. "Rube," he says, "where are you going?"

"Well," I says, "I ain't pinted nowhere in pertic'ler except away from that town we just left. Which my name ain't Rube, Doctor Kirby, but Danny."

"Danny what?" asts he.

"Nothing," says I, "jest Danny."

"Well, then, Danny," says he, "how would you like to be an Indian?"

"Medical?" asts I, "or real?"

"Like Looey," says he.

I tells him being a medical Injun and mixed up with a show like his'n would suit me down to the ground, and asts him what is the main duties of one besides the blankets and the feathers.

"Well," he says, "this camping-out scheme of mine will take a couple of Indians. Instead of paying hotel and feed bills we'll pitch our tent," he says, "at the edge of town in each sweet Auburn of the plains. We'll save money and we'll be near the throbbing heart of nature. And an Indian camp in each place will be a good advertisement for the Sagraw. You can look after the horses and learn to do the cooking and that kind o' thing. And maybe after while," he says, kind o' working himself up to where he thought it was going to be real nice, "maybe after while I will give you some insight into the hidden mysteries of selling Siwash Indian Sagraw."

"Well," says I, "I'd like to learn that."

"Would you?" says he, kind o' laughing at himself and me too, and yet kind o' enthusiastic, "well, then, the first thing you have to do is learn how to sell corn salve. Any one that can sell corn salve can sell anything. There's a farmhouse right over there, and I'll give you your first lesson right now. Rummage around in that satchel there under the seat and get me a tin box and some corn salve labels."

I found a lot of labels, and some boxes too. The labels was all different sizes, but barring that they all looked about the same to me. Whilst I was sizing them up he asts me agin was they any corn salve ones in there.

"What colour label is it, Doctor Kirby?" I asts him. Fur they was blue labels and white labels and pink labels.

He looks at me right queer. "Can't you read the labels?" he says, right sharp.

"Well," I says, "I never been much of a reader when it comes to different kind of medicines."

"Corn salve is spelled only one way," says he.

"That's right," I says, "and you'd think I orter be able to pick out a common, ordinary thing like corn salve right off, wouldn't you?"

"Danny," he says, "you don't mean to tell me you can't read anything at all?"

"I never told you nothing of the kind."

He picks out a label.

"If you can read so fast, what's that?" he asts.

She is a pink one. I thinks to myself; she either is corn salve or else she ain't corn salve. And it ain't natcheral he will pick corn salve, fur he would think I would say that first off. So I'm betting it ain't. I takes a chancet on it.

"That," says I, "is mighty easy reading. That is Siwash Injun Sagraw." I lost.

"It's corn salve," he says. "And Great Scott! They call this the twentieth century!"

"I never called it that," says I, sort o' mad-like. Fur I was feeling bad Doctor Kirby had found out I was such a ignoramus.

"Where ignorance is bliss," says he, "it is folly to be wise. But all the same, I'm going to take your education in hand and make you drink of life's Peruvian springs." Or some spring like that it was.

And the doctor, he done it. Looey said it wouldn't be no use learning to read. He'd done a lot of reading, he said, and it never helped him none. All he ever read showed him this feller Hamlet was right, he said, when he wrote Shakespeare's works, and they wasn't much use in anything, without you had a lot o' money. And they wasn't no chancet to get that with all these here trusts around gobbling up everything and stomping the poor man into the dirt, and they was lots of times he wisht he was a Injun sure enough, and not jest a medical one, fur then he'd be a free man and the bosses and the trusts and the railroads and the robber tariff couldn't touch him. And then he shut up, and didn't say nothing fur a hull hour, except oncet he laughed.

Fur Doctor Kirby, he says, winking at me: "Looey, here, is a nihilist."

"Is he," says I, "what's that?" And the doctor tells me about how they blow up dukes and czars and them foreign high-mucky-mucks with dynamite. Which is when Looey laughed.

THE SWEDE
"The doctor paid him fur everything in medicine"

Well, we jogged along at a pretty good gait fur several hours, and we stayed that night at a Swede's place, which the doctor paid him fur everything in medicine, only it took a long time to make the bargain, fur them Swedes is always careful not to get cheated, and hasn't many diseases. And the next night we showed in a little town, and done right well, and took in considerable money. We stayed there three days and bought a tent and a sheet-iron stove and some skillets and things and some provisions, and a suit of duds for me.

Well, we went on, and we kept going on, and they was bully times. We'd ease up careful toward a town, and pick us out a place on the edge, where the hosses could graze along the side of the road; and most ginerally by a piece of woods not fur from that town, and nigh a crick, if we could. Then we'd set up our tent. After we had everything fixed, I'd put on my Injun clothes and Looey his'n, and we'd drive through the main store street of the town at a purty good lick, me a-holt of the reins, and the doctor all togged out in his best clothes, and Looey doing a Injun dance in the midst of the wagon. I'd pull up the hosses sudden in front of the post-office or the depot platform or the hotel, and the people would come crowding around, and the doctor he'd make a little talk from the wagon, and tell everybody they would be a free show that night on that corner, and fur everybody to come to it. And then we'd drive back to camp, lickitysplit.

Purty soon every boy in town would be out there, kind o' hanging around, to see what a Injun camp was like. And the farmers that went into and out of town always stopped and passed the time of day, and the Injun camp got the hull town all worked up as a usual thing; and the doctor, he done well, fur when night come every one would be on hand. Looey and me, every time we went into town, had on our Injun suits, and the doctor, he wondered why he hadn't never thought up that scheme before. Sometimes, when they was lots of people ailing in a town, and they hadn't been no show fur quite a while, we'd stay five or six days, and make a good clean-up. The doctor, he sent to Chicago several times fur alcohol in barrels, 'cause he was selling it so fast he had to make new Sagraw. And he had to get more and more bottles, and a hull satchel full of new Sagraw labels printed.

And all the time the doctor was learning me education. And shucks! they wasn't nothing so hard about it oncet you'd got started in to reading things. I jest natcherally took to print like a duck to water, and inside of a month I was reading nigh everything that has ever been wrote. He had lots of books with him and every time a new sockdologer of a word come along and I learnt how to spell her and where she orter fit in to make sense it kind o' tickled me all over. And many's the time afterward, when me and the doctor had lost track of each other, and they was quite a spell people got to thinking I was a tramp, I've went into these here Andrew Carnegie libraries in different towns jest as much to see if they had anything fitten to read as fur to keep warm.

Well, we went easing over toward the Indiany line, and we was having a purty good time. They wasn't no work to do you could call really hard, and they was plenty of vittles. Afternoons we'd lazy around the camp and swap stories and make medicine if we needed a batch, and josh back and forth with the people that hung around, and loaf and doze and smoke; or mebby do a little fishing if we was nigh a crick.

And nights after the show was over it was fun, too. We always had a fire, even if it was a hot night, fur to cook by in the first place, and fur to keep mosquitoes off, and to make things seem more cheerful. They ain't nothing so good as hanging round a campfire. And they ain't nothing any better than sleeping outdoors, neither. You roll up in your blanket with your feet to the fire and you get to wondering things about things afore you go to sleep. The silentness jest natcherally swamps everything after a while, and then all them queer little noises you never hear in the daytime comes popping and poking through the silentness, or kind o' scratching their way through it sometimes, and makes it kind o' feel more silent than ever. And if you are nigh a crick, purty soon it will sort of get to talking to you, only you can't make out what it's trying to say, and you get to wondering about that, too. And if you are in a tent and it rains and the tent don't leak, that rain is a kind of a nice thing to listen to itself. But if you can see the stars you get to wondering more'n ever. They come out and they is so many of them and they are so fur away, and yet they are so kind o' friendly-like, too, if you happen to be feeling purty good. But if you ain't feeling purty good, jest lay there and look at them stars long enough; and then mebby you'll see it don't make no difference whether you're feeling good or not, fur they got a way o' making your private troubles look mighty small. And you get to wondering why that is, too, fur they ain't human; and it don't stand to reason you orter pay no attention to them, one way nor the other. They is jest there, like trees and cricks and hills. But I have often noticed that the things that is jest there has got a way of seeming more friendly than the things that has been built and put there. You can look at a big iron bridge or a grain elevator or a canal all day long, and if you're feeling blue it don't help you none. It was jest put there. Or a hay stack is the same way. But you go and lazy around in the grass when you're down on your luck and kind o' make remarks to a crick or a big, old walnut tree, and before long it gets you to feeling like it didn't make no difference how you felt, anyhow; fur you don't amount to nothing by the side of something that was always there. You get to thinking how the hull world itself was always here, and you sort o' see they ain't nothing important enough about yourself to worry about, and presently you will go to sleep and forget it. The doctor says to me one time them stars ain't any different from this world, and this is one of them. Which is a fool idea, as any one can see. He had a lot of queer ideas like that, Doctor Kirby had. But they ain't nothing like sleeping out of doors nights to make you wonder the kind of wonderings you never will get any answer to.

Well, I never cared so much fur houses after them days. They was bully times, them was. And I was kind of proud of being with a show, too. Many's the time I have went down the street in that there Injun suit, and seen how the young fellers would of give all they owned to be me. And every now and then you would hear one say when you went past:

"Huh, I know him! That's one of them show fellers!"

One afternoon we pitches our tent right on the edge of a little town called Athens. We was nigh the bank of a crick, and they was a grove there. We was camped jest outside of a wood-lot fence, and back in through the trees from us they was a house with a hedge fence all around it. They was apple trees and all kind of flower bushes and things inside of the hedge. The second day we was there I takes a walk back through the wood-lot, and along past the house, and they was one of these here early harvest apple trees spilling apples through a gap in the fence. Them is a mighty sweet and juicy kind of apple, and I picks one up and bites into it.

"I think you might have asked for it," says some one.

———————————————

CHAPTER VI

I looks up, and that was how I got acquainted with Martha. She was eating one herself, setting up in the tree like a boy. In her lap was a book she had been reading. She was leaning back into the fork two limbs made so as not to tumble.

"Well," I says, "can I have one?"

"You've eaten it already," she says, "so there isn't any use begging for it now."

I seen she was a tease, that girl, and I would of give anything to of been able to tease her right back agin. But I couldn't think of nothing to say, so I jest stands there kind o' dumb like, thinking what a dern purty girl she was, and thinking how dumb I must look, and I felt my face getting red. Doctor Kirby would of thought of something to say right off. And after I got back to camp I would think of something myself. But I couldn't think of nothing bright, so I says:

"Well, then, you give me another one!"

She gives the core of the one she has been eating a toss at me. But I ketched it, and made like I was going to throw it back at her real hard. She slung up her arm, and dodged back, and she dropped her book.

I thinks to myself I'll learn that girl to get sassy and make me feel like a dumb-head, even if she is purty. So I don't say a word. I jest picks up that book and sticks it under my arm and walks away slow with it to where they was a stump a little ways off, not fur from the crick, and sets down with my back to her and opens it. And I was trying all the time to think of something smart to say to her. But I couldn't of done it if I was to be shot. Still, I thinks to myself, no girl can sass me and not get sassed back, neither.

I hearn a scramble behind me which I knowed was her getting out of that tree. And in a minute she was in front of me, mad.

"Give me my book," she says.

But I only reads the name of the book out loud, fur to aggervate her. I had on purty good duds, but I kind of wisht I had on my Injun rig then. You take the girls that always comes down to see the passenger train come into the depot in them country towns and that Injun rig of mine and Looey's always made 'em turn around and look at us agin. I never wisht I had on them Injun duds so hard before in my life. But I couldn't think of nothing bright to say, so

I jest reads the name of that book over to myself agin, kind o' grinning like I got a good joke I ain't going to tell any one.

"You give me my book," she says agin, red as one of them harvest apples, "or I'll tell Miss Hampton you stole it and she'll have you and your show arrested."

I reads the name agin. It was "The Lost Heir." I seen I had her good and teased now, so I says: "It must be one of these here love stories by the way you take on over it."

"It's not," she says, getting ready to cry. "And what right have you got in our wood-lot, anyhow?"

"Well," I says, "I was jest about to move on and climb out of it when you hollered to me from that tree."

"I didn't!" she says. But she was mad because she knowed she *had* spoke to me first, and she was awful sorry she had.

"I thought I hearn you holler," I says, "but I guess it must of been a squirrel." I said it kind o' sarcastic like, fur I was still mad with myself fur being so dumb when we first seen each other. I hadn't no idea it would hurt her feelings as hard as it did. But all of a sudden she begins to wink, and her chin trembled, and she turned around short, and started to walk off slow. She was mad with herself fur being ketched in a lie, and she was wondering what I would think of her fur being so bold as to of spoke first to a feller she didn't know.

I got up and follered her a little piece. And it come to me all to oncet I had teased her too hard, and I was down on myself fur it.

"Say," I says, kind of tagging along beside of her, "here's your old book."

But she didn't make no move to take it, and her hands was over her face, and she wouldn't pull 'em down to even look at it.

So I tried agin.

"Well," I says, feeling real mean, "I wisht you wouldn't cry. I didn't go to make you do that."

She drops her hands and whirls around on me, mad as a wet hen right off.

"I'm not! I'm not!" she sings out, and stamps her feet. "I'm not crying!" But jest then she loses her holt on herself and busts out and jest natcherally bellers. "I hate you!" she says, like she could of killed me.

That made me kind of dumb agin. Fur it come to me all to oncet I liked that girl awful well. And here I'd up and made her hate me. I held the book out to her agin and says:

"Well, I'm mighty sorry fur that, fur I don't feel that-a-way about you a-tall. Here's your book."

Well, sir, she snatches that book and she gives it a sling. I thought it was going kersplash into the crick. But it didn't. It hit right into the fork of a limb that hung down over the crick, and it all spread out when it lit, and stuck in that crotch somehow. She couldn't of slung it that way on purpose in a million years. We both stands and looks at it a minute.

"Oh, oh!" she says, "what have I done? It's out of the town library and I'll have to pay for it."

"I'll get it fur you," I says. But it wasn't no easy job. If I shook that limb it would tumble into the crick. But I clumb the tree and eased out on that limb as fur as I dast to. And, of course, jest as I got holt of the book, that limb broke and I fell into the crick. But I had the book. It was some soaked, but I reckoned it could still be read.

I clumb out and she was jest splitting herself laughing at me. The wet on her face where she had cried wasn't dried up yet, and she was laughing right through it, kind o' like the sun does to one of these here May rainstorms sometimes, and she was the purtiest girl I ever seen. Gosh!—how I was getting to like that girl! And she told me I looked like a drowned rat.

Well, that was how Martha and me was interduced. She wasn't more'n sixteen, and when she found out I was a orphan she was glad, fur she was one herself. Which Miss Hampton that lived in that house had took her to raise. And when I tells her how I been travelling around the country all summer she claps her hands and she says:

"Oh, you are on a quest! How romantic!"

I asts her what is a quest. And she tells me. She knowed all about them, fur Martha was considerable of a reader. Some of them was longer and some of them was shorter, them quests, but mostly, Martha says, they was fur a twelvemonth and a day. And then you are released from your vow and one of these here queens gives you a whack over the shoulder with a sword and says: "Arise, Sir Marmeluke, I dub you a night." And then it is legal fur you to go out and rescue people and reform them and spear them if they don't see things your way, and come between husband and wife when they row, and do a heap of good in the world. Well, they was other kind of quests too, but mostly you married somebody, or was dubbed a night, or found the party you was looking fur, in the end. And Martha had it all fixed up in her own mind I was in a quest to find my father. Fur, says she, he is purty certain to be a powerful rich man and more'n likely a earl.

"'Arise, Sir Marmeluke, I dub you a night'"

The way I was found, Martha says, kind o' pints to the idea they was a earl mixed up in it somewhere. She had read a lot about earls, and knew their ways. Mebby my mother was a earl's daughter. Earl's daughters is the worst fur leaving you out in baskets, going by what Martha said. It is a kind of a habit with them, fur they is awful proud people. But it was a lucky way to start life, from all she said, that basket way. There was Moses was left out that way, and when he growed up he was made a kind of a president of the hull human race, the same as Ruzevelt, and figgered out the twelve commandments. Martha would of give anything if she could of only been found in a basket like me, I could see that. But she wasn't. She had jest been left a orphan when her folks died. They wasn't even no hopes she had been changed at birth fur another one. But I seen down in under everything Martha kind o' thought mebby one of them nights might come a-prancing along and wed her in spite of herself, or she would be carried off, or something. She was a very romanceful kind of girl.

When I seen she had it figgered out I was in a quest fur some high-mucky-muck fur a dad, I didn't tell her no different. I didn't take much stock in them earls and nights myself. So fur as I could see they was all furriners of one kind or another. But that thing of being into a quest kind of interested me, too.

"How would I know him if I was to run acrost him?" I asts her.

"You would feel an Intangible Something," she says, "drawing you toward him."

I asts her what kind of a something. I make out from what she says it is some like these fellers that can find water with a piece of witch hazel switch.

You take a switch of it between your thumbs and point it up. Then you shut your eyes and walk backwards. When you get over where the water is the witch hazel stick twists around and points to the ground. You dig there and you get a good well. Nobody knows jest why that stick is drawed to the ground. It is like one of these little whirlygig compasses is drawed to the north. It is the same, Martha says, if you is on a quest fur a father or a mother, only you have got to be worthy of that there quest, she says. The first time you meet the right one you are drawed jest like the witch hazel. That is the Intangible Something working on you, she says. Martha had learnt a lot about that. The book that had fell in the crick was like that. She lent it to me.

Well, that all sounded kind of reasonable to me. I seen that witch hazel work myself. Old Blindy Wolfe, whose eyes had been dead fur so many years they had turned plumb white, had that gift, and picked out all the places fur wells that was dug in our neighbourhood at home. And I makes up my mind I will watch out fur that feeling of being drawed wherever I goes after this. You can't tell what will come of them kind of things. So purty soon Martha has to milk the cow, and I goes along back to camp thinking about that quest and about what a purty girl she is, which we had set there talking so long it was nigh sundown and my clothes had dried onto me.

When I got over to camp I seen they must be something wrong. Looey was setting in the grass under the wagon looking kind of sour and kind of worried and watching the doctor. The doctor was jest inside the tent, and he was looking queer too, and not cheerful, which he was usually.

The doctor looks at me like he don't skeercly know me. Which he don't. He has one of them quiet kind of drunks on. Which Looey explains is bound to come every so often. He don't do nothing mean, but jest gets low-sperrited and won't talk to no one. Then all of a sudden he will go down town and walk up and down the main streets, orderly, but looking hard into people's faces, mostly women's faces. Oncet, Looey says, they was big trouble over it. They was in a store in a good-sized town, and he took hold of a woman's chin, and tilted her face back, and looked at her hard, and most scared her to death, and they was nearly being a riot there. And he was jailed and had to pay a big fine. Since then Looey always follers him around when he is that-a-way.

Well, that night Doctor Kirby is too fur gone fur us to have our show. He jest sets and stares and stares at the fire, and his eyes looks like they is another fire inside of his head, and he is hurting outside and in. Looey and me watches him from the shadders fur a long time before we turns in, and the last thing I seen before I went to sleep was him setting there with his face in his hands, staring, and his lips moving now and then like he was talking to himself.

The next day he is asleep all morning. But that day he don't drink any more, and Looey says mebby it ain't going to be one of the reg'lar pifflicated kind. I seen Martha agin that day, too—twicet I has talks with her. I told her about the doctor.

"Is he into a quest, do you think?" I asts her.

She says she thinks it is remorse fur some crime he has done. But I couldn't figger Doctor Kirby would of done none. So that night after the show I says to him, innocent-like:

"Doctor Kirby, what is a quest?" He looks at me kind of queer.

"Wherefore," says he, "this sudden thirst for enlightenment?"

"I jest run acrost the word accidental-like," I told him.

He looks at me awful hard, his eyes jest natcherally digging into me. I felt like he knowed I had set out to pump him. I wisht I hadn't tried it. Then he tells me a quest is a hunt. And I'm glad that's over with. But it ain't. Fur purty soon he says:

"Danny, did you ever hear of Lady Clara Vere de Vere?"

"No," I says, "who is she?"

"A lady friend of Lord Tennyson's," he says, "whose manners were above reproach."

"Well," I says, "she sounds kind of like a medicine to me."

"Lady Clara," he says, "and all the other Vere de Veres, were people with manners we should try to imitate. If Lady Clara had been here last night when I was talking to myself, Danny, her manners wouldn't have let her listen to what I was talking about."

"I didn't listen!" I says. Fur I seen what he was driving at now with them Vere de Veres. He thought I had ast him what a quest was because he was on one. I was certain of that, now. He wasn't quite sure what he had been talking about, and he wanted to see how much I had hearn. I thinks to myself it must be a awful funny kind of hunt he is on, if he only hunts when he is in that fix. But I acted real innocent and like my feelings was hurt, and he believed me. Purty soon he says, cheerful like:

"There was a girl talking to you to-day, Danny."

"Mebby they was," I says, "and mebby they wasn't." But I felt my face getting red all the same, and was mad because it did. He grinned kind of aggervating at me and says some poetry at me about in the spring a young man's frenzy likely turns to thoughts of love.

48

"Well," I says, kind of sheepish-like, "this is summer-time, and purty nigh autumn." Then I seen I'd jest as good as owned up I liked Martha, and was kind of mad at myself fur that. But I told him some more about her, too. Somehow I jest couldn't help it. He laughs at me and goes on into the tent.

I laid there and looked at the fire fur quite a spell, outside the tent. I was thinking, if all them tales wasn't jest dern foolishness, how I wisht I would really find a dad that was a high-muckymuck and could come back in an automobile and take her away. I laid there fur a long, long time; it must of been fur a couple of hours. I supposed the doctor had went to sleep.

But all of a sudden I looks up, and he is in the door of the tent staring at me. I seen he had been in there at it hard agin, and thinking, quiet-like, all this time. He stood there in the doorway of the tent, with the firelight onto his face and his red beard, and his arms stretched out, holding to the canvas and looking at me strange and wild. Then he moved his hand up and down at me, and he says:

"If she's fool enough to love you, treat her well—treat her well. For if you don't, you can never run away from the hell you'll carry in your own heart."

And he kind of doubled up and pitched forward when he said that, and if I hadn't ketched him he would of fell right acrost the fire. He was plumb pifflicated.

CHAPTER VII

Martha wouldn't of took anything fur being around Miss Hampton, she said. Miss Hampton was kind of quiet and sweet and pale looking, and nobody ever thought of talking loud or raising any fuss when she was around. She had enough money of her own to run herself on, and she kep' to herself a good deal. She had come to that town from no one knowed where, years ago, and bought that place. Fur all of her being so gentle and easy and talking with one of them soft, drawly kind of voices, Martha says, no one had ever dared to ast her about herself, though they was a lot of women in that town that was wishful to.

But Martha said she knowed what Miss Hampton's secret was, and she hadn't told no one, neither. Which she told me, and all the promising I done about not telling would of made the cold chills run up your back, it was so solemn. Miss Hampton had been jilted years ago, Martha said, and the name of the jilter was David Armstrong. Well, he must of been a low down sort of man. Martha said if things was only fixed in this country like they ought to be, she would of sent a night to find that David Armstrong. And that would of ended up in a mortal combat, and the night would have cleaved him.

"Yes," says I, "and then you would of married that there night, I suppose."

She says she would of.

"Well," says I, "mebby you would of and mebby you wouldn't of. If he cleaved David Armstrong, that night would likely be arrested fur it."

Martha says if he was she would wait outside his dungeon keep fur years and years, till she was a old woman with gray in her hair, and every day they would give lingering looks at each other through the window bars. And they would be happy thata-way. And she would get her a white dove and train it so it would fly up to that window and take in notes to him, and he would send notes back that-away, and they would both be awful sad and romanceful and contented doing that-a-way fur ever and ever.

Well, I never took no stock in them mournful ways of being happy. I couldn't of riz up to being a night fur Martha. She expected too much of one. I thought it over fur a little spell without saying anything, and I tried to make myself believe I would of liked all that dove business. But it wasn't no use pertending. I knowed I would get tired of it.

"Martha," I says, "mebby these here nights is all right, and mebby they ain't. I never seen one, and I don't know. And, mind you, I ain't saying a word agin their way of acting. I can't say how I would of been myself, if I had been brung up like them. But it looks to me, from some of the things you've said about 'em, they must have a dern fool streak in 'em somewheres."

I was kind of jealous of them nights, I guess, or I wouldn't of run 'em down that-a-way behind their backs. But the way she was always taking on over them was calkelated to make me see I wasn't knee-high to a duck in Martha's mind when one of them nights popped into her head. When I run 'em down that-a-way, she says to the blind all things is blind, and if I had any chivalry into me myself I'd of seen they wasn't jest dern fools, but noble, and seen it easy. And she sighed, like she'd looked fur better things from me. When I hearn her do that I felt sorry I hadn't come up to her expectances. So I says:

"Martha, it's no use pertending I could stay in one of them jails and keep happy at it. I got to be outdoors. But I tell you what I can do, if it will make you feel any better. If I ever happen to run acrost this here David Armstrong, and he is anywheres near my size, I'll lick him fur you. And if he's too hefty fur me to lick him fair," I says, "and I get a good chancet I will hit him with a piece of railroad iron fur you."

Of course, I knowed I would never find him. But what I said seemed to brighten her up a little.

"But," says I, "if I went too fur with it, and was hung fur it, how would you feel then, Martha?"

Well, sir, that didn't jar Martha none. She looked kind of dreamy and said mebby she would go and jine a convent and be a nun. And when she got to be the head nun she would build a chapel over the tomb where I was buried in. And every year, on the day of the month I was hung on, she would lead all the other nuns into that chapel, and the organ would play mournful, and each nun as passed would lay down a bunch of white roses onto my tomb. I reckon that orter made me feel good, but somehow it didn't.

So I changed the subject, and asts her why I ain't seen Miss Hampton around the place none. Martha says she has a bad sick headache and ain't been outside the house fur four or five days. I asts her why she don't wait on her. But she don't want her to, Martha says. She's been staying in the house ever since we been in town, and jest wants to be let alone. I thinks all that is kind of funny. And then I seen from the way Martha is answering my questions that she is holding back something she would like to tell, but don't think she orter tell. I leaves her alone and purty soon she says:

"Do you believe in ghosts?"

I tell her sometimes I think I don't believe in 'em, and sometimes I think I do, but anyhow I would hate to see one. I asts her why does she ast.

"Because," she says, "because—but I hadn't ought to tell you."

"It's daylight," I says; "it's no use being scared to tell now."

"It ain't that," she says, "but it's a secret."

When she said it was a secret, I knowed she would tell. Martha liked having her friends help her to keep a secret.

"I think Miss Hampton has seen one," she says, finally, "and that her staying indoors has something to do with that."

Then she tells me. The night of the day after we camped there, her and Miss Hampton was out fur a walk. We didn't have any show that night. They passed right by our camp, and they seen us there by the fire, all three of us. But they was in the road in the dark, and we was all in the light, so none of the three of us seen them. Miss Hampton was kind of scared of us, first glance, fur she gasped and grabbed holt of Martha's arm all of a sudden so tight she pinched it. Which it was very natcheral that she would be startled, coming across three strange men all of a sudden at night around a turn in the road. They went along home, and Martha went inside and lighted a lamp, but Miss Hampton lingered on the porch fur a minute. Jest as she lit the lamp Martha hearn another little gasp, or kind of sigh, from Miss Hampton out there on the porch. Then they was the sound of her falling down. Martha ran out with the lamp, and she was laying there. She had fainted and keeled over. Martha said jest in the minute she had left her alone on the porch was when Miss Hampton must of seen the ghost. Martha brung her to, and she was looking puzzled and wild-like both to oncet. Martha asts her what is the matter.

"Nothing," she says, rubbing her fingers over her forehead in a helpless kind of way, "nothing."

"You look like you had seen a ghost," Martha tells her.

Miss Hampton looks at Martha awful funny, and then she says mebby she *has* seen a ghost, and goes along upstairs to bed. And since then she ain't been out of the house. She tells Martha it is a sick headache, but Martha says she knows it ain't. She thinks she is scared of something.

"Scared?" I says. "She wouldn't see no more ghosts in the daytime."

Martha says how do I know she wouldn't? She knows a lot about ghosts of all kinds, Martha does.

Horses and dogs can see them easier than humans, even in the daytime, and it makes their hair stand up when they do. But some humans that have the gift can see them in the daytime like an animal. And Martha asts me how can I tell but Miss Hampton is like that?

"Well, then," I says, "she must be a witch. And if she is a witch why is she scared of them a-tall?"

But Martha says if you have second sight you don't need to be a witch to see them in the daytime.

Well, you can never tell about them ghosts. Some says one thing and some says another. Old Mis' Primrose, in our town, she always believed in 'em firm till her husband died. When he was dying they fixed it up he was to come back and visit her. She told him he had to, and he promised. And she left the front door open fur him night after night fur nigh a year, in all kinds of weather; but Primrose never come. Mis' Primrose says he never lied to her, and he always done jest as she told him, and if he could of come she knowed he would; and when he didn't she quit believing in ghosts. But they was others in our town said it didn't prove nothing at all. They said Primrose had really been lying to her all his life, because she was so bossy he had to lie to keep peace in the fambly, and she never ketched on. Well, if I was a ghost and had of been Mis' Primrose's husband when I was a human, I wouldn't of come back neither, even if she had of bully-ragged me into one of them death-bed promises. I guess Primrose figgered he had earnt a rest.

If they is ghosts, what comfort they can get out of coming back where they ain't wanted and scaring folks is more'n I can see. It's kind of low down, I think, and foolish too. Them kind of ghosts is like these here overgrown smart alecs that scares kids. They think they are mighty cute, but they ain't. They are jest foolish. A human, or a ghost either, that does things like that is jest simply got no principle to him. I hearn a lot of talk about 'em, first and last, and I ain't ready to say they ain't no ghosts, nor yet ready to say they is any. To say they is any is to say something that is too plumb unlikely. And too many people has saw them fur me to say they ain't any. But if they is, or they ain't, so fur as I can see, it don't make much difference. Fur they never do nothing, besides scaring you, except to rap on tables and tell fortunes, and such fool things. Which a human can do it all better and save the expense of paying money to one of these here sperrit mediums that travels around and makes 'em perform. But all the same they has been nights I has felt different about 'em myself, and less hasty to run 'em down. Well, it don't do no good to speak harsh of no one, not even a ghost or a ordinary dead man, and if I was to see a ghost, mebby I would be all the scareder fur what I have jest wrote.

Well, with all the talking back and forth we done about them ghosts we couldn't agree. That afternoon it seemed like we couldn't agree about anything. I knowed we would be going away from there before long, and I says to myself before I go I'm going to have that girl fur my girl, or else know the reason why. No matter what I was talking about, that idea was in the back of my head, and somehow it kind of made me want to pick fusses with her, too. We was setting on a log, purty deep into the woods, and there come a time when neither of us had said nothing fur quite a spell. But after a while I says:

"Martha, we'll be going away from here in two, three days now."

She never said nothing.

"Will you be sorry?" I asts her.

She says she will be sorry.

"Well," I says, "*why* will you be sorry?"

I thought she would say because *I* was going. And then I would be finding out whether she liked me a lot. But she says the reason she will be sorry is because there will be no one new to talk to about things both has read. I was considerable took down when she said that.

"Martha," I says, "it's more'n likely I won't never see you agin after I go away."

She says that kind of parting comes between the best of friends.

I seen I wasn't getting along very fast, nor saying what I wanted to say. I reckon one of them Sir Marmeluke fellers would of knowed what to say. Or Doctor Kirby would. Or mebby even Looey would of said it better than I could. So I was kind of mad with myself, and I says, mean-like:

"If you don't care, of course, I don't care, neither."

She never answered that, so I gets up and makes like I am starting off.

"I was going to give you some of them there Injun feathers of mine to remember me by," I tells her, "but if you don't want 'em, there's plenty of others would be glad to take 'em."

But she says she would like to have them.

"Well," I says, "I will bring them to you tomorrow afternoon."

She says, "Thank you."

Finally I couldn't stand it no longer. I got brave all of a sudden, and busted out: "Martha, I—I—I—"

But I got to stuttering, and my braveness stuttered itself away. And I finishes up by saying:

"I like you a hull lot, Martha." Which wasn't jest exactly what I had planned fur to say.

Martha, she says she kind of likes me, too.

"Martha," I says, "I like you more'n any girl I ever run acrost before."

She says, "Thank you," agin. The way she said it riled me up. She said it like she didn't know what I meant, nor what I was trying to get out of me. But she did know all the time. I knowed she did. She knowed I knowed it, too. Gosh-dern it, I says to myself, here I am wasting all this time jest *talking* to her. The right thing to do come to me all of a sudden, and like to took my breath away. But I done it. I grabbed her and I kissed her.

Twice. And then agin. Because the first was on the chin on account of her jerking her head back. And the second one she didn't help me none. But the third time she helped me a little. And the ones after that she helped me considerable.

Well, they ain't no use trying to talk about the rest of that afternoon. I couldn't rightly describe it if I wanted to. And I reckon it's none of anybody's business.

Well, it makes you feel kind of funny. You want to go out and pick on somebody about four sizes bigger'n you are and knock the socks off'n him. It stands to reason others has felt that-a-way, but you don't believe it. You want to tell people about it one minute. The next minute you have got chills and ague fur fear some one will guess it. And you think the way you are about her is going to last fur always.

That evening, when I was cooking supper, I laughed every time I was spoke to. When Looey and I was hitching up to drive down town to give the show, one of the hosses stepped on his foot and I laughed at that, and there was purty nigh a fight. And I was handling some bottles and broke one and cut my hand on a piece of glass. I held it out fur a minute dumb-like, with the blood and medicine dripping off of it, and all of a sudden I busted out laughing agin. The doctor asts if I am crazy. And Looey says he has thought I was from the very first, and some night him and the doctor will be killed whilst asleep. One of the things we have every night in the show is an Injun dance, and Looey and I sings what the doctor calls the Siwash war chant, whirling round and round each other, and making licks at each other with our tommyhawks, and letting out sudden wild yips in the midst of that chant. That night I like to of killed Looey with that tommyhawk, I was feeling so good. If it had been a real one, instead of painted-up wood, I would of killed Looey, the lick I give him. The worst part of that was that, after the show, when we got back to camp and the hosses was picketed out fur the night, I had to tell Looey all about how I felt fur an explanation of why I hit him.

"One of the things we have every night in the show is an Injun dance"

Which it made Looey right low in his sperrits, and he shakes his head and says no good will come of it.

"Did you ever hear of Romeo and Joliet?" he says:

"Mebby," I says, "but what it was I hearn I can't remember. What about them?"

"Well," he says, "they carried on the same as you. And now where are they?"

"Well," I says, "where are they?"

"In the tomb," says Looey, very sad, like they was closte personal friends of his'n. And he told me all about them and how Young Cobalt had done fur them. But from what I could make out it all happened away back in the early days. And shucks!—I didn't care a dern, anyhow. I told him so.

"Well," he says, "It's been the history of the world that it brings trouble." And he says to look at Damon and Pythias, and Othello and the Merchant of Venus. And he named about a hundred prominent couples like that out of Shakespeare's works.

"But it ends happy sometimes," I says.

"Not when it is true love it don't," says Looey. "Look at Anthony and Cleopatra."

"Yes," I says, sarcastic like, "I suppose they are in the tomb, too?"

"They are," says Looey, awful solemn.

"Yes," I says, "and so is Adam and Eve and Dan and Burrsheba and all the rest of them old-timers. But I bet they had a good time while they lasted."

Looey shakes his head solemn and sighs and goes to sleep very mournful, like he has to give me up fur lost. But I can't sleep none myself. So purty soon I gets up and puts on my shoes and sneaks through the wood-lot and through the gap in the fence by the apple tree and into Miss Hampton's yard.

It was a beauty of a moonlight night, that white and clear and clean you could almost see to read by it, like all of everything had been scoured as bright as the bottom of a tin pan. And the shadders was soft and thick and velvety and laid kind of brownish-greeney on the grass. I flopped down in the shadder of some lilac bushes and wondered which was Martha's window. I knowed she would be in bed long ago, but—— Well, I was jest plumb foolish that night, and I couldn't of kept away fur any money. That moonlight had got into my head, it seemed like, and made me drunk. But I would rather be looney that-a-way than to have as much sense as King Solomon and all his adverbs. I was that looney that if I had knowed any poetry I would of said it out loud, right up toward that window. I never knowed why poetry was made up before that night. But the only poetry I could think of was about there was a man named Furgeson that lived on Market Street, and he had a one-eyed Thomas cat that couldn't well be beat. Which it didn't seem to fit the case, so I didn't say her.

The porch of that house was part covered with vines, but they was kind of gaped apart at one corner. As I laid there in the shadder of the bushes I hearn a fluttering movement, light and gentle, on that porch. Then, all of a sudden, I seen some one standing on the edge of the porch where the vines was gaped apart, and the moonlight was falling onto them. They must of come there awful soft and still. Whoever it was couldn't see into the shadder where I laid, that is, if it was a human and not a ghost. Fur my first thought was it might be one of them ghosts I had been running down so that very day, and mebby the same one Miss Hampton seen on that very same porch. I thought I was in fur it then, mebby, and I felt like some one had whispered to the back of my neck it ought to be scared. And I *was* scared clean up into my hair. I stared hard, fur I couldn't take my eyes away. Then purty soon I seen if it was a ghost it must be a woman ghost. Fur it was dressed in light-coloured clothes that moved jest a little in the breeze, and the clothes was so near the colour of the moonlight they seemed to kind of silver into it. You would of said it had jest floated there, and was waiting fur to float away agin when the breeze blowed a little stronger, or the moon drawed it.

It didn't move fur ever so long. Then it leaned forward through the gap in the vines, and I seen the face real plain. It wasn't no ghost, it was a lady. Then I knowed it must be Miss Hampton standing there. Away off through the trees our camp fire sent up jest a dull kind of a glow. She was standing there looking at that. I wondered why.

CHAPTER VIII

The next day we broke camp and was gone from that place, and I took away with me the half of a ring me and Martha had chopped in two. We kept on going, and by the time punkins and county fairs was getting ripe we was into the upper left-hand corner of Ohio. And there Looey left us.

One day Doctor Kirby and me was walking along the main street of a little town and we seen a bang-up funeral percession coming. It must of been one of the Grand Army of the Republicans, fur they was some of the old soldiers in buggies riding along behind, and a big string of people follering in more buggies and some on foot. Everybody was looking mighty sollum. But they was one man setting beside the undertaker on the seat of the hearse that was looking sollumer than them all. It was Looey, and I'll bet the corpse himself would of felt proud and happy and contented if he could of knowed the style Looey was giving that funeral.

It wasn't nothing Looey done, fur he didn't do nothing but jest set there with his arms folded onto his bosom and look sad. But he done *that* better than any one else. He done it so well that you forgot the corpse was the chief party to that funeral. Looey took all the glory from him. He had jest natcherally stole that funeral away from its rightful owner with his enjoyment of it. He seen the doctor and me as the hearse went by our corner, but he never let on. A couple of hours later Looey comes into camp and says he is going to quit.

The doctor asts him if he has inherited money.

"No," says Looey, "but my aunt has given me a chancet to go into business."

Looey says he was born nigh there, and was prowling around town the day before and run acrost an old aunt of his'n he had forgot all about. She is awful respectable and religious and ashamed of him being into a travelling show. And she has offered to lend him enough to buy a half-share in a business.

"Well," says the doctor, "I hope it will be something you are fitted for and will enjoy. But I've noticed that after a man gets the habit of roaming around this terrestial ball it's mighty hard to settle down and watch his vine and fig tree grow."

Looey smiles in a sad sort of a way, which he seldom smiled fur anything, and says he guesses he'll like the business. He says they ain't many businesses he could take to. Most of them makes you forget this world is but a fleeting show. But he has found a business which keeps you reminded all the time that dust is dust and ash to ashes shalt return. When he first went into the medicine business, he said, he was drawed to it by the diseases and the sudden dyings-off it always kept him in mind of. He thought they wasn't no other business could lay over it fur that kind of comfort. But he has found out his mistake.

"What kind of business are you going into?" asts the doctor.

"I am going to be an undertaker," says Looey. "My aunt says this town needs the right kind of an undertaker bad."

Mr. Wilcox, the undertaker that town has, is getting purty old and shaky, Looey says, and young Mr. Wilcox, his son, is too light-minded and goes at things too brisk and airy to give it the right kind of a send-off. People don't want him joking around their corpses and he is a fat young man and can't help making puns even in the presence of the departed. Old Mr. Wilcox's eyesight is getting so poor he made a scandal in that town only the week before. He was composing a departed's face into a last smile, but he went too fur with it, and give the departed one of them awful mean, devilish kind of grins, like he had died with a bad temper on. By the time the departed's fambly had found it out, things had went too fur, and the face had set that-a-way, so it wasn't safe to try to change it any.

Old Mr. Wilcox had several brands of last looks. One was called: "Bear Up, for We Will Meet Again." The one that had went wrong was his favourite look, named: "O Death, Where is Thy Victory?"

Looey's aunt says she will buy him a partnership if she is satisfied he can fill the town's needs. They have a talk with the Wilcoxes, and he rides on the hearse that day fur a try-out. His aunt peeks out behind her bedroom curtains as the percession goes by her house, and when she sees the style Looey is giving to that funeral, and how easy it comes to him, that settles it with her on the spot. And it seems the hull dern town liked it, too, including the departed's fambly.

Looey says they is a lot of chancet fur improvements in the undertaking game by one whose heart is in his work, and he is going into that business to make a success of it, and try and get all the funeral trade fur miles around. He reads us an advertisement of the new firm he has been figgering out fur that town's weekly paper. I cut a copy out when it was printed, and it is about the genteelest thing like that I even seen, as follers:

WILCOX AND SIMMS Invite Your Patronage

This earth is but a fleeting show, and the blank-winged angels wait for all. It is always a satisfaction to remember that all possible has been done for the deceased.

```
See Our New Line of Coffins
   Lined Caskets a Specialty
   Lodge Work Solicited
```

Time and tide wait for no man, and his days are few and full of troubles. The paths of glory lead but to the grave, and none can tell when mortal feet may stumble.

When in Town Drop in and Inspect Our New Embalming Outfit. It is a Pleasure to Show Goods and Tools Even if Your Family Needs no Work Done Just Yet.

Outfits for mourners who have been bereaved on short notice a specialty. We take orders for tombstones. Look at our line of shrouds, robes, and black suits for either sex and any age. Give us just one call, and you will entrust future embalmings and obsequies in your family to no other firm.

WILCOX AND SIMMS Main Street, Near Depot

The doctor, he reads it over careful and says she orter drum up trade, all right. Looey tells us that mebby, if he can get that town educated up to it, he will put in a creamatory, where he will burn them, too, but will go slow, fur that there sollum and beautiful way of returning ash to ashes might make some prejudice in such a religious town.

The last we seen of Looey was a couple of days later when we told him good-bye in his shop. Old Mr. Wilcox was explaining to him the science of them last looks he was so famous at when he was a younger man. Young Mr. Wilcox was laying on a table fur Looey to practise on, and Looey was learning fast. But he nearly broke down when he said good-bye, fur he liked the doctor.

"Doc," he says, "you've been a good friend, and I won't never forget you. They ain't much I can do, and in this deceitful world words is less than actions. But if you ever was to die within a hundred miles of me, I'd go," he says, "and no other hands but mine should lay you out. And it wouldn't cost you a cent, either. Nor you neither, Danny."

We thanked him kindly fur the offer, and went.

The next town we come to there was a county fair, and the doctor run acrost an old pal of his'n who had a show on the grounds and wanted to hire him fur what he called a ballyhoo man. Which was the first I ever hearn them called that, but I got better acquainted with them since. They are the fellers that stands out in front and gets you all excited about the Siamese twins or the bearded lady or the snake-charmer or the Circassian beauties or whatever it is inside the tent, as represented upon the canvas. The doctor says he will do it fur a week, jest fur fun, and mebby pick up another feller to take Looey's place out there.

This feller's name is Watty Sanders, and his wife is a fat lady in his own show and very good-natured when not intoxicated nor mad at Watty. She was billed on the curtains outside fur five hundred and fifty pounds, and Watty says she really does weigh nigh on to four hundred. But being a fat lady's husband ain't no bed of rosy ease at that, Watty tells the doctor. It's like every other trade—it has its own pertic'ler responsibilities and troubles. She is a turrible expense to Watty on account of eating so much. The tales that feller told of how hard he has to hustle showing her off in order to support her appetite would of drawed tears from a pawnbroker's sign, as Doctor Kirby says. Which he found it cheaper fur his hull show to board and sleep in the tent, and we done likewise.

Well, I got a job with that show myself. Watty had a wild man canvas but no wild man, so he made me an offer and I took him up. I was from Borneo, where they're all supposed to be captured. Jest as Doctor Kirby would get to his talk about how the wild man had been ketched after great struggle and expense, with four men killed and another crippled, there would be an awful rumpus on the inside of the tent, with wild howlings and the sound of revolvers shot off and a woman screaming. Then I would come busting out all blacked up from head to heel with no more clothes on than the law pervided fur, yipping loud and shaking a big spear and rolling my eyes, and Watty would come rushing after me firing his revolver. I would make fur the doctor and draw my spear back to jab it clean through him, and Watty would grab my arm. And the doctor would whirl round and they would wrastle me to the ground and I would be handcuffed and dragged back into the tent, still howling and struggling to break loose. On the inside my part of the show was to be wild in a cage. I would be chained to the floor, and every now and then I would get wilder and rattle my chains and shake the bars and make jumps at the crowd and carry on, and make believe I was too mad to eat the pieces of raw meat Watty throwed into the cage.

Watty had a snake-charmer woman, with an awful long, bony kind of neck, working fur him, and another feller that was her husband and eat glass. The show opened up with them two doing what they said was a comic turn. Then the fat lady come on. Whilst everybody was admiring her size, and looking at the number of pounds on them big cheat scales Watty weighed her on, the long-necked one would be changing to her snake clothes. Which she only had one snake, and he had been in the business so long, and was so kind of worn out and tired with being charmed so much, it always seemed like a pity to me the way she would take and twist him around. I guess they never was a snake was worked harder fur the little bit he got to eat, nor got no sicker of a woman's society than poor old Reginald did. After Reginald had been charmed a while, it would be the glass eater's turn. Which he really eat it, and the doctor says that kind always dies before they is fifty. I never knowed his right name, but what he went by was The Human Ostrich.

Watty's wife was awful jealous of Mrs. Ostrich, fur she got the idea she was carrying on with Watty. One night I hearn an argument from the fenced-off part of the tent Watty and his wife slept in. She was setting on Watty's chest and he was gasping fur mercy.

"You know it ain't true," says Watty, kind of smothered-like.

"It is," says she, "you own up it is!" And she give him a jounce.

"No, darling," he gets out of him, "you know I never could bear them thin, scrawny kind of women." And he begins to call her pet names of all kinds and beg her please, if she won't get off complete, to set somewheres else a minute, fur his chest he can feel giving way, and his ribs caving in. He called her his plump little woman three or four times and she must of softened up some, fur she moved and his voice come stronger, but not less meek and lowly. And he follers it up:

"Dolly, darling," he says, "I bet I know something my little woman don't know."

"What is it?" the fat lady asts him.

"'You don't know what a cruel, weak stomach your hubby has got . . . . or you wouldn't bear down quite so hard onto it—please, Dolly!'"

"You don't know what a cruel, weak stomach your hubby has got," Watty says, awful coaxing like, "or you wouldn't bear down quite so hard onto it— please, Dolly!"

She begins to blubber and say he is making fun of her big size, and if he is mean to her any more or ever looks at another woman agin she will take anti-fat and fade away to nothing and ruin his show, and it is awful hard to be made a joke of all her life and not have no steady home nor nothing like other women does.

"You know I worship every pound of you, little woman," says Watty, still coaxing. "Why can't you trust me? You know, Dolly, darling, I wouldn't take your weight in gold for you." And he tells her they never was but once in all his life he has so much as turned his head to look at another woman, and that was by way of a plutonic admiration, and no flirting intended, he says. And even then it was before he had met his own little woman. And that other woman, he says, was plump too, fur he wouldn't never look at none but a plump woman.

"What did she weigh?" asts Watty's wife. He tells her a measly little three hundred pound.

"But she wasn't refined like my little woman," says Watty, "and when I seen that I passed her up." And inch by inch Watty coaxed her clean off of him.

But the next day she hearn him and Mrs. Ostrich giggling about something, and she has a reg'lar tantrum, and jest fur meanness goes out and falls down on the race track, pertending she has fainted, and they can't move her no ways, not even roll her. But finally they rousted her out of that by one of these here sprinkling carts backing up agin her and turning loose.

But aside from them occasional mean streaks Dolly was real nice, and I kind of got to liking her. She tells me that because she is so fat no one won't take her serious like a human being, and she wisht she was like other women and had a fambly. That woman wanted a baby, too, and I bet she would of been good to it, fur she was awful good to animals. She had been big from a little girl, and never got no sympathy when sick, nor nothing, and even whilst she played with dolls as a kid she knowed she looked ridiculous, and was laughed at. And by jings!—they was the funniest thing come to light before we left that crowd. That poor, derned, old, fat fool *had* a doll yet, all hid away, and when she was alone she used to take it out and cuddle it. Well, Dolly never had many friends, and you couldn't blame her much if she did drink a little too much now and then, or get mad at Watty fur his goings-on and kneel down on him whilst he was asleep. Them was her only faults and I liked the old girl. Yet I could see Watty had his troubles too.

That show busted up before the fair closed. Fur one day Watty's wife gets mad at Mrs. Ostrich and tries to set on her. And then Mrs. Ostrich gets mad too, and sicks Reginald onto her. Watty's wife is awful scared of Reginald, who don't really have ambition enough to bite no one, let alone a lady built so round everywhere he couldn't of got a grip on her. And as fur as wrapping himself around her and squashing her to death, Reginald never seen the day he could reach that fur. Reginald's feelings is plumb friendly toward Dolly when he is turned loose, but she don't know that, and she has some hysterics and faints in earnest this time. Well, they was an awful hullaballo when she come to, and fur the sake of peace in the fambly Watty has to fire Mr. and Mrs. Ostrich and poor old Reginald out of their jobs, and the show is busted. So Doctor Kirby and me lit out fur other parts agin.

CHAPTER IX

W e was jogging along one afternoon not fur from a good-sized town at the top of Ohio, right on the lake, when we run acrost some remainders of a busted circus riding in a stake and chain wagon. They was two fellers—both jugglers, acrobats, and tumblers—and a balloon. The circus had busted without paying them nothing but promises fur months and months, and they had took the team and wagon and balloon by attachment, they said. They was carting her from the little burg the show busted in to that good-sized town on the lake. They would sell the team and wagon there and get money enough to put an advertisement in the Billboard, which is like a Bible to them showmen, that they had a balloon to sell and was at liberty.

One of them was the slimmest, lightest-footed, quickest feller you ever seen, with a big nose and dark complected, and his name was Tobias. The other was heavier and blonde complected. His name was Dobbs, he said, and they was the Blanchet Brothers. Doctor Kirby and them got real well acquainted in about three minutes. We drove on ahead and got into the town first.

The doctor says that balloon is jest wasted on them fellers. They can't go up in her, not knowing that trade, but still they ought to be some way fur them to make a little stake out of it before it was sold.

The next evening we run acrost them fellers on the street, and they was feeling purty blue. They hadn't been able to sell that team and wagon, which it was eating its meals reg'lar in a livery stable, and they had been doing stunts in the street that day and passing around the hat, but not getting enough fur to pay expenses.

"Where's the balloon?" asts the doctor. And I seen he was sicking his intellects onto the job of making her pay.

"In the livery stable with the wagon," they tells him.

He says he is going to figger out a way to help them boys. They is like all circus performers, he says—they jest knows their own acts, and talks about 'em all the time, and studies up ways to make 'em better, and has got no more idea of business outside of that than a rabbit. We all went to the livery stable and overhauled that balloon. It was an awful job, too. But they wasn't a rip in her, and the parachute was jest as good as new.

"There's no reason why we can't give a show of our own," says Doctor Kirby, "with you boys and Danny and me and that balloon. What we want is a lot with a high board fence around it, like a baseball grounds, and the chance to tap a gas main." He says he'll be willing to take a chancet on it, even paying the gas company real money to fill her up.

What the Doctor didn't know about starting shows wasn't worth knowing. He had even went in for the real drama in his younger days now and then.

"One of my theatrical productions came very near succeeding, too," he says.

It was a play he says, in which the hero falls in love with a pair of Siamese twins and commits suicide because he can't make a choice between them.

"We played it as comedy in the big towns and tragedy in the little ones," he says. "But like a fool I booked it for two weeks of middle-sized towns and it broke us."

The next day he finds a lot that will do jest fine. It has been used fur a school playgrounds, but the school has been moved and the old building is to be tore down. He hired the place cheap. And he goes and talks the gas company into giving him credit to fill that balloon. Which I kept wondering what was the use of filling her, fur none of the four of us had ever went up in one. And when I seen the handbills he had had printed I wondered all the more. They read as follers:

Kirby's Komedy Kompany and Open Air Circus

Presenting a Peerless Personnel of Artistic Attractions

Greatest in the Galaxy of Gaiety, is

Hartley L. Kirby

Monologuist and minstrel, dancer and vaudevillian in his terpsichorean travesties, buoyant burlesques, inimitable imitations, screaming impersonations, refined comedy sketches and popular song hits of the day.

The Blanchet Brothers

Daring, Dazzling, Danger-Loving, Death-Defying Demons

Joyous jugglers, acrobatic artists, constrictorial contortionists, exquisite equilibrists, in their marvellous, mysterious, unparalleled performances.

Umslopogus The Patagonian Chieftain

The lowest type of human intellect

This formerly ferocious fiend has so far succumbed to the softer wiles of civilization that he is no longer a cannibal, and it is now safe to put him on exhibition. But to prevent accidents he is heavily manacled, and the public is warned not to come too near.

```
Balloon! Balloon!! Balloon!!!

    The management also presents the balloon of

    Prof. Alonzo Ackerman The Famous Aeronaut

    in which he has made his

    Wonderful Ascension and Parachute Drop

    many times, reaching remarkable altitudes

    Balloon! Balloon!! Balloon!!!

    Saturday, 3 P. M. Old Vandegrift School Lot
Admission 50 Cents
```

Well, fur a writer he certainly laid over Looey, Doctor Kirby did—more cheerful-like, you might say. I seen right off I was to be the Patagonian Chieftain. I was getting more and more of an actor right along—first an Injun, then a wild Borneo, and now a Patagonian.

"But who is this Alonzo Ackerman?" I asts him.

"Celebrated balloonist," says he, "and the man that invented parachutes. They eat out of his hand."

"Where is he?" asts I.

"How should I know?" he says.

"How is he going up, then?" I asts.

The doctor chuckles and says it is a good bill, a better bill than he thought; that it is getting in its work already. He says to me to read it careful and see if it says Alonzo Ackerman is going up. Well, it don't. But any one would of thought so the first look. I reckon that bill was some of a liar herself, not lying outright, but jest hinting a lie. They is a lot of mean, stingy-souled kind of people wouldn't never lie to help a friend, but Doctor Kirby wasn't one of 'em.

"But," I says, "when that crowd finds out Alonzo ain't going up they will be purty mad."

"Oh," says he, "I don't think so. The American public are a good-natured set of chuckle-heads, mostly. If they get sore I'll talk 'em out of it."

If he had any faults at all—and mind you, I ain't saying Doctor Kirby had any—the one he had hardest was the belief he could talk any crowd into any notion, or out of it, either. And he loved to do it jest fur the fun of it. He'd rather have the feeling he was doing that than the money any day. He was powerful vain about that gab of his'n, Doctor Kirby was.

The four of us took around about five thousand bills. The doctor says they is nothing like giving yourself a chancet. And Saturday morning we got the balloon filled up so she showed handsome, tugging away there at her ropes. But we had a dern mean time with that balloon, too.

The doctor says if we have good luck there may be as many as three, four hundred people.

But Jerusalem! They was two, three times that many. By the time the show started I reckon they was nigh a thousand there. The doctor and the Blanchet Brothers was tickled. When they quit coming fast the doctor left the gate and made a little speech, telling all about the wonderful show, and the great expense it was to get it together, and all that.

They was a rope stretched between the crowd and us. Back of that was the Blanchet Brothers' wagon and our wagon, and our little tent. I was jest inside the tent with chains on. Back of everything else was the balloon.

Well, the doctor he done a lot of songs and things as advertised. Then the Blanchet Brothers done some of their acts. They was really fine acts, too. Then come some more of Doctor Kirby's refined comedy, as advertised. Next, more Blanchet. Then a lecture about me by the doctor. All in all it takes up about an hour and a half. Then the doctor makes a mighty nice little talk, and wishes them all good afternoon, thanking them fur their kind intentions and liberal patronage, one and all.

"But when will the balloon go up?" asts half a dozen at oncet.

"The balloon?" asts Doctor Kirby, surprised.

"Balloon! Balloon!" yells a kid. And the hull crowd took it up and yelled: "Balloon! Balloon! Balloon!" And they crowded up closte to that rope.

Doctor Kirby has been getting off the wagon, but he gets back on her, and stretches his arms wide, and motions of 'em all to come close.

"Ladies and gentlemen," he says, "please to gather near—up here, good people—and listen! Listen to what I have to say—harken to the utterings of my voice! There has been a misunderstanding here! There has been a misconstruction! There has been, ladies and gentlemen, a woeful lack of comprehension here!"

It looked to me like they was beginning to understand more than he meant them to. I was wondering how it would all come out, but he never lost his nerve.

"Listen," he says, very earnest, "listen to me. Somehow the idea seems to have gone forth that there would be a balloon ascension here this afternoon. How, I do not know, for what we advertised, ladies and gentlemen, was that the balloon used by Prof. Alonzo Ackerman, the illustrious aeronaut, would be *UPON EXHIBITION*. And there she is, ladies and gentlemen, there she is, for every eye to see and gladden with the sight of—right before you, ladies and gentlemen—the balloon of Alonzo Ackerman, the wonderful voyager of the air, exactly as represented. During their long career Kirby and Company have never deceived the public. Others may, but Kirby and Company are like Caesar's wife—Kirby and Company are above suspicion. It is the province of Kirby's Komedy Kompany, ladies and gentlemen, to spread the glad tidings of innocent amusement throughout the length and breadth of this fair land of ours. And there she is before you, the balloon as advertised, the gallant ship of the air in which the illustrious Ackerman made so many voyages before he sailed at last into the Great Beyond! You can see her, ladies and gentlemen, straining at her cords, anxious to mount into the heavens and be gone! It is an education in itself, ladies and gentlemen, a moral education, and well worth coming miles to see. Think of it—think of it—the Ackerman balloon—and then think that the illustrious Ackerman himself—he was my personal friend, ladies and gentlemen, and a true friend sticketh closer than a brother—the illustrious Ackerman is dead. The balloon, ladies and gentlemen, is there, but Ackerman is gone to his reward. Look at that balloon, ladies and gentlemen, and tell me if you can, why should the spirit of mortals be proud? For the man that rode her like a master and tamed her like she was a dove lies cold and dead in a western graveyard, ladies and gentlemen, and she is here, a useless and an idle vanity without the mind that made her go!"

Well, he went on and he told a funny story about Alonzo, which I don't believe they ever was no Alonzo Ackerman, and a lot of 'em laughed; and he told a pitiful story, and they got sollum agin, and then another funny story. Well, he had 'em listening, and purty soon most of the crowd is feeling in a good humour toward him, and one feller yells out:

"Go it—you're a hull show yourself!" And some joshes him, but they don't seem to be no trouble in the air. When they all look to be in a good humour he holds up a bill and asts how many has them. Many has. He says that is well, and then he starts to telling another story. But in the middle of the story that hull dern crowd is took with a fit of laughing. They has looked at the bill closet, and seen they is sold, and is taking it good-natured. And still shouting and laughing most of them begins to start along off. And I thought all chancet of trouble was over with. But it wasn't.

Fur they is always a natcheral born kicker everywhere, and they was one here, too.

He was a lean feller with a sticking out jaw, and one of his eyes was in a kind of a black pocket, and he was jest natcherally laying it off to about a dozen fellers that was in a little knot around him.

The doctor sees the main part of the crowd going and climbs down off'n the wagon. As he does so that hull bunch of about a dozen moves in under the rope, and some more that was going out seen it, and stopped and come back.

"Perfessor," says the man with the patch over his eye to Doctor Kirby, "you say this man Ackerman is dead?"

"Yes," says the doctor, eying him over, "he's dead."

"How did he die?" asts the feller.

"He died hard, I understand," says the doctor, careless-like.

"Fell out of his balloon?"

"Yes."

"This aeronaut trade is a dangerous trade, I hear," says the feller with the patch on his eye.

"They say so," says Doctor Kirby, easy-like.

"Was you ever an aeronaut yourself?" asts the feller.

"No," says the doctor.

"Never been up in a balloon?"

"No."

"Well, you're going up in one this afternoon!"

"What do you mean?" asts Doctor Kirby.

"We've come out to see a balloon ascension—and we're going to see it, too."

And with that the hull crowd made a rush at the doctor.

Well, I been in fights before that, and I been in fights since then. But I never been in no harder one. The doctor and the two Blanchet brothers and me managed to get backed up agin the fence in a row when the rush come. I guess I done my share, and I guess the Blanchet brothers done theirn, too. But they was too many of 'em for us—too dern many. It wouldn't of ended as quick as it did if Doctor Kirby hadn't gone clean crazy. His back was to the fence, and he cleaned out everything in front of him, and then he give a wild roar jest like a bull and rushed that hull gang—twenty men, they was—with his head down. He caught two fellers, one in each hand, and he cracked their heads together, and he caught two more, and done the same. But he orter never took his back away from that fence. The hull gang closed in on him, and down he went at the bottom of a pile. I was awful busy myself, but I seen that pile moving and churning. Then I made a big mistake myself. I kicked a feller in the stomach, and another feller caught my leg, and down I went. Fur a half a minute I never knowed nothing. And when I come to I was all mashed about the face, and two fellers was sitting on me.

The crowd was tying Doctor Kirby to that parachute. They straddled legs over the parachute bar, and tied his feet below it. He was still fighting, but they was too many fur him. They left his arms untied, but they held 'em, and then—

Then they cut her loose. She went up like she was shot from a gun, and as she did Doctor Kirby took a grip on a feller's arm that hadn't let loose quick enough and lifted him plumb off'n the ground. He slewed around on the trapeze bar with the feller's weight, and slipped head downward. And as he slipped he give that feller a swing and let loose of him, and then ketched himself by the crook of one knee. The feller turned over twicet in the air and landed in a little crumpled-up pile on the ground, and never made a sound.

The fellers that had holt of me forgot me and stood up, and I stood up too, and looked. The balloon was rising fast. Doctor Kirby was trying to pull himself up to the trapeze bar, twisting and squirming and having a hard time of it, and shooting higher every second. I reckoned he couldn't fall complete, fur where his feet was tied would likely hold even if his knee come straight— but he would die mebby with his head filling up with blood. But finally he made a squirm and raised himself a lot and grabbed the rope at one side of the bar. And then he reached and got the rope on the other side, and set straddle of her. And jest as he done that the wind ketched the balloon good and hard, and she turned out toward Lake Erie. It was too late fur him to pull the rope that sets the parachute loose then, and drop onto the land.

I rushed out of that schoolhouse yard and down the street toward the lake front, and run, stumbling along and looking up. She was getting smaller every minute. And with my head in the air looking up I was running plumb to the edge of the water before I knowed it.

She was away out over the lake now, and awful high, and going fast before the wind, and the doctor was only a speck. And as I stared at that speck away up in the sky I thought this was a mean world to live in. Fur there was the only real friend I ever had, and no way fur me to help him. He had learnt me to read, and bought me good clothes, and made me know they was things in the world worth travelling around to see, and made me feel like I was something more than jest Old Hank Walters's dog. And I guessed he would be

73

drownded and I would never see him agin now. And all of a sudden something busted loose inside of me, and I sunk down there at the edge of the water, sick at my stomach, and weak and shivering.

CHAPTER X

I didn't exactly faint there, but things got all mixed fur me, and when they was straightened out agin I was in a hospital. It seems I had been considerable stepped on in that fight, and three ribs was broke. I knowed I was hurting, but I was so interested in what was happening to the doctor the hull hurt never come to me till the balloon was way out over the lake.

But now I was in a plaster cast, and before I got out of that I was in a fever. I was some weeks getting out of there.

I tried to get some word of Doctor Kirby, but couldn't. Nothing had been heard of him or the balloon. The newspapers had had stuff about it fur a day or two, and they guessed the body might come to light sometime. But that was all. And I didn't know where to hunt nor how.

The hosses and wagon and tent and things worried me some, too. They wasn't mine, and so I couldn't sell 'em. And they wasn't no good to me without Doctor Kirby. So I tells the man that owns the livery stable to use the team fur its board and keep it till Doctor Kirby calls fur it, and if he never does mebby I will sometime.

I didn't want to stay in that town or I could of got a job in the livery stable. They offered me one, but I hated that town. I wanted to light out. I didn't much care where to.

Them Blanchet Brothers had left a good share of the money we took in at the balloon ascension with the hospital people fur me before they cleared out. But before I left that there town I seen they was one thing I had to do to make myself easy in my mind. So I done her.

That was to hunt up that feller with his eye in the patch. It took me a week to find him. He lived down near some railroad yards. I might of soaked him with a coupling link and felt a hull lot better. But I didn't guess it would do to pet and pamper my feelings too much. So I does it with my fists in a quiet place, and does it very complete, and leaves that town in a cattle car, feeling a hull lot more contented in my mind.

Then they was a hull dern year I didn't stay nowhere very long, nor work at any one job too long, neither. I jest worked from place to place seeing things —big towns and rivers and mountains. Working here and there, and loafing and riding blind baggages and freight trains between jobs, I covered a lot of ground that year, and made some purty big jumps, and got acquainted with some awful queer folks, first and last.

75

But the worst of that is lots of people gets to thinking I am a hobo. Even one or two judges in police courts I got acquainted with had that there idea of me. I always explains that I am not one, and am jest travelling around to see things, and working when I feels like it, and ain't no bum. But frequent I am not believed. And two, three different times I gets to the place where I couldn't hardly of told myself from a hobo, if I hadn't of knowed I wasn't one.

I got right well acquainted with some of them hobos, too. As fur as I can see, they is as much difference in them as in other humans. Some travels because they likes to see things, and some because they hates to work, and some because they is in the habit and can't stop it. Well, I know myself it's purty hard after while to stop it, fur where would you stop at? What excuse is they to stop one place more'n another? I met all kinds of 'em, and oncet I got in fur a week with a couple of real Johnny Yeggs that is both in the pen now. I hearn a feller say one time there is some good in every man. I went the same way as them two yeggmen a hull dern week to try and find out where the good in 'em was. I guess they must be some mistake somewheres, fur I looked hard and I watched closet and I never found it. They is many kinds of hobos and tramps, perfessional and amachure, and lots of kinds of bums, and lots of young fellers working their way around to see things, like I was, and lots of working men in hard luck going from place to place, and all them kinds is humans. But the real yeggman ain't even a dog.

And oncet I went all the way from Chicago to Baltimore with a serious, dern fool that said he was a soshyologest, whatever them is, and was going to put her all into a book about the criminal classes. He worked hard trying to get at the reason I was a hobo. Which they wasn't no reason, fur I wasn't no hobo. But I didn't want to disappoint that feller and spoil his book fur him. So I tells him things. Things not overly truthful, but very full of crime. About a year afterward I was into one of these here Andrew Carnegie lib'aries with the names of the old-time presidents all chiselled along the top and I seen the hull dern thing in print. He said of me the same thing I have said about them yeggmen. If all he met joshed that feller the same as me, that book must of been what you might call misleading in spots.

One morning I woke up in a good-sized town in Illinoise, not a hundred miles from where I was raised, without no money, and my clothes not much to look at, and no job. I had been with a railroad show fur about two weeks, driving stakes and other rough work, and it had went off and left me sleeping on the ground. Circuses never waits fur nothing nor cares a dern fur no one. I tried all day around town fur to get some kind of a job. But I was looking purty rough and I couldn't land nothing. Along in the afternoon I was awful hungry.

I was feeling purty low down to have to ast fur a meal, but finally I done it.

I dunno how I ever come to pick out such a swell-looking house, but I makes a little talk at the back door and the Irish girl she says, "Come in," and into the kitchen I goes.

"It's Minnesota you're working toward?" asts she, pouring me out a cup of coffee.

She is thinking of the wheat harvest where they is thousands makes fur every fall. But none of 'em fur me. That there country is full of them Scandiluvian Swedes and Norwegians, and they gets into the field before daylight and stays there so long the hired man's got to milk the cows by moonlight.

"I been acrost the river into I'way," I says, "a-working at my trade, and now I'm going back to Chicago to work at it some more."

"What might your trade be?" she asts, sizing me up careful; and I thinks I'll hand her one to chew on she ain't never hearn tell of before.

"I'm a agnostic by trade," I says. I spotted that there word in a religious book one time, and that's the first chancet I ever has to try it on any one. You can't never tell what them reg'lar sockdologers is going to do till you tries them.

"I see," says she. But I seen she didn't see. And I didn't help her none. She would of ruther died than to let on she didn't see. The Irish is like that. Purty soon she says:

"Ain't that the dangerous kind o' work, though!"

"It is," I says. And says nothing further.

She sets down and folds her arms, like she was thinking of it, watching my hands closet all the time I was eating, like she's looking fur scars where something slipped when I done that agnostic work. Purty soon she says:

"Me brother Michael was kilt at it in the old country. He was the most vinturesome lad of thim all!"

"Did it fly up and hit him?" I asts her. I was wondering w'ether she is making fun of me or am I making fun of her. Them Irish is like that, you can never tell which.

"No," says she, "he fell off of it. And I'm thinking you don't know what it is yourself." And the next thing I know I'm eased out o' the back door and she's grinning at me scornful through the crack of it.

So I was walking slow around toward the front of the house thinking how the Irish was a great nation, and what shall I do now, anyhow? And I says to myself: "Danny, you was a fool to let that circus walk off and leave you asleep in this here town with nothing over you but a barbed wire fence this morning. Fur what *are* you going to do next? First thing you know, you *will* be a reg'lar tramp, which some folks can't be made to see you ain't now." And jest when I was thinking that, a feller comes down the front steps of that house on the jump and nabs me by the coat collar.

"Did you come out of this house?" he asts.

"I did," I says, wondering what next.

"Back in you go, then," he says, marching me forward toward them front steps, "they've got smallpox in there."

I like to of jumped loose when he says that.

"Smallpox ain't no inducement to me, mister," I tells him. But he twisted my coat collar tight and dug his thumbs into my neck, all the time helping me onward with his knee from behind, and I seen they wasn't no use pulling back. I could probable of licked that man, but they's no system in mixing up with them well-dressed men in towns where they think you are a tramp. The judge will give you the worst of it.

He rung the door bell and the girl that opened the door she looked kind o' surprised when she seen me, and in we went.

"Tell Professor Booth that Doctor Wilkins wants to see him again," says the man a-holt o' me, not letting loose none. And we says nothing further till the perfessor comes, which he does, slow and absent-minded. When he seen me he took off his glasses so's he could see me better, and he says:

"What is that you have there, Doctor Wilkins?"

"A guest for you," says Doctor Wilkins, grinning all over hisself. "I found him leaving your house. And you being under quarantine, and me being secretary to the board of health, and the city pest-house being crowded too full already, I'll have to ask you to keep him here till we get Miss Margery onto her feet again," he says. Or they was words to that effect, as the lawyers asts you.

"Dear me," says Perfesser Booth, kind o' helpless like. And he comes over closet to me and looks me all over like I was one of them amphimissourian lizards in a free museum. And then he goes to the foot of the stairs and sings out in a voice that was so bleached-out and flat-chested it would of looked jest like him himself if you could of saw it—"Estelle," he sings out, "oh,

Estelle!"

Estelle, she come down stairs looking like she was the perfessor's big brother. I found out later she was his old maid sister. She wasn't no spring chicken, Estelle wasn't, and they was a continuous grin on her face. I figgered it must of froze there years and years ago. They was a kid about ten or eleven years old come along down with her, that had hair down to its shoulders and didn't look like it knowed whether it was a girl or a boy. Miss Estelle, she looks me over in a way that makes me shiver, while the doctor and the perfessor jaws about whose fault it is the smallpox sign ain't been hung out. And when she was done listening she says to the perfessor: "You had better go back to your laboratory." And the perfessor he went along out, and the doctor with him.

"What are you going to do with him, Aunt Estelle?" the kid asts her.

"What would *you* suggest, William, Dear?" asts his aunt. I ain't feeling very comfortable, and I was getting all ready jest to natcherally bolt out the front door now the doctor was gone. Then I thinks it mightn't be no bad place to stay in fur a couple o' days, even risking the smallpox. Fur I had riccolected I couldn't ketch it nohow, having been vaccinated a few months before in Terry Hutt by compulsive medical advice, me being fur a while doing some work on the city pavements through a mistake about me in the police court.

William Dear looks at me like it was the day of judgment and his job was to keep the fatted calves separate from the goats and prodigals, and he says:

"If I were you, Aunt Estelle, the first thing would be to get his hair cut and his face washed and then get him some clothes."

"William Dear is my friend," thinks I.

JAMES

"Then he buttles me into a suit 'o somebody's clothes and into
a room at the top 'o the house next to his'n, and then he
comes back and buttles a comb and brush at me"

She calls James, which was a butler. James, he buttles me into a bathroom the like o' which I never seen afore, and then he buttles me into a suit o' somebody's clothes and into a room at the top o' the house next to his'n, and then he comes back and buttles a comb and brush at me. James was the most mournful-looking fat man I ever seen, and he says that account of me not being respectable I will have my meals alone in the kitchen after the servants has eat.

The first thing I knowed I been in that house more'n a week. I eat and I slept and I smoked and I kind of enjoyed not worrying about things fur a while. The only oncomfortable thing about being the perfessor's guest was Miss Estelle. Soon's she found out I was a agnostic she took charge o' my intellectuals and what went into 'em, and she makes me read things and asts me about 'em, and she says she is going fur to reform me. And whatever brand o' disgrace them there agnostics really is I ain't found out to this day, having come acrost the word accidental.

Biddy Malone, which was the kitchen mechanic, she says the perfessor's wife's been over to her mother's while this smallpox has been going on, and they is a nurse in the house looking after Miss Margery, the little kid that's sick. And Biddy, she says if she was Mrs. Booth she'd stay there, too. They's been some talk, anyhow, about Mrs. Booth and a musician feller around that there town. But Biddy, she likes Mrs. Booth, and even if it was true, which it ain't Biddy says, who could of blamed her? Fur things ain't joyous around that house the last year, since Miss Estelle's come there to live. The perfessor, he's so full of scientifics he don't know nothing with no sense to it, Biddy says. He's got more money'n you can shake a stick at, and he don't have to do no work, nor never has, and his scientifics gets worse and worse every year. But while scientifics is worrying to the nerves of a fambly, and while his labertory often makes the house smell like a sick drug store has crawled into it and died there, they wouldn't of been no serious row on between the perfessor and his wife, not *all* the time, if it hadn't of been fur Miss Estelle. She has jest natcherally made herself boss of that there house, Biddy says, and she's a she-devil. Between all them scientifics and Miss Estelle things has got where Mrs. Booth can't stand 'em much longer.

I didn't blame her none fur getting sore on her job, neither. You can't expect a woman that's purty, and knows it, and ain't no more'n thirty-two or three, and don't look it, to be serious intrusted in mummies and pickled snakes and chemical perfusions, not *all* the time. Mebby when Mrs. Booth would ast him if he was going to take her to the opery that night the perfessor would look up in an absent-minded sort of way and ast her did she know them Germans had invented a new germ? It wouldn't of been so bad if the perfessor had picked out jest one brand of scientifics and stuck to that reg'lar. Mrs. Booth could of got use to any *one* kind. But mebby this week the perfessor would be took hard with ornithography and he'd go chasing humming-birds all over the front yard, and the next he'd be putting gastronomy into William's breakfast feed.

They was always a row on over them kids, which they hadn't been till Miss Estelle come. Mrs. Booth, she said they could kill their own selves, if they wanted to, him and Miss Estelle, but she had more right than any one else to say what went into William's and Margery's digestive ornaments, and she didn't want 'em brung up scientific nohow, but jest human. But Miss Estelle's got so she runs that hull house now, and the perfessor too, but he don't know it, Biddy says, and her a-saying every now and then it was too bad Frederick couldn't of married a noble woman who would of took a serious intrust in his work. The kids don't hardly dare to kiss their ma in front of Miss Estelle no more, on account of germs and things. And with Miss Estelle taking care of their religious organs and their intellectuals and the things like that, and the perfessor filling them up on new invented feeds, I guess they never was two kids got more education to the square inch, outside and in. It hadn't worked none on Miss Margery yet, her being younger, but William Dear he took it hard and serious, and it made bumps all over his head, and he was kind o' pale and spindly. Every time that kid cut his finger he jest natcherally bled scientifics. One day I says to Miss Estelle, says I:

"It looks to me like William Dear is kind of peaked." She looks worried and she looks mad fur me lipping in, and then she says mebby it is true, but she don't see why, because he is being brung up like he orter be in every way and no expense nor trouble spared.

"Well," says I, "what a kid about that size wants to do is to get out and roll around in the dirt some, and yell and holler."

She sniffs like I wasn't worth taking no notice of. But it kind o' soaked in, too. She and the perfessor must of talked it over. Fur the next day I seen her spreading a oilcloth on the hall floor. And then James comes a buttling in with a lot of sand what the perfessor has baked and made all scientific down in his labertory. James, he pours all that nice, clean dirt onto the oilcloth and then Miss Estelle sends fur William Dear.

"William Dear," she says, "we have decided, your papa and I, that what you need is more romping around and playing along with your studies. You ought to get closer to the soil and to nature, as is more healthy for a youth of your age. So for an hour each day, between your studies, you will romp and play in this sand. You may begin to frolic now, William Dear, and then James will sweep up the dirt again for to-morrow's frolic."

But William didn't frolic none. He jest looked at that dirt in a sad kind o' way, and he says very serious but very decided:

"Aunt Estelle, I shall *not* frolic." And they had to let it go at that, fur he never would frolic none, neither. And all that nice clean dirt was throwed out in the back yard along with the unscientific dirt.

CHAPTER XI

One night when I've been there more'n a week, and am getting kind o' tired staying in one place so long, I don't want to go to bed after I eats, and I gets a-holt of some of the perfessor's cigars and goes into the lib'ary to see if he's got anything fit to read. Setting there thinking of the awful remarkable people they is in this world I must of went to sleep. Purty soon, in my sleep, I hearn two voices. Then I waked up sudden, and still hearn 'em, low and quicklike, in the room that opens right off of the lib'ary with a couple of them sliding doors like is onto a box car. One voice was a woman's voice, and it wasn't Miss Estelle's.

"But I *must* see them before we go, Henry," she says.

And the other was a man's voice and it wasn't no one around our house.

"But, my God," he says, "suppose you get it yourself, Jane!"

I set up straight then, fur Jane was the perfessor's wife's first name.

"You mean suppose *you* get it," she says. I like to of seen the look she must of give him to fit in with the way she says that *you*. He didn't say nothing, the man didn't; and then her voice softens down some, and she says, low and slow: "Henry, wouldn't you love me if I *did* get it? Suppose it marked and pitted me all up?"

"Oh, of course," he says, "of course I would. Nothing can change the way I feel. *You* know that." He said it quick enough, all right, jest the way they does in a show, but it sounded *too much* like it does on the stage to of suited me if *I*'d been her. I seen folks overdo them little talks before this.

I listens some more, and then I sees how it is. This is that musician feller Biddy Malone's been talking about. Jane's going to run off with him all right, but she's got to kiss the kids first. Women is like that. They may hate the kids' pa all right, but they's dad-burned few of 'em don't like the kids. I thinks to myself: "It must be late. I bet they was already started, or ready to start, and she made him bring her here first so's she could sneak in and see the kids. She jest simply couldn't get by. But she's taking a fool risk, too. Fur how's she going to see Margery with that nurse coming and going and hanging around all night? And even if she tries jest to see William Dear it's a ten to one shot he'll wake up and she'll be ketched at it."

And then I thinks, suppose she *is* ketched at it? What of it? Ain't a woman got a right to come into her own house with her own door key, even if they is a quarantine onto it, and see her kids? And if she is ketched seeing them, how would any one know she was going to run off? And ain't she got a right to have a friend of hern and her husband's bring her over from her mother's house, even if it is a little late?

Then I seen she wasn't taking no great risks neither, and I thinks mebby I better go and tell that perfessor what is going on, fur he has treated me purty white. And then I thinks: "I'll be gosh-derned if I meddle. So fur as I can see that there perfessor ain't getting fur from what's coming to him, nohow. And as fur *her*, you got to let some people find out what they want fur theirselves. Anyhow, where do *I* come in at?"

But I want to get a look at her and Henry, anyhow. So I eases off my shoes, careful-like, and I eases acrost the floor to them sliding doors, and I puts my eye down to the little crack. The talk is going backward and forward between them two, him wanting her to come away quick, and her undecided whether to risk seeing the kids. And all the time she's kind o' hoping mebby she will be ketched if she tries to see the kids, and she's begging off fur more time ginerally.

Well, sir, I didn't blame that musician feller none when I seen her. She was a peach.

And I couldn't blame her so much, neither, when I thought of Miss Estelle and all them scientics of the perfessor's strung out fur years and years world without end.

Yet, when I seen the man, I sort o' wished she wouldn't. I seen right off that Henry wouldn't do. It takes a man with a lot of gumption to keep a woman feeling good and not sorry fur doing it when he's married to her. But it takes a man with twicet as much to make her feel right when they ain't married. This feller wears one of them little, brown, pointed beards fur to hide where his chin ain't. And his eyes is too much like a woman's. Which is the kind that gets the biggest piece of pie at the lunch counter and fergits to thank the girl as cuts it big. She was setting in front of a table, twisting her fingers together, and he was walking up and down. I seen he was mad and trying not to show it, and I seen he was scared of the smallpox and trying not to show that, too. And jest about that time something happened that kind o' jolted me.

They was one of them big chairs in the room where they was that has got a high back and spins around on itself. It was right acrost from me, on the other side of the room, and it was facing the front window, which was a bow window. And that there chair begins to turn, slow and easy. First I thought she wasn't turning. Then I seen she was. But Jane and Henry didn't. They was all took up with each other in the middle of the room, with their backs to it.

Henry is a-begging of Jane, and she turns a little more, that chair does. Will she squeak, I wonders?

"Don't you be a fool, Jane," says the Henry feller.

Around she comes three hull inches, that there chair, and nary a squeak.

"A fool?" asts Jane, and laughs. "And I'm not a fool to think of going with you at all, then?"

That chair, she moved six inches more and I seen the calf of a leg and part of a crumpled-up coat tail.

"But I *am* going with you, Henry," says Jane. And she gets up jest like she is going to put her arms around him.

But Jane don't. Fur that chair swings clear around and there sets the perfessor. He's all hunched up and caved in and he's rubbing his eyes like he's jest woke up recent, and he's got a grin onto his face that makes him look like his sister Estelle looks all the time.

"Excuse me," says the perfessor.

They both swings around and faces him. I can hear my heart bumping. Jane never says a word. The man with the brown beard never says a word. But if they felt like me they both felt like laying right down there and having a fit. They looks at him and he jest sets there and grins at them.

But after a while Jane, she says:

"Well, now you *know!* What are you going to do about it?"

Henry, he starts to say something too. But—

"Don't start anything," says the perfessor to him. "*You* aren't going to do anything." Or they was words to that effect.

"Professor Booth," he says, seeing he has got to say something or else Jane will think the worse of him, "I am—"

"Keep still," says the perfessor, real quiet. "I'll tend to you in a minute or two. *You* don't count for much. This thing is mostly between me and my wife."

When he talks so decided I thinks mebby that perfessor has got something into him besides science after all. Jane, she looks kind o' surprised herself. But she says nothing, except:

"What are you going to do, Frederick?" And she laughs one of them mean kind of laughs, and looks at Henry like she wanted him to spunk up a little more, and says: "What *can* you do, Frederick?"

Frederick, he says, not excited a bit:

"There's quite a number of things I *could* do that would look bad when they got into the newspapers. But it's none of them, unless one of you forces me to it." Then he says:

"You *did* want to see the children, Jane?"

She nodded.

"Jane," he says, "can't you see I'm the better man?"

The perfessor, he was woke up after all them years of scientifics, and he didn't want to see her go. "Look at him," he says, pointing to the feller with the brown beard, "he's scared stiff right now."

Which I would of been scared myself if I'd a-been ketched that-a-way like Henry was, and the perfessor's voice sounding like you was chopping ice every time he spoke. I seen the perfessor didn't want to have no blood on the carpet without he had to have it, but I seen he was making up his mind about something, too. Jane, she says:

"*You* a better man? *You*? You think you've been a model husband just because you've never beaten me, don't you?"

"No," says the perfessor, "I've been a blamed fool all right. I've been a worse fool, maybe, than if I *had* beaten you." Then he turns to Henry and he says:

"Duels are out of fashion, aren't they? And a plain killing looks bad in the papers, doesn't it? Well, you just wait for me." With which he gets up and trots out, and I hearn him running down stairs to his labertory.

Henry, he'd rather go now. He don't want to wait. But with Jane a-looking at him he's shamed not to wait. It's his place to make some kind of a strong action now to show Jane he is a great man. But he don't do it. And Jane is too much of a thoroughbred to show him she expects it. And me, I'm getting the fidgets and wondering to myself, "What is that there perfessor up to now? Whatever it is, it ain't like no one else. He is looney, that perfessor is. And she is kind o' looney, too. I wonder if they is any one that ain't looney sometimes?" I been around the country a good 'eal, too, and seen and hearn of some awful remarkable things, and I never seen no one that wasn't more or less looney when the *search us the femm* comes into the case. Which is a Dago word I got out'n a newspaper and it means: "Who was the dead gent's lady friend?" And we all set and sweat and got the fidgets waiting fur that perfessor to come back.

Which he done with that Sister Estelle grin onto his face and a pill box in his hand. They was two pills in the box. He says, placid and chilly:

"Yes, sir, duels are out of fashion. This is the age of science. All the same, the one that gets her has got to fight for her. If she isn't worth fighting for, she isn't worth having. Here are two pills. I made 'em myself. One has enough poison in it to kill a regiment when it gets to working well—which it does fifteen minutes after it is taken. The other one has got nothing harmful in it. If you get the poison one, I keep her. If I get it, you can have her. Only I hope you will wait long enough after I'm dead so there won't be any scandal around town."

Henry, he never said a word. He opened his mouth, but nothing come of it. When he done that I thought I hearn his tongue scrape agin his cheek on the inside like a piece of sand-paper. He was scared, Henry was.

"But *you* know which is which," Jane sings out. "The thing's not fair!"

"That is the reason my dear Jane is going to shuffle these pills around each other herself," says the perfessor, "and then pick out one for him and one for me. *You* don't know which is which, Jane. And as he is the favourite, he is going to get the first chance. If he gets the one I want him to get, he will have just fifteen minutes to live after taking it. In that fifteen minutes he will please to walk so far from my house that he won't die near it and make a scandal. I won't have a scandal without I have to. Everything is going to be nice and quiet and respectable. The effect of the poison is similar to heart failure. No one can tell the difference on the corpse. There's going to be no blood anywhere. I will be found dead in my house in the morning with heart failure, or else he will be picked up dead in the street, far enough away so as to make no talk." Or they was words to that effect.

He is rubbing it in considerable, I thinks, that perfessor is. I wonder if I better jump in and stop the hull thing. Then I thinks: "No, it's between them three." Besides, I want to see which one is going to get that there loaded pill. I always been intrusted in games of chancet of all kinds, and when I seen the perfessor was such a sport, I'm sorry I been misjudging him all this time.

Jane, she looks at the box, and she breathes hard and quick.

"I won't touch 'em," she says. "I refuse to be a party to any murder of that kind."

"Huh? You do?" says the perfessor. "But the time when you might have refused has gone by. You have made yourself a party to it already. You're really the *main* party to it.

"But do as you like," he goes on. "I'm giving him more chance than I ought to with those pills. I might shoot him, and I would, and then face the music, if it wasn't for mixing the children up in the scandal, Jane. If you want to see him get a fair chance, Jane, you've got to hand out these pills, one to him and then one to me. *You* must kill one or the other of us, or else *I'll kill him* the other way. And *you* had better pick one out for him, because *I* know which is which. Or else let him pick one out for himself," he says.

Henry, he wasn't saying nothing. I thought he had fainted. But he hadn't. I seen him licking his lips. I bet Henry's mouth was all dry inside.

Jane, she took the box and she went round in front of Henry and she looked at him hard. She looked at him like she was thinking: "Fur God's sake, spunk up some, and take one if it *does* kill you!" Then she says out loud: "Henry, if you die I will die, too!"

And Henry, he took one. His hand shook, but he took it out'n the box. If she had of looked like that at me mebby I would of took one myself. Fur Jane, she was a peach, she was. But I don't know whether I would of or not. When she makes that brag about dying, I looked at the perfessor. What she said never fazed him. And I thinks agin: "Mebby I better jump in now and stop this thing." And then I thinks agin: "No, it is between them three and Providence." Besides, I'm anxious to see who is going to get that pill with the science in it. I gets to feeling jest like Providence hisself was in that there room picking out them pills with his own hands. And I was anxious to see what Providence's ideas of right and wrong was like. So fur as I could see they was all three in the wrong, but if I had of been in there running them pills in Providence's place I would of let them all off kind o' easy.

Henry, he ain't eat his pill yet. He is jest looking at it and shaking. The perfessor pulls out his watch and lays it on the table.

"It is a quarter past eleven," he says. "Mr. Murray, are you going to make me shoot you, after all? I didn't want a scandal," he says. "It's for you to say whether you want to eat that pill and get your even chance, or whether you want to get shot. The shooting method is sure, but it causes talk. These pills won't *which?*"

And he pulls a revolver. Which I suppose he had got that too when he went down after them pills.

Henry, he looks at the gun.

Then he looks at the pill.

Then he swallers the pill.

The perfessor puts his gun back into his pocket, and then he puts his pill into his mouth. He don't swaller it. He looks at the watch, and he looks at

Henry.

"Sixteen minutes past eleven," he says. "*At exactly twenty-nine minutes to twelve Mr. Murray will be dead*. I got the harmless one. I can tell by the taste."

And he put the pieces out into his hand, to show that he has chewed his'n up, not being willing to wait fifteen minutes fur a verdict from his digestive ornaments. Then he put them pieces back into his mouth and chewed 'em up and swallered 'em down like he was eating cough drops.

Henry has got sweat breaking out all over his face, and he tries to make fur the door, but he falls down onto a sofa.

"This is murder," he says, weak-like. And he tries to get up again, but this time he falls to the floor in a dead faint.

"It's a dern short fifteen minutes," I thinks to myself. "That perfessor must of put more science into Henry's pill than he thought he did fur it to of knocked him out this quick. It ain't skeercly three minutes."

When Henry falls the woman staggers and tries to throw herself on top of him. The corners of her mouth was all drawed down, and her eyes was turned up. But she don't yell none. She can't. She tries, but she jest gurgles in her throat. The perfessor won't let her fall acrost Henry. He ketches her. "Sit up, Jane," he says, with that Estelle look onto his face, "and let us have a talk."

She looks at him with no more sense in her face than a piece of putty has got. But she can't look away from him.

And I'm kind o' paralyzed, too. If that feller laying on the floor had only jest kicked oncet, or grunted, or done something, I could of loosened up and yelled, and I would of. I jest *needed* to fetch a yell. But Henry ain't more'n dropped down there till I'm feeling jest like he'd *always* been there, and I'd *always* been staring into that room, and the last word any one spoke was said hundreds and hundreds of years ago.

"You're a murderer," says Jane in a whisper, looking at the perfessor in that stare-eyed way. "You're a *murderer*," she says, saying it like she was trying to make herself feel sure he really was one.

"Murder!" says the perfessor. "Did you think I was going to run any chances for a pup like him? He's scared, that's all. He's just fainted through fright. He's a coward. Those pills were both just bread and sugar. He'll be all right in a minute or two. I've just been showing you that the fellow hasn't got nerve enough nor brains enough for a fine woman like you, Jane," he says.

Then Jane begins to sob and laugh, both to oncet, kind o' wild like, her voice clucking like a hen does, and she says:

"It's worse then, it's worse! It's worse for me than if it were a murder! Some farces can be more tragic than any tragedy ever was," she says. Or they was words to that effect.

And if Henry had of been really dead she couldn't of took it no harder than she begun to take it now when she saw he was alive, but jest wasn't no good. But I seen she was taking on fur herself now more'n fur Henry. Doctor Kirby always use to say women is made unlike most other animals in many ways. When they is foolish about a man they can stand to have that man killed a good 'eal better than to have him showed up ridiculous right in front of them. They will still be crazy about the man that is dead, even if he was crooked. But they don't never forgive the fellow that lets himself be made a fool and lets them look foolish, too. And when the perfessor kicks Henry in the ribs, and Henry comes to and sneaks out, Jane, she never even turns her head and looks at him.

"Jane," says the perfessor, when she quiets down some, "you have a lot o' things to forgive me. But do you suppose I have learned enough so that we can make a go of it if we start all over again?"

But Jane she never said nothing.

"Jane," he says, "Estelle is going back to New England, as soon as Margery gets well, and she will stay there for good."

Jane, she begins to take a little intrust then.

"Did Estelle tell you so?" she asts.

"No," says the perfessor. "Estelle doesn't know it yet. I'm going to break the news to her in the morning."

But Jane still hates him. She's making herself hate him hard. She wouldn't of been a human woman if she had let herself be coaxed up all to onct. Purty soon she says: "I'm tired." And she went out looking like the perfessor was a perfect stranger. She was a peace, Jane was.

After she left, the perfessor set there quite a spell and smoked. And he was looking tired out, too. They wasn't no mistake about me. I was jest dead all through my legs.

———————————————————

CHAPTER XII

I was down in the perfessor's labertory one day, and that was a queer place. They was every kind of scientifics that has ever been discovered in it. Some was pickled in bottles and some was stuffed and some was pinned to the walls with their wings spread out. If you took hold of anything, it was likely to be a skull and give you the shivers or some electric contraption and shock you; and if you tipped over a jar and it broke, enough germs might get loose to slaughter a hull town. I was helping the perfessor to unpack a lot of stuff some friends had sent him, and I noticed a bottle that had onto it, blowed in the glass:

DANIEL, DUNNE AND COMPANY

"That's funny," says I, out loud.

"What is?" asts the perfessor.

I showed him the bottle and told him how I was named after the company that made 'em. He says to look around me. They is all kinds of glassware in that room—bottles and jars and queer-shaped things with crooked tails and noses—and nigh every piece of glass the perfessor owns is made by that company.

"Why," says the perfessor, "their factory is in this very town."

And nothing would do fur me but I must go and see that factory. I couldn't till the quarantine was pried loose from our house. But when it was, I went down town and hunted up the place and looked her over.

It was a big factory, and I was kind of proud of that. I was glad she wasn't no measly, little, old-fashioned, run-down concern. Of course, I wasn't really no relation to it and it wasn't none to me. But I was named fur it, too, and it come about as near to being a fambly as anything I had ever had or was likely to find. So I was proud it seemed to be doing so well.

I thinks as I looks at her of the thousands and thousands of bottles that has been coming out of there fur years and years, and will be fur years and years to come. And one bottle not so much different from another one. And all that was really knowed about me was jest the name on one out of all them millions and millions of bottles. It made me feel kind of queer, when I thought of that, as if I didn't have no separate place in the world any more than one of them millions of bottles. If any one will shut his eyes and say his own name over and over agin fur quite a spell, he will get kind of wonderized and mesmerized a-doing it—he will begin to wonder who the dickens he is, anyhow, and what he is, and what the difference between him and the next feller is. He will wonder why he happens to be himself and the next feller *himself.* He wonders where himself leaves off and the rest of the world begins. I been that way myself—all wonderized, so that I felt jest like I was a melting piece of the hull creation, and it was all shifting and drifting and changing and flowing, and not solid anywhere, and I could hardly keep myself from flowing into it. It makes a person feel awful queer, like seeing a ghost would. It makes him feel like *he* wasn't no solider than a ghost himself. Well, if you ever done that and got that feeling, you *know* what I mean. All of a sudden, when I am trying to take in all them millions and millions of bottles, it rushed onto me, that feeling, strong. Thinking of them bottles had somehow brung it on. The bigness of the hull creation, and the smallness of me, and the gait at which everything was racing and rushing ahead, made me want to grab hold of something solid and hang on.

I reached out my hand, and it hit something solid all right. It was a feller who was wheeling out a hand truck loaded with boxes from the shipping department. I had been standing by the shipping department door, and I reached right agin him.

He wants to know if I am drunk or a blanked fool. So after some talk of that kind I borrows a chew of tobacco of him and we gets right well acquainted.

I helped him finish loading his wagon and rode over to the freight depot with him and helped him unload her. Lifting one of them boxes down from the wagon I got such a shock I like to of dropped her.

"Lifting one of them boxes down from the wagon I got such
a shock I like to of dropped her"

Fur she was marked so many dozen, glass, handle with care, and she was addressed to Dr. Hartley L. Kirby, Atlanta, Ga.

I managed to get that box onto the platform without busting her, and then I sets down on top of her awful weak.

"What's the matter?" asts the feller I was with.

"Nothing," says I.

"You look sick," he says. And I *was* feeling that-a-way.

"Mebby I do," says I, "and it's enough to shake a feller up to find a dead man come to life sudden like this."

"Great snakes, no!" says he, looking all around, "where?"

But I didn't stop to chew the rag none. I left him right there, with his mouth wide open, staring after me like I was crazy. Half a block away I looked back and I seen him double over and slap his knee and laugh loud, like he had hearn a big joke, but what he was laughing at I never knew.

I was tickled. Tickled? Jest so tickled I was plumb foolish with it. The doctor was alive after all—I kept saying it over and over to myself—he hadn't drownded nor blowed away. And I was going to hunt him up.

I had a little money. The perfessor had paid it to me. He had give me a job helping take care of his hosses and things like that, and wanted me to stay, and I had been thinking mebby I would fur a while. But not now!

I calkelated I could grab a ride that very night that would put me into Evansville the next morning. I figgered if I ketched a through freight from there on the next night I might get where he was almost as quick as them bottles did.

I didn't think it was no use writing out my resignation fur the perfessor. But I got quite a bit of grub from Biddy Malone to make a start on, fur I didn't figger on spending no more money than I had to on grub. She asts me a lot of questions, and I had to lie to her a good deal, but I got the grub. And at ten that night I was in an empty bumping along south, along with a cross-eyed feller named Looney Hogan who happened to be travelling the same way.

Riding on trains without paying fare ain't always the easy thing it sounds. It is like a trade that has got to be learned. They is different ways of doing it. I have done every way frequent, except one. That I give up after trying her two, three times. That is riding the rods down underneath the cars, with a piece of board put acrost 'em to lay yourself on.

I never want to go *anywheres* agin bad enough to ride the rods.

Because sometimes you arrive where you are going to partly smeared over the trucks and in no condition fur to be made welcome to our city, as Doctor Kirby would say. Sometimes you don't arrive. Every oncet in a while you read a little piece in a newspaper about a man being found alongside the tracks, considerable cut up, or laying right acrost them, mebby. He is held in the morgue a while and no one knows who he is, and none of the train crew knows they has run over a man, and the engineer says they wasn't none on the track. More'n likely that feller has been riding the rods, along about the middle of the train. Mebby he let himself go to sleep and jest rolled off. Mebby his piece of board slipped and he fell when the train jolted. Or mebby he jest natcherally made up his mind he rather let loose and get squashed then get any more cinders into his eyes. Riding the blind baggage or the bumpers gives me all the excitement I wants, or all the gambling chancet either; others can have the rods fur all of me. And they *is* some people ackshally says they likes 'em best.

A good place, if it is winter time, is the feed rack over a cattle car, fur the heat and steam from all them steers in there will keep you warm. But don't crawl in no lumber car that is only loaded about half full, and short lengths and bundles of laths and shingles in her; fur they is likely to get to shifting and bumping. Baled hay is purty good sometimes. Myself, not being like these bums that is too proud to work, I have often helped the fireman shovel coal and paid fur my ride that-a-way. But an empty, fur gineral purposes, will do about as well as anything.

This feller Looney Hogan that was with me was a kind of a harmless critter, and he didn't know jest where he was going, nor why. He was mostly scared of things, and if you spoke to him quick he shivered first and then grinned idiotic so you wouldn't kick him, and when he talked he had a silly little giggle. He had been made that-a-way in a reform school where they took him young and tried to work the cussedness out'n him by batting him around. They worked it out, and purty nigh everything else along with it, I guess. Looney had had a pardner whose name was Slim, he said; but a couple of years before Slim had fell overboard off'n a barge up to Duluth and never come up agin. Looney knowed Slim was drownded all right, but he was always travelling around looking at tanks and freight depots and switch shanties, fur Slim's mark to be fresh cut with a knife somewheres, so he would know where to foller and ketch up with him agin. He knowed he would never find Slim's mark, he said, but he kept a-looking, and he guessed that was the way he got the name of Looney.

Looney left me at Evansville. He said he was going east from there, he guessed. And I went along south. But I was hindered considerable, being put off of trains three or four times, and having to grab these here slow local freights between towns all the way down through Kentuckey. Anywheres south of the Ohio River and east of the Mississippi River trainmen is grouchier to them they thinks is bums than north of it, anyhow. And in some parts of it, if a real bum gets pinched, heaven help 'im, fur nothing else won't.

One night, between twelve and one o'clock, I was put off of a freight train fur the second time in a place in the northern part of Tennessee, right near the Kentuckey line. I set down in a lumber yard near the railroad track, and when she started up agin I grabbed onto the iron ladder and swung myself aboard. But the brakeman was watching fur me, and clumb down the ladder and stamped on my fingers. So I dropped off, with one finger considerable mashed, and set down in that lumber yard wondering what next.

It was a dark night, and so fur as I could see they wasn't much moving in that town. Only a few places was lit up. One was way across the town square from me, and it was the telephone exchange, with a man operator reading a book in there. The other was the telegraph room in the depot about a hundred yards from me, and they was only two fellers in it, both smoking. The main

95

business part of the town was built up around the square, like lots of old-fashioned towns is, and they was jest enough brightness from four, five electric lights to show the shape of the square and be reflected from the windows of the closed-up stores.

I knowed they was likely a watchman somewheres about, too. I guessed I wouldn't wander around none and run no chances of getting took up by him. So I was getting ready to lay down on top of a level pile of boards and go to sleep when I hearn a curious kind of noise a way off, like it must be at the edge of town.

It sounded like quite a bunch of cattle might shuffling along a dusty road. The night was so quiet you could hear things plain from a long ways off. It growed a little louder and a little nearer. And then it struck a plank bridge somewheres, and come acrost it with a clatter. Then I knowed it wasn't cattle. Cows and steers don't make that cantering kind of noise as a rule; they trot. It was hosses crossing that bridge. And they was quite a lot of 'em.

As they struck the dirt road agin, I hearn a shot. And then another and another. Then a dozen all to oncet, and away off through the night a woman screamed.

I seen the man in the telephone place fling down his book and grab a pistol from I don't know where. He stepped out into the street and fired three shots into the air as fast as he could pull the trigger. And as he done so they was a light flashed out in a building way down the railroad track, and shots come answering from there. Men's voices began to yell out; they was the noise of people running along plank sidewalks, and windows opening in the dark. Then with a rush the galloping noise come nearer, come closet; raced by the place where I was hiding, and nigh a hundred men with guns swept right into the middle of that square and pulled their hosses up.

CHAPTER XIII

I seen the feller from the telephone exchange run down the street a little ways as the first rush hit the square, and fire his pistol twice. Then he turned and made fur an alleyway, but as he turned they let him have it. He throwed up his arms and made one long stagger, right acrost the bar of light that streamed out of the windows, and he fell into the shadder, out of sight, jest like a scorched moth drops dead into the darkness from a torch.

Out of the middle of that bunch of riders come a big voice, yelling numbers, instead of men's names. Then different crowds lit out in all directions—some on foot, while others held their hosses—fur they seemed to have a plan laid ahead.

And then things began to happen. They happened so quick and with such a whirl it was all unreal to me—shots and shouts, and windows breaking as they blazed away at the store fronts all around the square—and orders and cuss-words ringing out between the noise of shooting—and those electric lights shining on them as they tossed and trampled, and showing up masked faces here and there—and pounding hoofs, and hosses scream—like humans with excitement—and spurts of flame squirted sudden out of the ring of darkness round about the open place—and a bull-dog shut up in a store somewheres howling himself hoarse—and white puffs of powder smoke like ghosts that went a-drifting by the lights—it was all unreal to me, as if I had a fever and was dreaming it. That square was like a great big stage in front of me, and I laid in the darkness on my lumber pile and watched things like a show—not much scared because it *was* so derned unreal.

From way down along the railroad track they come a sort of blunted roar, like blasting big stumps out—and then another and another. Purty soon, down that way, a slim flame licked up the side of a big building there, and crooked its tongue over the top. Then a second big building right beside it ketched afire, and they both showed up in their own light, big and angry and handsome, and the light showed up the men in front of 'em, too—guarding 'em, I guess, fur fear the town would get its nerve and make a fight to put 'em out. They begun to light the whole town up as light as day, and paint a red patch onto the sky, that must of been noticed fur miles around. It was a mighty purty sight to see 'em burn. The smoke was rolling high, too, and the sparks flying and other things in danger of ketching, and after while a lick of smoke come drifting up my way. I smelt her. It was tobacco burning in them warehouses.

But that town had some fight in her, in spite of being took unexpected that-a-way. It wasn't no coward town. The light from the burning buildings made all the shadders around about seem all the darker. And every once in a while, after the surprise of the first rush, they would come thin little streaks of fire out of the darkness somewheres, and the sound of shots. And then a gang of riders would gallop in that direction shooting up all creation. But by the time the warehouses was all lit up so that you could see they was no hope of putting them out the shooting from the darkness had jest about stopped.

It looked like them big tobacco warehouses was the main object of the raid. Fur when they was burning past all chancet of saving, with walls and floors a-tumbling and crashing down and sending up great gouts of fresh flame as they fell, the leader sings out an order, and all that is not on their hosses jumps on, and they rides away from the blaze. They come across the square—not galloping now, but taking it easy, laughing and talking and cussing and joking each other—and passed right by my lumber pile agin and down the street they had come. You bet I laid low on them boards while they was going by, and flattened myself out till I felt like a shingle.

As I hearn their hoof-sounds getting farther off, I lifts up my head agin. But they wasn't all gone, either. Three that must of been up to some pertic'ler deviltry of their own come galloping acrost the square to ketch up with the main bunch. Two was quite a bit ahead of the third one, and he yelled to them to wait. But they only laughed and rode harder.

And then fur some fool reason that last feller pulled up his hoss and stopped. He stopped in the road right in front of me, and wheeled his hoss acrost the road and stood up in his stirrups and took a long look at that blaze. You'd 'a' said he had done it all himself and was mighty proud of it, the way he raised his head and looked back at that town. He was so near that I hearn him draw in a slow, deep breath. He stood still fur most a minute like that, black agin the red sky, and then he turned his hoss's head and jabbed him with his stirrup edge.

Jest as the hoss started they come a shot from somewheres behind me. I s'pose they was some one hid in the lumber piles, where the street crossed the railway, besides myself. The hoss jumped forward at the shot, and the feller swayed sideways and dropped his gun and lost his stirrups and come down heavy on the ground. His hoss galloped off. I heard the noise of some one running off through the dark, and stumbling agin the lumber. It was the feller who had fired the shot running away. I suppose he thought the rest of them riders would come back, when they heard that shot, and hunt him down.

I thought they might myself. But I laid there, and jest waited. If they come, I didn't want to be found running. But they didn't come. The two last ones had caught up with the main gang, I guess, fur purty soon I hearn them all crossing that plank bridge agin, and knowed they was gone.

At first I guessed the feller on the ground must be dead. But he wasn't, fur purty soon I hearn him groan. He had mebby been stunned by his fall, and was coming to enough to feel his pain.

I didn't feel like he orter be left there. So I clumb down and went over to him. He was lying on one side all kind of huddled up. There had been a mask on his face, like the rest of them, with some hair onto the bottom of it to look like a beard. But now it had slipped down till it hung loose around his neck by the string. They was enough light to see he wasn't nothing but a young feller. He raised himself slow as I come near him, leaning on one arm and trying to set up. The other arm hung loose and helpless. Half setting up that-away he made a feel at his belt with his good hand, as I come near. But that good arm was his prop, and when he took it off the ground he fell back. His hand come away empty from his belt.

The big six-shooter he had been feeling fur wasn't in its holster, anyhow. It had fell out when he tumbled. I picked it up in the road jest a few feet from his shot-gun, and stood there with it in my hand, looking down at him.

"Well," he says, in a drawly kind of voice, slow and feeble, but looking at me steady and trying to raise himself agin, "yo' can finish yo' little job now— yo' shot me from the darkness, and now yo' done got my pistol. I reckon yo' better shoot *agin*."

"I don't want to rub it in none," I says, "with you down and out, but from what I seen around this town to-night I guess you and your own gang got no *great* objections to shooting from the dark yourselves."

"Why don't yo' shoot then?" he says. "It most suttinly is *yo'* turn now." And he never batted an eye.

"Bo," I says, "you got nerve. I *like* you, Bo. I didn't shoot you, and I ain't going to. The feller that did has went. I'm going to get you out of this. Where you hurt?"

"Hip," he says, "but that ain't much. The thing that bothers me is this arm. It's done busted. I fell on it."

I drug him out of the road and back of the lumber pile I had been laying on, and hurt him considerable a-doing it.

"Now," I says, "what can I do fur you?"

"I reckon yo' better leave me," he says, "without yo' want to get yo'self mixed up in all this."

"If I do," I says, "you may bleed to death here: or anyway you would get found in the morning and be run in."

"Yo' mighty good to me," says he, "considering yo' are no kin to this here part of the country at all. I reckon by yo' talk yo' are one of them damn Yankees, ain't yo'?"

In Illinoise a Yankee is some one from the East, but down South he is anybody from north of the Ohio, and though that there war was fought forty years ago some of them fellers down there don't know damn and Yankee is two words yet. But shucks!—they don't mean no harm by it! So I tells him I am a damn Yankee and asts him agin if I can do anything fur him.

"Yes," he says, "yo' can tell a friend of mine Bud Davis has happened to an accident, and get him over here quick with his wagon to tote me home."

I was to go down the railroad track past them burning warehouses till I come to the third street, and then turn to my left. "The third house from the track has got an iron picket fence in front of it," says Bud, "and it's the only house in that part of town which has. Beauregard Peoples lives there. He is kin to me."

"Yes," I says, "and Beauregard is jest as likely as not going to take a shot out of the front window at me, fur luck, afore I can tell him what I want. It seems to be a kind of habit in these here parts to-night—I'm getting homesick fur Illinoise. But I'll take a chancet."

"He won't shoot," says Bud, "if yo' go about it right. Beauregard ain't going to be asleep with all this going on in town to-night. Yo' rattle on the iron gate and he'll holler to know what yo' all want."

"If he don't shoot first," I says.

"When he hollers, yo' cry back at him yo' have found his *Old Dead Hoss* in the road. It won't hurt to holler that loud, and that will make him let you within talking distance."

"His old *dead hoss*?"

"Yo' don't need to know what that is. *He* will." And then Bud told me enough of the signs and words to say, and things to do, to keep Beauregard from shooting—he said he reckoned he had trusted me so much he might as well go the hull hog. Beauregard, he says, belongs to them riders too; they have friends in all the towns that watches the lay of the land fur them, he says.

I made a long half-circle around them burning buildings, keeping in the dark, fur people was coming out in bunches, now that it was all over with, watching them fires burning, and talking excited, and saying the riders should be follered—only not follering.

I found the house Bud meant, and they was a light in the second-story window. I rattled on the gate. A dog barked somewheres near, but I hearn his chain jangle and knowed he was fast, and I rattled on the gate agin.

The light moved away from the window. Then another front window opened quiet, and a voice says:

"Doctor, is that yo' back agin?"

"No," I says, "I ain't a doctor."

"Stay where you are, then. *I got you covered.*"

"I am staying," I says, "don't shoot."

"Who are yo'?"

"A feller," I says, kind of sensing his gun through the darkness as I spoke, "who has found your *old dead hoss* in the road."

He didn't answer fur several minutes. Then he says, using the words *dead hoss* as Bud had said he would.

"A *dead hoss* is fitten fo' nothing but to skin."

"Well," I says, using the words fur the third time, as instructed, "it is a *dead hoss* all right."

I hearn the window shut and purty soon the front door opened.

"Come up here," he says. I come.

"Who rode that hoss yo' been talking about?" he asts.

"One of the *Silent Brigade*," I tells him, as Bud had told me to say. I give him the grip Bud had showed me with his good hand.

"Come on in," he says.

He shut the door behind us and lighted a lamp agin. And we looked each other over. He was a scrawny little feller, with little gray eyes set near together, and some sandy-complected whiskers on his chin. I told him about Bud, and what his fix was.

"Damn it—oh, damn it all," he says, rubbing the bridge of his nose, "I don't see how on *airth* I kin do it. My wife's jest had a baby. Do yo' hear that?"

And I did hear a sound like kittens mewing, somewheres up stairs. Beauregard, he grinned and rubbed his nose some more, and looked at me like he thought that mewing noise was the smartest sound that ever was made.

"Boy," he says, grinning, "bo'n five hours ago. I've done named him Burley—after the tobaccer association, yo' know. Yes, *sir*, Burley Peoples is his name—and he shore kin squall, the derned little cuss!"

"Yes," I says, "you better stay with Burley. Lend me a rig of some sort and I'll take Bud home."

So we went out to Beauregard's stable with a lantern and hitched up one of his hosses to a light road wagon. He went into the house and come back agin with a mattress fur Bud to lie on, and a part of a bottle of whiskey. And I drove back to that lumber pile. I guess I nearly killed Bud getting him into there. But he wasn't bleeding much from his hip—it was his arm was giving him fits.

We went slow, and the dawn broke with us four miles out of town. It was broad daylight, and early morning noises stirring everywheres, when we drove up in front of an old farmhouse, with big brick chimbleys built on the outside of it, a couple of miles farther on.

━━━━━━━━━━━━━

CHAPTER XIV

As I drove into the yard, a bare-headed old nigger with a game leg throwed down an armful of wood he was gathering and went limping up to the veranda as fast as he could. He opened the door and bawled out, pointing to us, before he had it fairly open:

"O Marse *Will*yum! O Miss *Lucy*! Dey've brung him home! *Dar* he!"

"A bare-headed old nigger with a game leg . . . . went limping up to the veranda as fast as he could"

A little, bright, black-eyed old lady like a wren comes running out of the house, and chirps:

"O Bud—O my honey boy! Is he dead?"

"I reckon not, Miss Lucy," says Bud raising himself up on the mattress as she runs up to the wagon, and trying to act like everything was all a joke. She was jest high enough to kiss him over the edge of the wagon box. A worried-looking old gentleman come out the door, seen Bud and his mother kissing each other, and then says to the old nigger man:

"George, yo' old fool, what do yo' mean by shouting out like that?"

"Marse Willyum—" begins George, explaining.

"Shut up," says the old gentleman, very quiet. "Take the bay mare and go for Doctor Po'ter." Then he comes to the wagon and says:

"So they got yo', Bud? Yo' *would* go nightriding like a rowdy and a thug! Are yo' much hurt?"

He said it easy and gentle, more than mad. But Bud, he flushed up, pale as he was, and didn't answer his dad direct. He turned to his mother and said:

"Miss Lucy, dear, it would 'a' done yo' heart good to see the way them trust warehouses blazed up!"

And the old lady, smiling and crying both to oncet, says, "God bless her brave boy." But the old gentleman looked mighty serious, and his worry settled into a frown between his eyes, and he turns to me and says:

"Yo' must pardon us, sir, fo' neglecting to thank yo' sooner." I told him that would be all right, fur him not to worry none. And him and me and Mandy, which was the nigger cook, got Bud into the house and into his bed. And his mother gets that busy ordering Mandy and the old gentleman around, to get things and fix things, and make Bud as easy as she could, that you could see she was one of them kind of woman that gets a lot of satisfaction out of having some one sick to fuss over. And after quite a while George gets back with Doctor Porter.

He sets Bud's arm, and he locates the bullet in him, and he says he guesses he'll do in a few weeks if nothing like blood poisoning nor gangrene nor inflammation sets in.

Only the doctor says he "reckons" instead of he "guesses," which they all do down there. And they all had them easy-going, wait-a-bit kind of voices, and didn't see no pertic'ler importance in their "r's." It wasn't that you could spell it no different when they talked, but it sounded different.

I eat my breakfast with the old gentleman, and then I took a sleep until time fur dinner. They wouldn't hear of me leaving that night. I fully intended to go on the next day, but before I knowed it I been there a couple of days, and have got very well acquainted with that fambly.

Well, that was a house divided agin itself. Miss Lucy, she is awful favourable to all this nightrider business. She spunks up and her eyes sparkles whenever she thinks about that there tobaccer trust.

She would of like to been a night-rider herself. But the old man, he says law and order is the main pint. What the country needs, he says, ain't burning down tobaccer warehouses, and shooting your neighbours, and licking them with switches, fur no wrong done never righted another wrong.

"But you were in the Ku Klux Klan yo'self," says Miss Lucy.

The old man says the Ku Kluxes was working fur a principle—the principle of keeping the white supremacy on top of the nigger race. Fur if you let 'em quit work and go around balloting and voting it won't do. It makes 'em biggity. And a biggity nigger is laying up trouble fur himself. Because sooner or later he will get to thinking he is as good as one of these here Angle-Saxtons you are always hearing so much talk about down South. And if the Angle-Saxtons was to stand fur that, purty soon they would be sociable equality. And next the hull dern country would be niggerized. Them there Angle-Saxtons, that come over from Ireland and Scotland and France and the Great British Islands and settled up the South jest simply couldn't afford to let that happen, he says, and so they Ku Kluxed the niggers to make 'em quit voting. It was *their* job to *make* law and order, he says, which they couldn't be with niggers getting the idea they had a right to govern. So they Ku Kluxed 'em like gentlemen. But these here night-riders, he says, is *agin* law and order —they can shoot up more law and order in one night than can be manufactured agin in ten years. He was a very quiet, peaceable old man, Mr. Davis was, and Bud says he was so dern foolish about law and order he had to up and shoot a man, about fifteen years ago, who hearn him talking that-a-way and said he reminded him of a Boston school teacher.

But Miss Lucy and Bud, they tells me what all them night-ridings is fur. It seems this here tobaccer trust is jest as mean and low-down and unprincipled as all the rest of them trusts. The farmers around there raised considerable tobaccer—more'n they did of anything else. The trust had shoved the price so low they couldn't hardly make a living. So they organized and said they would all hold their tobaccer fur a fair price. But some of the farmers wouldn't organize—said they had a right to do what they pleased with their own tobaccer. So the night-riders was formed to burn their barns and ruin their crops and whip 'em and shoot 'em and make 'em jine. And also to burn a few trust warehouses now and then, and show 'em this free American people, composed mainly out of the Angle-Saxton races, wasn't going to take no sass from anybody.

An old feller by the name of Rufe Daniels who wouldn't jine the night-riders had been shot to death on his own door step, jest about a mile away,

105

only a week or so before. The night-riders mostly used these here automatic shot-guns, but they didn't bother with birdshot. They mostly loaded their shells with buckshot. A few bicycle ball bearings dropped out of old Rufe when they gathered him up and got him into shape to plant. They is always some low-down cuss in every crowd that carries things to the point where they get brutal, Bud says; and he feels like them bicycle bearings was going a little too fur, though he wouldn't let on to his dad that he felt that-a-way.

So fur as I could see they hadn't hurt the trust none to speak of, them night-riders. But they had done considerable damage to their own county, fur folks was moving away, and the price of land had fell. Still, I guess they must of got considerable satisfaction out of raising the deuce nights that-away; and sometimes that is worth a hull lot to a feller. As fur as I could make out both the trust and the night-riders was in the wrong. But, you take 'em one at a time, personal-like, and not into a gang, and most of them night-riders is good-dispositioned folks. I never knowed any trusts personal, but mebby if you could ketch 'em the same way they would be similar.

I asts George one day what he thought about it. George, he got mighty serious right off, like he felt his answer was going to be used to decide the hull thing by. He was carrying a lot of scraps on a plate to a hound dog that had a kennel out near George's cabin, and he walled his eyes right thoughtful, and scratched his head with the fork he had been scraping the plate with, but fur a while nothing come of it. Finally George says:

"I'se 'spec' mah jedgment des about de same as Marse *Will*yum's an' Miss *Lucy*'s. I'se notice hit mos' ingin'lly am de same."

"That can't be, George," says I, "fur they think different ways."

"Den if *dat* am de case," says George, "dey ain't NO ONE kin settle hit twell hit settles hise'f."

"'I'se mos' ingin'lly notice a thing *do* settle hitse'f arter a while'"
[PAGE 108]

"I'se mos' ingin'lly notice a thing *do* settle hitse'f arter a while. Yass, *sah*, I'se notice dat! Long time ago dey was consid'ble gwines-on in dis hyah county, Marse Daniel. I dunno ef yo' evah heah 'bout dat o' not, Marse Daniel, but dey was a wah fit right hyah in dis hyah county. Such gwines-on as nevah was—dem dar Yankees a-ridin' aroun' an' eatin' up de face o' de yearth, like de plagues o' Pha'aoah, Marse Daniel, and rippin' and rarin' an' racin' an' stealin' evehything dey could lay dey han's on, Marse Daniel. An' ouah folks a-ridin' and a racin' and projickin' aroun' in de same onsettled way.

"Marse Willyum, he 'low *he* gwine settle dat dar wah he-se'f—yass, *sah!* An' he got on he hoss, and he ride away an' jine Marse Jeb Stuart. But dey don' settle hit. Marse Ab'ham Linkum, he 'low *he* gwine settle hit, an' sen' millyums an' millyums mo' o' dem Yankees down hyah, Marse Daniel. But dey des *on*settle hit wuss'n evah! But arter a while it des settle *hit*se'f.

"An' den freedom broke out among de niggers, and dey was mo' gwines-*on*, an' talkin', an' some on 'em 'lowed dey was gwine ter be no mo' wohk, Marse Daniel. But arter a while dat settle *hit*se'f, and dey all went back to wohk agin. Den some on de niggers gits de notion, Marse Daniel, dey gwine foh to *vote*. An' dey was mo' gwines-on, an' de Ku Kluxes come a projickin' aroun' nights, like de grave-yahds done been resu'rected, Marse Daniel, an' den arter a while dat trouble settle *hit*se'f.

"Den arter de Ku Kluxes dey was de time Miss Lucy Buckner gwine ter mahy Marse Prent McMakin. An' she don' want to ma'hy him, if dey give her her druthers about hit. But Ol' Marse Kunnel Hampton, her gram-pa, and her aunt, *my* Miss Lucy hyah, dey ain't gwine give her no druthers. And dey was mo' gwines-*on*. But dat settle *hit*se'f, too."

George, he begins to chuckle, and I ast him how.

"Yass, *sah*, dat settle *hit*se'f. But I 'spec' Miss Lucy Buckner done he'p some in de settle*ment*. Foh de day befoh de weddin' was gwine ter be, she ups an' she runs off wid a Yankee frien' of her brother, Kunnel Tom Buckner. An' I'se 'spec' Kunnel Tom an' Marse Prent McMakin would o' settle' *him* ef dey evah had o' cotched him—dat dar David Ahmstrong!"

"Who?" says I.

"David Ahmstrong was his entitlement," says George, "an' he been gwine to de same college as Marse Tom Buckner, up no'th somewhah. Dat's how-come he been visitin' Marse Tom des befoh de weddin' trouble done settle *hit* se'f dat-away."

Well, it give me quite a turn to run onto the mention of that there David Armstrong agin in this part of the country. Here he had been jilting Miss Hampton way up in Indiany, and running away with another girl down here in Tennessee. Then it struck me mebby it is jest different parts of the same story I been hearing of, and Martha had got her part a little wrong.

"George," I says, "what did you say Miss Lucy Buckner's gran-dad's name was?"

"Kunnel Hampton—des de same as *my* Miss Lucy befo' *she* done ma'hied Marse Willyum."

That made me sure of it. It was the same woman. She had run away with David Armstrong from this here same neighbourhood. Then after he got her up North he had left her—or her left him. And then she wasn't Miss Buckner no longer. And she was mad and wouldn't call herself Mrs. Armstrong. So she moved away from where any one was lible to trace her to, and took her mother's maiden name, which was Hampton.

"Well," I says, "what ever become of 'em after they run off, George?"

But George has told about all he knows. They went North, according to what everybody thinks, he says. Prent McMakin, he follered and hunted. And

Col. Tom Buckner, he done the same. Fur about a year Colonel Tom, he was always making trips away from there to the North. But whether he ever got any track of his sister and that David Armstrong nobody knowed. Nobody never asked him. Old Colonel Hampton, he grieved and he grieved, and not long after the runaway he up and died. And Tom Buckner, he finally sold all he owned in that part of the country and moved further south. George said he didn't rightly know whether it was Alabama or Florida. Or it might of been Georgia.

I thinks to myself that mebby Mrs. Davis would like to know where her niece is, and that I better tell her about Miss Hampton being in that there little Indiany town, and where it is. And then I thinks to myself I better not butt in. Fur Miss Hampton has likely got her own reasons fur keeping away from her folks, or else she wouldn't do it. Anyhow, it's none of *my* affair to bring the subject up to 'em. It looks to me like one of them things George has been gassing about—one of them things that has settled itself, and it ain't fur me to meddle and unsettle it.

It set me to thinking about Martha, too. Not that I hadn't thought of her lots of times. I had often thought I would write her. But I kept putting it off, and purty soon I kind of forgot Martha. I had seen a lot of different girls of all kinds since I had seen Martha. Yet, whenever I happened to think of Martha, I had always liked her best. Only moving around the country so much makes it kind of hard to keep thinking steady of the same girl. Besides, I had lost that there half of a ring, too.

But knowing what I did now about Miss Hampton being Miss Buckner—or Mrs. Armstrong—and related to these Davises made me want to get away from there. Fur that secret made me feel kind of sneaking, like I wasn't being frank and open with them. Yet if I had of told 'em I would of felt sneakinger yet fur giving Miss Hampton away. I never got into a mix up that-a-way betwixt my conscience and my duty but what it made me feel awful uncomfortable. So I guessed I would light out from there. They wasn't never no kinder, better people than them Davises, either. They was so pleased with my bringing Bud home the night he was shot they would of jest natcherally give me half their farm if I had of ast them fur it. They wanted me to stay there—they didn't say fur how long, and I guess they didn't give a dern. But I was in a sweat to ketch up with Doctor Kirby agin.

CHAPTER XV

I made purty good time, and in a couple of days I was in Atlanta. I knowed the doctor must of gone back into some branch of the medicine game—the bottles told me that. I knowed it must be something that he needed some special kind of bottles fur, too, or he wouldn't of had them shipped all that distance, but would of bought them nearer. I seen I was a dern fool fur rushing off and not inquiring what kind of bottles, so I could trace what he was into easier.

It's hard work looking fur a man in a good-sized town. I hung around hotel lobbies and places till I was tired of it, thinking he might come in. And I looked through all the office buildings and read all the advertisements in the papers. Then the second day I was there the state fair started up and I went out to it.

I run acrost a couple I knowed out there the first thing—it was Watty and the snake-charmer woman. Only she wasn't charming them now. Her and Watty had a Parisian Models' show. I ast Watty where Dolly was. He says he don't know, that Dolly has quit him. By which I guess he means he has quit her. I ast where Reginald is, and the Human Ostrich. But from the way they answered my questions I seen I wasn't welcome none around there. I suppose that Mrs. Ostrich and Watty had met up agin somewheres, and had jest natcherally run off with each other and left their famblies. Like as not she had left poor old Reginald with that idiotic ostrich feller to sell to strangers that didn't know his disposition. Or mebby by now Reginald was turned loose in the open country to shift fur himself, among wild snakes that never had no human education nor experience; and what chancet would a friendly snake like Reginald have in a gang like that? Some women has jest simply got no conscience at all about their husbands and famblies, and that there Mrs. Ostrich was one of 'em.

Well, a feller can be a derned fool sometimes. Fur all my looking around I wasted a lot of time before I thought of going to the one natcheral place—the freight depot of the road them bottles had been shipped by. I had lost a week coming down. But freight often loses more time than that. And it was at the freight depot that I found him.

Tickled? Well, yes! Both of us.

"Well, by George," says he, "you're good for sore eyes."

Before he told me how he happened not to of drownded or blowed away or anything he says we better fix up a bit. Which he meant I better. So he buys me duds from head to heel, and we goes to a Turkish bath place and I puts 'em on. And then we goes and eats. Hearty.

"Now," he says, "Fido Cut-up, how did you find me?" *

I told him about the bottles.

"A dead loss, those bottles," he says. "I wanted some non-refillable ones for a little scheme I had in mind, and I had to get them at a certain place—and now the scheme's up in the air and I can't use 'em."

The doctor had changed some in looks in the year or more that had passed since I saw him floating away in that balloon. And not fur the better. He told me how he had blowed clean acrost Lake Erie in that there balloon. And then when he got over land agin and went to pull the cord that lets the parachute loose it wouldn't work at first. He jest natcherally drifted on into the midst of nowhere, he said—miles and miles into Canada. When he lit the balloon had lost so much gas and was flying so low that the parachute didn't open out quick enough to do much floating. So he lit hard, and come near being knocked out fur good. But—

*Author's Note—Can it be that Danny struggles vaguely to report some reference to *fidus achates*?

that wasn't the worst of it, fur the exposure had crawled into his lungs by the time he found a house, and he got newmonia into them also, and like to of died. Whilst I was laying sick he had been sick also, only his'n lasted much longer.

But he tells me he has jest struck an idea fur a big scheme. No little schemes go fur him any more, he says. He wants money. Real money.

"How you going to get it?" I asts him.

"Come along and I'll tell you," he says. "We'll take a walk, and I'll show you how I got my idea."

We left the restaurant and went along the brag street of that town, which it is awful proud of, past where the stores stops and the houses begins. We come to a fine-looking house on a corner—a swell place it was, with lots of palms and ferns and plants setting on the verandah and showing through the windows. And stables back of it; and back of the stables a big yard with noises coming from it like they was circus animals there. Which I found out later they really was, kept fur pets. You could tell the people that lived there had money.

"This," says Doctor Kirby, as we walked by, "is the house that Jackson built. Dr. Julius Jackson—*old* Doctor Jackson, the man with an idea! The idea made all the money you smell around here."

"Old Doctor Jackson, the man with an idea — the glorious
humanitarian and philanthropic idea of taking the kinks
and curls out of the hair of the Afro-American brother"

"What idea?"

"The idea—the glorious humanitarian and philanthropic idea—of taking the kinks and curls out of the hair of the Afro-American brother," says Doctor Kirby, "at so much per kink."

This Doctor Jackson, he says, sells what he calls Anti-Curl to the niggers. It is to straighten out their hair so it will look like white people's hair. They is millions and millions of niggers, and every nigger has millions and millions of kinks, and so Doctor Jackson has got rich at it. So rich he can afford to keep that there personal circus menagerie in his back yard, for his little boy to play with, and many other interesting things. He must be worth two, three million dollars, Doctor Kirby says, and still a-making it, with more niggers growing up all the time fur to have their hair unkinked. Especially mulattoes and yaller niggers. Doctor Kirby says thinking what a great idea that Anti-Curl was give him his own great idea. They is a gold mine there, he says, and Dr. Julius Jackson has only scratched a little off the top of it, but *he* is going to dig deeper.

"Why is it that the Afro-American brother buys Anti-Curl?" he asts.

"Why?" I asts.

"Because," he says, "he wants to be as much like a white man as he possibly can. He strives to burst his birth's invidious bar, Danny. They talk about progress and education for the Afro-American brother, and uplift and advancement and industrial education and manual training and all that sort of thing. Especially we Northerners. But what the Afro-American brother thinks about and dreams about and longs for and prays to be—when he thinks at all —is to be white. Education, to his mind, is learning to talk like a white man. Progress means aping the white man. Religion is dying and going to heaven and being a *white* angel—listen to his prayers and sermons and you'll find that out. He'll do anything he can, or give anything he can get his Ethiopian grubhooks on, for something that he thinks is going to make him more like a white man. Poor devil! Therefore the millions of Doctor Jackson Anti-Curl.

"All this Doctor Jackson Anti-Curl has discovered and thought out and acted upon. If he had gone just one step farther the Afro-American brother would have hailed him as a greater man than Abraham Lincoln, or either of the Washingtons, George or Booker. It remains for me, Danny—for *us*—to carry the torch ahead—to take up the work where the imagination of Doctor Jackson Anti-Curl has laid it down."

"How?" asts I.

"We'll put up and sell a preparation to turn the negroes white!"

That was his great idea. He was more excited over it than I ever seen him before about anything.

It sounded like so easy a way to get rich it made me wonder why no one had ever done it before, if it could really be worked. I didn't believe much it could be worked.

But Doctor Kirby, he says he has begun his experiments already, with arsenic. Arsenic, he says, will bleach anything. Only he is kind of afraid of arsenic, too. If he could only get hold of something that didn't cost much, and that would whiten them up fur a little while, he says, it wouldn't make no difference if they did get black agin. This here Anti-Curl stuff works like that —it takes the kinks out fur a little while, and they come back agin. But that don't seem to hurt the sale none. It only calls fur *more* of Doctor Jackson's medicine.

The doctor takes me around to the place he boards at, and shows me a nigger waiter he has been experimenting on. He had paid the nigger's fine in a police court fur slashing another nigger some with a knife, and kept him from going into the chain-gang. So the nigger agreed he could use his hide to try different kinds of medicines on. He was a velvety-looking, chocolate-coloured kind of nigger to start with, and the best Doctor Kirby had been able to do so fur was to make a few little liver-coloured spots come onto him. But it was making the nigger sick, and the doctor was afraid to go too fur with it, fur Sam might die and we would be at the expense of another nigger. Peroxide of hidergin hadn't even phased him. Nor a lot of other things we tried onto him.

You never seen a nigger with his colour running into him so deep as Sam's did. Sam, he was always apologizing about it, too. You could see it made him feel real bad to think his colour was so stubborn. He felt like it wasn't being polite to the doctor and me, Sam did, fur his skin to act that-a-way. He was a willing nigger, Sam was. The doctor, he says he will find out the right stuff if he has to start at the letter A and work Sam through every drug in the hull blame alphabet down to Z.

Which he finally struck it. I don't exactly know what she had in her, but she was a mixture of some kind. The only trouble with her was she didn't work equal and even—left Sam's face looking peeled and spotty in places. But still, in them spots, Sam was six shades lighter. The doctor says that is jest what he wants, that there passing on-to-the-next-cage-we-have-the-spotted-girocutus-look, as he calls it. The chocolate brown and the lighter spots side by side, he says, made a regular Before and After out of Sam's face, and was the best advertisement you could have.

Then we goes and has a talk with Doctor Jackson himself. Doctor Kirby has the idea mebby he will put some money into it. Doctor Jackson was setting on his front veranda with his chair tilted back, and his feet, with red carpet slippers on 'em, was on the railing, and he was smoking one of these long black cigars that comes each one in a little glass tube all by itself. He looks Sam over very thoughtful, and he says:

"Yes, it will do the work well enough. I can see that. But will it sell?"

Doctor Kirby makes him quite a speech. I never hearn him make a better one. Doctor Jackson he listens very calm, with his thumbs in the armholes of his vest, and moving his eyebrows up and down like he enjoyed it. But he don't get excited none. Finally Doctor Kirby says he will undertake to show that it will sell—me and him will take a trip down into the black country

114

ourselves and show what can be done with it, and take Sam along fur an object lesson.

Well, they was a lot of rag-chewing. Doctor Jackson don't warm up none, and he asts a million questions. Like how much it costs a bottle to make it, and what was our idea how much it orter sell fur. He says finally if we can sell a certain number of bottles in so long a time he will put some money into it. Only, he says, they will be a stock company, and he will have to have fifty-one per cent. of the stock, or he won't put no money into it. He says if things go well he will let Doctor Kirby be manager of that company, and let him have some stock in it too, and he will be president and treasurer of it himself.

Doctor Kirby, he didn't like that, and said so. Said *he* was going to organize that stock company, and control it himself. But Doctor Jackson said he never put money into nothing he couldn't run. So it was settled we would give the stuff a try-out and report to him. Before we went away from there it looked to me like Doctor Kirby and me was going to work fur this here Doctor Jackson, instead of making all them there millions fur ourselves. Which I didn't take much to that Anti-Curl man myself; he was so cold-blooded like.

I didn't like the scheme itself any too well, neither. Not any way you could look at it. In the first place it seemed like a mean trick on the niggers. Then I didn't much believe we could get away with it.

The more I looked him over the more I seen Doctor Kirby had changed considerable. When I first knowed him he liked to hear himself talking and he liked to live free and easy and he liked to be running around the country and all them things, more'n he liked to be making money. Of course, he wanted it; but that wasn't the *only* thing he was into the Sagraw game fur. If he had money, he was free with it and would help most any one out of a hole. But he wasn't thinking it and talking it all the time then.

But now he was thinking money and dreaming money and talking of nothing but how to get it. And planning to make it out of skinning them niggers. He didn't care a dern how he worked on their feelings to get it. He didn't even seem to care whether he killed Sam trying them drugs onto him. He wanted *money*, and he wanted it so bad he was ready and willing to take up with most any wild scheme to make it.

They was something about him now that didn't fit in much with the Doctor Kirby I had knowed. It seemed like he had spells when he saw himself how he had changed. He wasn't gay and joking all the time like he had been before, neither. I guess the doctor was getting along toward fifty years old. I suppose he thought if he was ever going to get anything out of his gift of the gab he better settle down to something, and quit fooling around, and do it right away. But it looked to me like he might never turn the trick. Fur he was drinking right smart all the time. Drinking made him think a lot, and thinking was making him look old. He was more'n one year older than he had been a year ago.

He kept a quart bottle in his room now. The night after we had took Sam to see Doctor Jackson we was setting in his room, and he was hitting it purty hard.

"Danny," he says to me, after a while, like he was talking out loud to himself too, "what did you think of Doctor Jackson?"

"I don't like him much," I says.

"Nor I," he says, frowning, and takes a drink. Then he says, after quite a few minutes of frowning and thinking, under his breath like: "He's a blame sight more decent than I am, for all of that."

"Why?" I asts him.

"Because Doctor Jackson," he says, "hasn't the least idea that he *isn't* decent, and getting his money in a decent way. While at one time I was—"

He breaks off and don't say what he was. I asts him. "I was going to say a gentleman," he says, "but on reflection, I doubt if I was ever anything but a cheap imitation. I never heard a man say that he was a gentleman at one time, that I didn't doubt him. Also," he goes on, working himself into a better humour again with the sound of his own voice, "if I *had* ever been a gentleman at any time, enough of it would surely have stuck to me to keep me out of partnership with a man who cheats niggers."

He takes another drink and says even twenty years of running around the country couldn't of took all the gentleman out of him like this, if he had ever been one, fur you can break, you can scatter the vase if you will, but the smell of the roses will stick round it still.

I seen now the kind of conversations he is always having with himself when he gets jest so drunk and is thinking hard. Only this time it happens to be out loud.

"What is a gentleman?" I asts him, thinking if he wasn't one it might take his mind off himself a little to tell me. "What *makes* one?"

"Authorities differ," says Doctor Kirby, slouching down in his chair, and grinning like he knowed a joke he wasn't going to tell no one. "I heard Doctor Jackson describe himself that way the other day."

Well, speaking personal, I never had smelled none of roses. I wasn't nothing but trash myself, so being a gentleman didn't bother me one way or the other. The only reason I didn't want to see them niggers bunked so very bad was only jest because it was such a low-down, ornery kind of trick.

"It ain't too late," I says, "to pull out of this nigger scheme yet and get into something more honest."

"I don't know," he says thoughtful. "I think perhaps it *is* too late." And he sets there looking like a man that is going over a good many years of life in his mind. Purty soon he says:

"As far as honesty goes—it isn't that so much, O Daniel-come-to-judgment! It's about as honest as most medicine games. It's—" He stopped and frowned agin.

"What is it?"

"It's their being *niggers*," he says.

That made the difference fur me, too. I dunno how, nor why.

"I've tried nearly everything but blackmail," he says, "and I'll probably be trying that by this time next year, if this scheme fails. But there's something about their being niggers that makes me sick of this thing already—just as the time has come to make the start. And I don't know *why* it should, either." He slipped another big slug of whiskey into him, and purty soon he asts me:

"Do you know what's the matter with me?"

I asts him what.

"I'm too decent to be a crook," he says, "and too crooked to be decent. You've got to be one thing or the other steady to make it pay."

Then he says:

"Did you ever hear of the descent to Avernus, Danny?"

"I might," I tells him, "and then agin I mightn't, but if I ever did, I don't remember what she is. What is she?"

"It's the chute to the infernal regions," he says. "They say it's greased. But it isn't. It's really no easier sliding down than it is climbing back."

Well, I seen this nigger scheme of our'n wasn't the only thing that was troubling Doctor Kirby that night. It was thinking of all the schemes like it in the years past he had went into, and how he had went into 'em light-hearted and more'n half fur fun when he was a young man, and now he wasn't fitten fur nothing else but them kind of schemes, and he knowed it. He was seeing himself how he had been changing, like another person could of seen it. That's the main trouble with drinking to fergit yourself. You fergit the wrong part of yourself.

I left him purty soon, and went along to bed. My room was next to his'n, and they was a door between, so the two could be rented together if wanted, I suppose. I went to sleep and woke up agin with a start out of a dream that had in it millions and millions and millions of niggers, every way you looked, and their mouths was all open red and their eyes walled white, fit to scare you out of your shoes.

I hearn Doctor Kirby moving around in his room. But purty soon he sets down and begins to talk to himself. Everything else was quiet. I was kind of worried about him, he had taken so much, and hoped he wouldn't get a notion to go downtown that time o' night. So I thinks I will see how he is acting, and steps over to the door between the rooms.

The key happened to be on my side, and I unlocked it. But she only opens a little ways, fur his wash stand was near to the hinge end of the door.

I looked through. He is setting by the table, looking at a woman's picture that is propped up on it, and talking to himself. He has never hearn me open the door, he is so interested. But somehow, he don't look drunk. He looks like he had fought his way up out of it, somehow—his forehead was sweaty, and they was one intoxicated lock of hair sticking to it; but that was the only un-sober-looking thing about him. I guess his legs would of been unsteady if he had of tried to walk, but his intellects was uncomfortable and sober.

He is still keeping up that same old argument with himself, or with the picture.

"It isn't any use," I hearn him say, looking at the picture.

Then he listened like he hearn it answering him. "Yes, you always say just that—just that," he says. "And I don't know why I keep on listening to you."

The way he talked, and harkened fur an answer, when they was nothing there to answer, give me the creeps.

"You don't help me," he goes on, "you don't help me at all. You only make it harder. Yes, this thing is worse than the others. I know that. But I want money—and fool things like this *have* sometimes made it. No, I won't give it up. No, there's no use making any more promises now. I know myself now. And you ought to know me by this time, too. Why can't you let me alone altogether? I should think, when you see what I am, you'd let me be.

"God help you! if you'd only stay away it wouldn't be so hard to go to hell!"

CHAPTER XVI

There's a lot of counties in Georgia where the blacks are equal in number to the whites, and two or three counties where the blacks number over the whites by two to one. It was fur a little town in one of the latter that we pinted ourselves, Doctor Kirby and me and Sam—right into the blackest part of the black belt.

That country is full of big-sized plantations, where they raise cotton, cotton, cotton, and then *more* cotton. Some of 'em raises fruit, too, and other things, of course; but cotton is the main stand-by, and it looks like it always will be.

Some places there shows that things can't be so awful much changed since slavery days, and most of the niggers are sure enough country niggers yet. Some rents their land right out from the owners, and some of 'em crops it on the shares, and very many of 'em jest works as hands. A lot of 'em don't do nigh so well now as they did when their bosses was their masters, they tell me; and then agin, some has done right well on their own hook. They intrusted me, because I never had been use to looking at so many niggers. Every way you turn there they is niggers and then more niggers.

Them that thinks they is awful easy to handle out of a natcheral respect fur white folks has got another guess coming. They ain't so bad to get along with if you keep it most pintedly shoved into their heads they *is* niggers. You got to do that especial in the black belt, jest because they *is* so many of 'em. They is children all their lives, mebby, till some one minute of craziness may strike one of them, and then he is a devil temporary. Mebby, when the crazy fit has passed, some white woman is worse off than if she was dead, or mebby she *is* dead, or mebby a loonatic fur life, and that nigger is a candidate fur a lynching bee and ginerally elected by an anonymous majority.

Not that *all* niggers is that-a-way, nor *half* of 'em, nor very *many* of 'em, even—but you can never tell *which* nigger is going to be. So in the black belt the white folks is mighty pertic'ler who comes along fooling with their niggers. Fur you can never tell what turn a nigger's thoughts will take, once anything at all stirs 'em up.

We didn't know them things then, Doctor Kirby and me didn't. We didn't know we was moving light-hearted right into the middle of the biggest question that has ever been ast. Which I disremember exactly how that nigger question is worded, but they is always asting it in the South, and answering of it different ways. We hadn't no idea how suspicious the white people in them awful black spots on the map can get over any one that comes along talking to their niggers. We didn't know anything about niggers much, being both from the North, except what Doctor Kirby had counted on when he made his medicine, and *that* he knowed second-handed from other people. We didn't take 'em very serious, nor all the talk we hearn about 'em down South.

But even at that we mightn't of got into any trouble if it hadn't of been fur old Bishop Warren. But that is getting ahead of the story.

We got into that little town—I might jest as well call it Cottonville—jest about supper time. Cottonville is a little place of not more'n six hundred people. I guess four hundred of 'em must be niggers.

After supper we got acquainted with purty nigh all the prominent citizens in town. They was friendly with us, and we was friendly with them. Georgia had jest went fur prohibition a few months before that, and they hadn't opened up these here near-beer bar-rooms in the little towns yet, like they had in Atlanta and the big towns. Georgia had went prohibition so the niggers couldn't get whiskey, some said; but others said they didn't know *what* its excuse was. Them prominent citizens was loafing around the hotel and every now and then inviting each other very mysterious into a back room that use to be a pool parlour. They had been several jugs come to town by express that day. We went back several times ourselves, and soon began to get along purty well with them prominent citizens.

Talking about this and that they finally edges around to the one thing everybody is sure to get to talking about sooner or later in the South—niggers. And then they gets to telling us about this here Bishop Warren I has mentioned.

He was a nigger bishop, Bishop Warren was, and had a good deal of white blood into him, they say. An ashy-coloured nigger, with bumps on his face, fat as a possum, and as cunning as a fox. He had plenty of brains into his head, too; but his brains had turned sour in his head the last few years, and the bishop had crazy streaks running through his sense now, like fat and lean mixed in a slab of bacon. He used to be friends with a lot of big white folks, and the whites depended on him at one time to preach orderliness and obedience and agriculture and being in their place to the niggers. Fur years they thought he preached that-a-way. He always *did* preach that-a-way when any whites was around, and he set on platforms sometimes with white preachers, and he got good donations fur schemes of different kinds. But gradual the suspicion got around that when he was alone with a lot of niggers his nigger blood would get the best of him, and what he preached wasn't white supremacy at all, but hopefulness of being equal.

So the whites had fell away from him, and then his graft was gone, and then his brains turned sour in his head and got to working and fermenting in it like cider getting hard, and he made a few bad breaks by not being careful what he said before white people. But the niggers liked him all the better fur that.

They always had been more or less hell in the bishop's heart. He had brains and he knowed it, and the white folks had let him see *they* knowed it, too. And he was part white, and his white forefathers had been big men in their day, and yet, in spite of all of that, he had to herd with niggers and to pertend he liked it. He was both white and black in his feelings about things, so some of his feelings counterdicted others, and one of these here race riots went on all the time in his own insides. But gradual he got to the place where they was spells he hated both whites and niggers, but he hated the whites the worst. And now, in the last two or three years, since his crazy streaks had growed as big as his sensible streaks, or bigger, they was no telling what he would preach to them niggers. But whatever he preached most of them would believe. It might be something crazy and harmless, or it might be crazy and harmful.

He had been holding some revival meetings in nigger churches right there in that very county, and was at it not fur away from there right then. The idea had got around he was preaching some most unusual foolishness to the blacks. Fur the niggers was all acting like they knowed something too good to mention to the white folks, all about there. But some white men had gone to one of the meetings, and the bishop had preached one of his old-time sermons whilst they was there, telling the niggers to be orderly and agriculturous—he was considerable of a fox yet. But he and the rest of the niggers was so *derned* anxious to be thought agriculturous and servitudinous that the whites smelt a rat, and wished he would go, fur they didn't want to chase him without they had to.

Jest when we was getting along fine one of them prominent citizens asts the doctor was we there figgering on buying some land?

"No," says the doctor, "we wasn't."

They was silence fur quite a little spell. Each prominent citizen had mebby had his hopes of unloading some. They all looks a little sad, and then another prominent citizen asts us into the back room agin.

When we returns to the front room another prominent citizen makes a little speech that was quite beautiful to hear, and says mebby we represents some new concern that ain't never been in them parts and is figgering on buying cotton.

"No," the doctor says, "we ain't cotton buyers."

Another prominent citizen has the idea mebby we is figgering on one of these here inter-Reuben trolley lines, so the Rubes in one village can ride over and visit the Rubes in the next. And another one thinks mebby we is figgering on a telephone line. And each one makes a very eloquent little speech about them things, and rings in something about our fair Southland. And when both of them misses their guess it is time fur another visit to the back room.

Was we selling something?

We was.

Was we selling fruit trees?

We wasn't.

Finally, after every one has a chew of natcheral leaf tobacco all around, one prominent citizen makes so bold as to ast us very courteous if he might enquire what it was we was selling.

The doctor says medicine.

Then they was a slow grin went around that there crowd of prominent citizens. And once agin we has to make a trip to that back room. Fur they are all sure we must be taking orders fur something to beat that there prohibition game. When they misses that guess they all gets kind of thoughtful and sad. A couple of 'em don't take no more interest in us, but goes along home sighing-like, as if it wasn't no difference *what* we sold as long as it wasn't what they was looking fur.

But purty soon one of them asts:

"What *kind* of medicine?"

The doctor, he tells about it.

When he finishes you never seen such a change as had come onto the faces of that bunch. I never seen such disgusted prominent citizens in my hull life. They looked at each other embarrassed, like they had been ketched at something ornery. And they went out one at a time, saying good night to the hotel-keeper and in the most pinted way taking no notice of us at all. It certainly was a chill. We sees something is wrong, and we begins to have a notion of what it is.

The hotel-keeper, he spits out his chew, and goes behind his little counter and takes a five-cent cigar out of his little show case and bites the end off careful. Then he leans his elbows onto his counter and reads our names to himself out of the register book, and looks at us, and from us to the names, and from the names to us, like he is trying to figger out how he come to let us write 'em there. Then he wants to know where we come from before we come to Atlanta, where we had registered from. We tells him we is from the North. He lights his cigar like he didn't think much of that cigar and sticks it in his mouth and looks at us so long in an absent-minded kind of way it goes out.

Then he says we orter go back North.

"Why?" asts the doctor.

He chewed his cigar purty nigh up to the middle of it before he answered, and when he spoke it was a soft kind of a drawl—not mad or loud—but like they was sorrowful thoughts working in him.

"Yo' all done struck the wo'st paht o' the South to peddle yo' niggah medicine in, sah. I reckon yo' must love 'em a heap to be that concerned over the colour of their skins."

And he turned his back on us and went into the back room all by himself.

We seen we was in wrong in that town. The doctor says it will be no use trying to interduce our stuff there, and we might as well leave there in the morning and go over to Bairdstown, which was a little place about ten miles off the railroad, and make our start there.

So we got a rig the next morning and drove acrost the country. No one bid us good-bye, neither, and Doctor Kirby says it's a wonder they rented us the rig.

But before we started that morning we noticed a funny thing. We hadn't so much as spoke to any nigger, except our own nigger Sam, and he couldn't of told *all* the niggers in that town about the stuff to turn niggers white, even if he had set up all night to do it. But every last nigger we saw looked like he knowed something about us. Even after we left town our nigger driver hailed two or three niggers in the road that acted that-away. It seemed like they was all awful polite to us. And yet they was different in their politeness than they was to them Georgia folks, which is their natcheral-born bosses—acted more familiar, somehow, as if they knowed we must be thinking about the same thing they was thinking about.

About half-way to Bairdstown we stopped at a place to get a drink of water. Seemingly the white folks was away fur the day, and an old nigger come up and talked to our driver while Sam and us was at the well.

I seen them cutting their eyes at us, whilst they was unchecking the hosses to let them drink too, and then I hearn the one that belonged there say:

"Is yo' *suah* dat hit air dem?"

123

"*Suah!*" says the driver.

"How-come yo' so all-powerful *suah* about hit?"

The driver pertended the harness needed some fixing, and they went around to the other side of the team and tinkered with one of the traces, a-talking to each other. I hearn the old nigger say, kind of wonderized:

"Is dey a-gwine dar *now*?"

Sam, he was pulling a bucket of water up out of the well fur us with a windlass. The doctor says to him:

"Sam, what does all this mean?"

Sam, he pertends he don't know what the doctor is talking about. But Doctor Kirby he finally pins him down. Sam hemmed and hawed considerable, making up his mind whether he better lie to us or not. Then, all of a sudden, he busted out into an awful fit of laughing, and like to of fell in the well. Seemingly he decided fur to tell us the truth.

From what Sam says that there bishop has been holding revival meetings in Big Bethel, which is a nigger church right on the edge of Bairdstown, and niggers fur miles around has been coming night after night, and some of them whooping her up daytimes too. And the bishop has worked himself up the last three or four nights to where he has been perdicting and prophesying, fur the spirit has hit the meeting hard.

What he has been prophesying, Sam says, is the coming of a Messiah fur the nigger race—a new Elishyah, he says, as will lead them from out'n their inequality and bring 'em up to white standards right on the spot. The whites has had their Messiah, the bishop says, but the niggers ain't never had none of their *special own* yet. And they needs one bad, and one is sure a-coming.

It seems the whites don't know yet jest what the bishop's been a-preaching. But every nigger fur miles on every side of Big Bethel is a-listening and a-looking fur signs and omens, and has been fur two, three days now. This here half-crazy bishop has got 'em worked up to where they is ready to believe anything, or do anything.

So the night before when the word got out in Cottonville that we had some scheme to make the niggers white, the niggers there took up with the idea that the doctor was mebby the feller the bishop had been prophesying about, and for a sign and a omen and a miracle of his grace and powers was going out to Big Bethel to turn 'em white. Poor devils, they didn't see but what being turned white orter be a part of what they was to get from the coming of that there Messiah.

News spreads among niggers quicker than among whites. No one knows how they do it. But I've hearn tales about how when war times was there, they would frequent have the news of a big fight before the white folks' papers would. Soldiers has told me that in them there Philippine Islands we conquered from Spain, where they is so much nigger blood mixed up with other kinds in the islanders, this mysterious spreading around of news is jest the same. And jest since nine o'clock the night before, the news had spread fur miles around that Bishop Warren's Messiah was on his way, and was going fur to turn the bishop white to show his power and grace, and he had with him one he had turned part white, and that was Sam, and one he had turned clear white, and that was me. And they was to be signs and wonders to behold at Big Bethel, with pillars of cloud and sounds of trumpets and fire squirting down from heaven, like it always use to be in them old Bible days, and them there niggers to be led singing and shouting and rejoicing into a land of milk and honey, forevermore, *Amen!*

That's what Sam says they are looking fur, dozens and scores and hundreds of them niggers round about. Sam, he had lived in town five or six years, and he looked down on all these here ignoramus country niggers. So he busts out laughing at first, and he pertends like he don't take no stock in any of it. Besides, he knowed well enough he wasn't spotted up by no Messiah, but it was the dope in the bottles done it. But as he told about them goings-on Sam got more and more interested and warmed up to it, and his voice went into a kind of a sing-song like he was prophesying himself. And the other two niggers quit pertending to fool around the team and edged a little closer, and a little closer yet, with their mouths open and their heads a-nodding and the whites of their eyes a-rolling.

Fur my part, I never hearn such a lot of dern foolishness in all my life. But the doctor, he says nothing at all. He listens to Sam ranting and rolling out big words and raving, and only frowns. He climbs back into the buggy agin silent, and all the rest of the way to Bairdstown he set there with that scowl on his face. I guesses he was thinking now, the way things had shaped up, he wouldn't sell none of his stuff at all without he fell right in with the reception chance had planned fur him. But if he did fall in with it, and pertend like he was a Messiah to them niggers, he could get all they had. He was mebby thinking how much ornerier that would make the hull scheme.

CHAPTER XVII

We got to Bairdstown early enough, but we didn't go to work there. We wasted all that day. They was something working in the doctor's head he wasn't talking about. I supposed he was getting cold feet on the hull proposition. Anyhow, he jest set around the little tavern in that place and done nothing all afternoon.

The weather was fine, and we set out in front. We hadn't set there more'n an hour till I could tell we was being noticed by the blacks, not out open and above board. But every now and then one or two or three would pass along down the street, and lazy about and take a look at us. They pertended they wasn't noticing, but they was. The word had got around, and they was a feeling in the air I didn't like at all. Too much caged-up excitement among the niggers. The doctor felt it too, I could see that. But neither one of us said anything about it to the other.

Along toward dusk we takes a walk. They was a good-sized crick at the edge of that little place, and on it an old-fashioned worter mill. Above the mill a little piece was a bridge. We crossed it and walked along a road that follered the crick bank closte fur quite a spell.

It wasn't much of a town—something betwixt a village and a settlement—although they was going to run a branch of the railroad over to it before very long. It had had a chancet to get a railroad once, years before that. But it had said then it didn't want no railroad. So until lately every branch built through that part of the country grinned very sarcastic and give it the go-by.

They was considerable woods standing along the crick, and around a turn in the road we come onto Sam, all of a sudden, talking with another nigger. Sam was jest a-laying it off to that nigger, but he kind of hushed as we come nearer. Down the road quite a little piece was a good-sized wooden building that never had been painted and looked like it was a big barn. Without knowing it the doctor and me had been pinting ourselves right toward Big Bethel.

The nigger with Sam he yells out, when he sees us:

"Glory be! *Hyah* dey comes! Hyah dey comes *now!*"

"'Glory be! *Hyah* dey comes! Hyah dey comes *now!*'"

And he throwed up his arms, and started on a lope up the road toward the church, singing out every ten or fifteen yards. A little knot of niggers come out in front of the church when they hearn him coming.

Sam, he stood his ground, and waited fur us to come up to him, kind of apologetic and sneaking—looking about something or other.

"What kind of lies have you been telling these niggers, Sam?" says the doctor, very sharp and short and mad-like.

Sam, he digs a stone out'n the road with the toe of his shoe, and kind of grins to himself, still looking sheepish. But he says he opinionates he been telling them nothing at all.

"I dunno how-come dey get all dem nigger notions in dey fool haid," Sam says, "but dey all waitin' dar inside de chu'ch do'—some of de mos' faiful an' de mos' pra'rful ones o' de Big Bethel cong'gation been dar fo' de las' houah a-waitin' an' a-watchin', spite o' de fac' dat reg'lah meetin' ain't gwine ter be called twell arter supper. De bishop, he dar too. Dey got some dese hyah coal-ile lamps dar des inside de chu'ch do' an' dey been keepin' on 'em lighted,

127

daytimes an' night times, fo' two days now, kaze dey say dey ain't gwine fo' ter be cotched napping when de bridegroom *com*eth. Yass, *sah!*—dey's ten o' dese hyah vergims dar, five of 'em sleepin' an' five of 'em watchin', an' a-takin' tuhns at hit, an' mebby dat how-come free or fouah dey bes' young colo'hed mens been projickin' aroun' dar all arternoon, a-helpin' dem dat's a-waitin' twell de bridegroom *com*eth!"

We seen a little knot of them, down the road there in front of the church, gathering around the nigger that had been with Sam. They all starts toward us. But one man steps out in front of them all, and turns toward them and holds his hands up, and waves them back. They all stops in their tracks.

Then he turns his face toward us, and comes slow and sollum down the road in our direction, walking with a cane, and moving very dignified. He was a couple of hundred yards away.

But as he come closeter we gradually seen him plainer and plainer. He was a big man, and stout, and dressed very neat in the same kind of rig as white bishops wear, with one of these white collars that buttons in the back. I suppose he was coming on to meet us alone, because no one was fitten fur to give us the first welcome but himself.

Well, it was all dern foolishness, and it was hard to believe it could all happen, and they ain't so many places in this here country it *could* happen. But fur all of it being foolishness, when he come down the road toward us so dignified and sollum and slow I ketched myself fur a minute feeling like we really had been elected to something and was going to take office soon. And Sam, as the bishop come closeter and closeter, got to jerking and twitching with the excitement that he had been keeping in—and yet all the time Sam knowed it was dope and works and not faith that had made him spotted that-a-way.

He stops, the bishop does, about ten yards from us and looks us over.

"Ah yo' de gennleman known ter dis hyah sinful genehation by de style an' de entitlemint o' Docto' Hahtley Kirby?" he asts the doctor very ceremonious and grand.

The doctor give him a look that wasn't very encouraging, but he nodded to him.

"Will yo' dismiss yo' sehvant in ordeh dat we kin hol' convehse an' communion in de midst er privacy?"

The doctor, he nods to Sam, and Sam moseys along toward the church.

"Now, then," says the doctor, sudden and sharp, "take off your hat and tell me what you want."

The bishop's hand goes up to his head with a jerk before he thought. Then it stops there, while him and the doctor looks at each other. The bishop's mouth opens like he was wondering, but he slowly pulls his hat off and stands there bare-headed in the road. But he wasn't really humble, that bishop.

"Now," says the doctor, "tell me in as straight talk as you've got what all this damned foolishness among you niggers means."

A queer kind of look passed over the bishop's face. He hadn't expected to be met jest that way, mebby. Whether he himself had really believed in the coming of that there new Messiah he had been perdicting, I never could settle in my mind. Mebby he had been getting ready to pass *Himself* off fur one before we come along and the niggers all got the fool idea Doctor Kirby was it. Before the bishop spoke agin you could see his craziness and his cunningness both working in his face. But when he did speak he didn't quit being ceremonious nor dignified.

"De wohd has gone fo'th among de faiful an' de puah in heaht," he says, "dat er man has come accredited wi' signs an' wi' mahvels an' de poweh o' de sperrit fo' to lay his han' on de sons o' Ham an' ter make 'em des de same in colluh as de yuther sons of ea'th."

"Then that word is a lie," says the doctor. "I *did* come here to try out some stuff to change the colour of negro skins. That's all. And I find your idiotic followers are all stirred up and waiting for some kind of a miracle monger. What you have been preaching to them, you know best. Is that all you want to know?"

The bishop hems and haws and fiddles with his stick, and then he says:

"Suh, will dish yeah prepa'shun *sho'ly* do de wohk?" Doctor Kirby tells him it will do the work all right.

And then the bishop, after beating around the bush some more, comes out with his idea. Whether he expected there would be any Messiah come or not, of course he knowed the doctor wasn't him. But he is willing to boost the doctor's game as long as it boosts *his* game. He wants to be in on the deal. He wants part of the graft. He wants to get together with the doctor on a plan before the doctor sees the niggers. And if the doctor don't want to keep on with the miracle end of it, the bishop shows him how he could do him good with no miracle attachment. Fur he has an awful holt on them niggers, and his say-so will sell thousands and thousands of bottles. What he is looking fur jest now is his little take-out.

That was his craftiness and his cunningness working in him. But all of a

129

sudden one of his crazy streaks come bulging to the surface. It come with a wild, eager look in his eyes.

"Suh," he cries out, all of a sudden, "ef yo' kin make me white, fo' Gawd sakes, do hit! Do hit! Ef yo' does, I gwine ter bless yo' all yo' days!

"Yo' don' know—no one kin guess or comperhen'—what des bein' white would mean ter me! Lawd! Lawd!" he says, his voice soft-spoken, but more eager than ever as he went on, and pleading something pitiful to hear, "des think of all de Caucasian blood in me! Gawd knows de nights er my youth I'se laid awake twell de dawn come red in de Eas' a-cryin' out ter Him only fo' ter be white! *Des ter be white!* Don' min' dem black, black niggers dar—don' think er *dem*—dey ain't wuth nothin' nor fitten fo' no fate but what dey got—But me! What's done kep' me from gwine ter de top but dat one thing: *I wasn't white!* Hit air too late now—too late fo' dem ambitions I done trifle with an' shove behin' me—hit's too late fo' dat! But ef I was des ter git one li'l year o' hit—*one li'l year o' bein' white!*—befo' I died—"

And he went on like that, shaking and stuttering there in the road, like a fit had struck him, crazy as a loon. But he got hold of himself enough to quit talking, in a minute, and his cunning come back to him before he was through trembling. Then the doctor says slow and even, but not severe:

"You go back to your people now, bishop, and tell them they've made a mistake about me. And if you can, undo the harm you've done with this Messiah business. As far as this stuff of mine is concerned, there's none of it for you nor for any other negro. You tell them that. There's none of it been sold yet—and there never will be."

Then we turned away and left him standing there in the road, still with his hat off and his face working.

Walking back toward the little tavern the doctor says:

"Danny, this is the end of this game. These people down here and that half-cracked, half-crooked old bishop have made me see a few things about the Afro-American brother. It wasn't a good scheme in the first place. And this wasn't the place to start it going, anyhow—I should have tried the niggers in the big towns. But I'm out of it now, and I'm glad of it. What we want to do is to get away from here to-morrow—go back to Atlanta and fix up a scheme to rob some widows and orphans, or something half-way respectable like that."

Well, I drew a long breath. I was with Doctor Kirby in everything he done, fur he was my friend, and I didn't intend to quit him. But I was glad we was out of this, and hadn't sold none of that dope. We both felt better because we hadn't. All them millions we was going to make—shucks! We didn't neither one of us give a dern about them getting away from us. All we wanted was jest to get away from there and not get mixed up with no nigger problems any more. We eat supper, and we set around a while, and we went to bed purty middling early, so as to get a good start in the morning.

We got up early, but early as it was the devil had been up earlier in that neighbourhood. About four o'clock that morning a white woman about a half a mile from the village had been attacked by a nigger. They was doubt as to whether she would live, but if she lived they wasn't no doubts she would always be more or less crazy. Fur besides everything else, he had beat her insensible. And he had choked her nearly to death. The country-side was up, with guns and pistols looking fur that nigger. It wasn't no trouble guessing what would happen to him when they ketched him, neither.

"And," says Doctor Kirby, when we hearn of it, "I hope to high heaven they *do* catch him!"

They wasn't much doubt they would, either. They was already beating up the woods and bushes and gangs was riding up and down the roads, and every nigger's house fur miles around was being searched and watched.

We soon seen we would have trouble getting hosses and a rig in the village to take us to the railroad. Many of the hosses was being ridden in the man-hunt. And most of the men who might have done the driving was busy at that too. The hotel-keeper himself had left his place standing wide open and went out. We didn't get any breakfast neither.

"Danny," says the doctor, "we'll just put enough money to pay the bill in an envelope on the register here, and strike out on shank's ponies. It's only nine or ten miles to the railroad—we'll walk."

"But how about our stuff?" I asts him. We had two big cases full of sample bottles of that dope, besides our suit cases.

"Hang the dope!" says the doctor, "I don't ever want to see it or hear of it again! We'll leave it here. Put the things out of your suit case into mine, and leave that here too. Sam can carry mine. I want to be on the move."

So we left, with Sam carrying the one suit case. It wasn't nine in the morning yet, and we was starting out purty empty fur a long walk.

"Sam," says the doctor, as we was passing that there Big Bethel church—and it showed up there silent and shabby in the morning, like a old coloured man that knows a heap more'n he's going to tell—"Sam, were you at the meeting here last night?"

"Yass, suh!"

131

"I suppose it was a pretty tame affair after they found out their Elisha wasn't coming after all?"

Sam, he walled his eyes, and then he kind of chuckled.

"Well, suh," he says, "I 'spicions de mos' on 'em don' know dat *yit!*"

The doctor asts him what he means.

It seems the bishop must of done some thinking after we left him in the road or on his way back to that church. They had all begun to believe that there Elishyah was on the way to 'em, and the bishop's credit was more or less wrapped up with our being it. It was true he hadn't started that belief; but it was believed, and he didn't dare to stop it now. Fur, if he stopped it, they would all think he had fell down on his prophetics, even although he hadn't prophesied jest exactly us. He was in a tight place, that bishop, but I bet you could always depend on him to get out of it with his flock. So what he told them niggers at the meeting last night was that he brung 'em a message from Elishyah, Sam says, the Elishyah that was to come. And the message was that the time was not ripe fur him to reveal himself as Elishyah unto the eyes of all men, fur they had been too much sinfulness and wickedness and walking into the ways of evil, right amongst that very congregation, and disobedience of the bishop, which was their guide. And he had sent 'em word, Elishyah had, that the bishop was his trusted servant, and into the keeping of the bishop was give the power to deal with his people and prepare them fur the great day to come. And the bishop would give the word of his coming. He was a box, that bishop was, in spite of his crazy streaks; and he had found a way to make himself stronger than ever with his bunch out of the very kind of thing that would have spoiled most people's graft. They had had a big meeting till nearly morning, and the power had hit 'em strong. Sam told us all about it.

But the thing that seemed to interest the doctor, and made him frown, was the idea that all them niggers round about there still had the idea he was the feller that had been prophesied to come. All except Sam, mebby. Sam had spells when he was real sensible, and other spells when he was as bad as the believingest of them all.

It was a fine day, and really joyous to be a-walking. It would of been a good deal joyouser if we had had some breakfast, but we figgered we would stop somewheres at noon and lay in a good, square, country meal.

That wasn't such a very thick settled country. But everybody seemed to know about the manhunt that was going on, here, there, and everywhere. People would come down to the road side as we passed, and gaze after us. Or mebby ast us if we knowed whether he had been ketched yet. Women and kids mostly, or old men, but now and then a younger man too. We noticed they wasn't no niggers to speak of that wasn't busier'n all get out, working at something or other, that day.

They is considerable woods in that country yet, though lots has been cut off. But they was sometimes right long stretches where they would be woods on both sides of the road, more or less thick, with underbrush between the trees. We tramped along, each busy thinking his own thoughts, and having a purty good time jest doing that without there being no use of talking. I was thinking that I liked the doctor better fur turning his back on all this game, jest when he might of made some sort of a deal with the bishop and really made some money out of it in the end. He never was so good a business man as he thought he was, Doctor Kirby wasn't. He always could make himself think he was. But when it come right down to brass tacks he wasn't. You give him a scheme that would *talk* well, the kind of a josh talk he liked to get off fur his own enjoyment, and he would take up with it every time instead of one that had more promise of money to it if it was worked harder. He was thinking of the *talk* more'n he was of the money, mostly; and he was always saying something about art fur art's sake, which was plumb foolishness, fur he never painted no pictures. Well, he never got over being more or less of a puzzle to me. But fur some reason or other this morning he seemed to be in a better humour with himself, after we had walked a while, than I had seen him in fur a long time.

We come to the top of one long hill, which it had made us sweat to climb, and without saying nothing to each other we both stopped and took off our hats and wiped our foreheads, and drawed long breaths, content to stand there fur jest a minute or two and look around us. The road run straight ahead, and dipped down, and then clumb up another hill about an eighth of a mile in front of us. It made a little valley. Jest about the middle, between the two hills, a crick meandered through the bottom land. Woods growed along the crick, and along both sides of the road we was travelling. Right nigh the crick they was another road come out of the woods to the left-hand side, and switched into the road we was travelling, and used the same bridge to cross the crick by. They was three or four houses here and there, with chimbleys built up on the outside of them, and blue smoke coming out. We stood and looked at the sight before us and forgot all the troubles we had left behind, fur a couple of minutes—it all looked so peaceful and quiet and homeyfied and nice.

"Well," says the doctor, after we had stood there a piece, "I guess we better be moving on again, Danny."

But jest as Sam, who was follering along behind with that suit case, picks it up and puts it on his head agin, they come a sound, from away off in the distance somewheres, that made him set it down quick. And we all stops in our tracks and looks at each other.

It was the voice of a hound dog—not so awful loud, but clear and mellow and tuneful, and carried to us on the wind. And then in a minute it come agin, sharper and quicker. They yells like that when they have struck a scent.

As we stood and looked at each other they come a crackle in the underbrush, jest to the left of us. We turned our heads that-a-way, jest as a nigger man give a leap to the top of a rail fence that separated the road from the woods. He was going so fast that instead of climbing that fence and balancing on the top and jumping off he jest simply seemed to hit the top rail and bounce on over, like he had been throwed out of the heart of the woods, and he fell sprawling over and over in the road, right before our feet.

He was onto his feet in a second, and fur a minute he stood up straight and looked at us—an ashes-coloured nigger, ragged and bleeding from the underbrush, red-eyed, and with slavers trickling from his red lips, and sobbing and gasping and panting fur breath. Under his brown skin, where his shirt was torn open acrost his chest, you could see that nigger's heart a-beating.

But as he looked at us they come a sudden change acrost his face—he must of seen the doctor before, and with a sob he throwed himself on his knees in the road and clasped his hands and held 'em out toward Doctor Kirby.

"*Elishyah! Elishyah!*" he sings out, rocking of his body in a kind of tune, "reveal yo'se'f, reveal yo'se'f an' he'p me *now!* Lawd Gawd *Elishyah*, beckon fo' a *Cha'iot*, yo' cha'iot of *fiah!* Lif' me, lif' me—lif' me away f'um hyah in er cha'iot o' *fiah!*"

The doctor, he turned his head away, and I knowed the thought working in him was the thought of that white woman that would always be an idiot for life, if she lived. But his lips was dumb, and his one hand stretched itself out toward that nigger in the road and made a wiping motion, like he was trying fur to wipe the picture of him, and the thought of him, off'n a slate forevermore.

Jest then, nearer and louder and sharper, and with an eager sound, like they knowed they almost had him now, them hounds' voices come ringing through the woods, and with them come the mixedup shouts of men.

"*Run!*" yells Sam, waving of that suit case round his head, fur one nigger will always try to help another no matter what he's done. "Run fo' de branch —git yo' foots in de worter an' fling 'em off de scent!"

He bounded down the hill, that red-eyed nigger, and left us standing there. But before he reached the crick the whole man-hunt come busting through the woods, the dogs a-straining at their straps. The men was all on foot, with guns and pistols in their hands. They seen the nigger, and they all let out a yell, and was after him. They ketched him at the crick, and took him off along that road that turned off to the left. I hearn later he was a member of Bishop Warren's congregation, so they hung him right in front of Big Bethel church.

We stood there on top of the hill and saw the chase and capture. Doctor Kirby's face was sweating worse than when we first clumb the hill. He was thinking about that nigger that had pleaded with him. He was thinking also of the woman. He was glad it hadn't been up to him personal right then and there to butt in and stop a lynching. He was glad, fur with them two pictures in front of him he didn't know what he would of done.

"Thank heaven!" I hearn him say to himself. "Thank heaven that it wasn't *really* in my power to choose!"

CHAPTER XVIII

Well, we had pork and greens fur dinner that day, with the best corn-bread I ever eat anywheres, and buttermilk, and sweet potato pie. We got 'em at the house of a feller named Withers—Old Daddy Withers. Which if they was ever a nicer old man than him, or a nicer old woman than his wife, I never run acrost 'em yet.

They lived all alone, them Witherses, with only a couple of niggers to help them run their farm. After we eats our dinner and Sam gets his'n out to the kitchen, we sets out in front of the house and gets to talking with them, and gets real well acquainted. Which we soon found out the secret of old Daddy Withers's life—that there innocent-looking old jigger was a poet. He was kind of proud of it and kind of shamed of it both to oncet. The way it come out was when the doctor says one of them quotations he is always getting off, and the old man he looks pleased and says the rest of the piece it dropped out of straight through.

Then they had a great time quoting it at each other, them two, and I seen the doctor is good to loaf around there the rest of the day, like as not. Purty soon the old lady begins to get mighty proud-looking over something or other, and she leans over and whispers to the old man:

"Shall I bring it out, Lemuel?"

The old man, he shakes his head, no. But she slips into the house anyhow, and fetches out a little book with a pale green cover to it, and hands it to the doctor.

"Bless my soul," says Doctor Kirby, looking at the old man, "you don't mean to say you write verse yourself?"

The old man, he gets red all over his face, and up into the roots of his white hair, and down into his white beard, and makes believe he is a little mad at the old lady fur showing him off that-a-way.

"Mother," he says, "yo' shouldn't have done that!" They had had a boy years before, and he had died, but he always called her mother the same as if the boy was living. He goes into the house and gets his pipe, and brings it out and lights it, acting like that book of poetry was a mighty small matter to him. But he looks at Doctor Kirby out of the corner of his eyes, and can't keep from getting sort of eager and trembly with his pipe; and I could see he was really anxious over what the doctor was thinking of them poems he wrote. The doctor reads some of 'em out loud.

Well, it was kind of home-made poetry, Old Daddy Withers's was. It wasn't like no other poetry I ever struck. And I could tell the doctor was thinking the same about it. It sounded somehow like it hadn't been jointed together right. You would keep listening fur it to rhyme, and get all worked up watching and waiting fur it to, and make bets with yourself whether it would rhyme or it wouldn't. And then it ginerally wouldn't. I never hearn such poetry to get a person's expectances all worked up, and then go back on 'em. But if you could of told what it was all about, you wouldn't of minded that so much. Not that you can tell what most poetry is about, but you don't care so long as it keeps hopping along lively. What you want in poetry to make her sound good, according to my way of thinking, is to make her jump lively, and then stop with a bang on the rhymes. But Daddy Withers was so independent-like he would jest natcherally try to force two words to rhyme whether the Lord made 'em fur mates or not—like as if you would try to make a couple of kids kiss and make up by bumping their heads together. They jest simply won't do it. But Doctor Kirby, he let on like he thought it was fine poetry, and he read them pieces over and over agin, out loud, and the old man and the old woman was both mighty tickled with the way he done it. He wouldn't of had 'em know fur anything he didn't believe it was the finest poetry ever wrote, Doctor Kirby wouldn't.

They was four little books of it altogether. Slim books that looked as if they hadn't had enough to eat, like a stray cat whose ribs is rubbing together. It had cost Daddy Withers five hundred dollars apiece to get 'em published. A feller in Boston charged him that much, he said. It seems he would go along fur years, raking and scraping of his money together, so as to get enough ahead to get out another book. Each time he had his hopes the big newspapers would mebby pay some attention to it, and he would get recognized.

"But they never did," said the old man, kind of sad, "it always fell flat."

"Why, *father!*"—the old lady begins, and finishes by running back into the house agin. She is out in a minute with a clipping from a newspaper and hands it over to Doctor Kirby, as proud as a kid with copper-toed boots. The doctor reads it all the way through, and then he hands it back without saying a word. The old lady goes away to fiddle around about the housework purty soon and the old man looks at the doctor and says:

"Well, you see, don't you?"

"Yes," says the doctor, very gentle.

"I wouldn't have *her* know for the world," says Daddy Withers. "*I* know and *you* know that newspaper piece is just simply poking fun at my poetry, and making a fool of me, the whole way through. As soon as I read it over

137

careful I saw it wasn't really praise, though there was a minute or two I thought my recognition had come. But *she* don't know it ain't serious from start to finish. *She* was all-mighty pleased when that piece come out in print. And I don't intend she ever shall know it ain't real praise."

His wife was so proud when that piece come out in that New York paper, he said, she cried over it. She said now she was glad they had been doing without things fur years and years so they could get them little books printed, one after the other, fur now fame was coming. But sometimes, Daddy Withers says, he suspicions she really knows he has been made a fool of, and is pertending not to see it, fur his sake, the same as he is pertending fur *her* sake. Well, they was a mighty nice old couple, and the doctor done a heap of pertending fur both their sakes—they wasn't nothing else to do.

"How'd you come to get started at it?" he asts.

Daddy Withers says he don't rightly know. Mebby, he says, it was living there all his life and watching things growing—watching the cotton grow, and the corn and getting acquainted with birds and animals and trees and things. Helping of things to grow, he says, is a good way to understand how God must feel about humans. For what you plant and help to grow, he says, you are sure to get to caring a heap about. You can't help it. And that is the reason, he says, God can be depended on to pull the human race through in the end, even if appearances do look to be agin His doing it sometimes, fur He started it to growing in the first place and that-a-way He got interested personal in it. And that is the main idea, he says, he has all the time been trying to get into that there poetry of his'n. But he reckons he ain't got her in. Leastways, he says, no one has never seen her there but the doctor and the old lady and himself. Well, for my part, I never would of seen it there myself, but when he said it out plain like that any one could of told what he meant.

You hadn't orter lay things up agin folks if the folks can't help 'em. And I will say Daddy Withers was a fine old boy in spite of his poetry. Which it never really done any harm, except being expensive to him, and lots will drink that much up and never figger it an expense, but one of the necessities of life. We went all over his place with him, and we noticed around his house a lot of tin cans tacked up to posts and trees. They was fur the birds to drink out of, and all the birds around there had found out about it, and about Daddy Withers, and wasn't scared of him at all. He could get acquainted with animals, too, so that after a long spell sometimes they would even let him handle them. But not if any one was around. They was a crow he had made a pet of, used to hop around in front of him, and try fur to talk to him. If he went to sleep in the front yard whilst he was reading, that crow had a favourite trick of stealing his spectacles off'n his nose and flying up to the ridgepole of the house, and cawing at him. Once he had been setting out a row of tomato plants very careful, and he got to the end of the row and turned around, and that there crow had been hopping along behind very sollum, pulling up each plant as he set it out. It acted like it had done something mighty smart, and knowed it, that crow. So after that the old man named him Satan, fur he said it was Satan's trick to keep things from growing. They was some blue and white pigeons wasn't scared to come and set on his shoulders; but you could see the old man really liked that crow Satan better'n any of them.

Well, we hung around all afternoon listening to the old man talk, and liking him better and better. First thing we knowed it was getting along toward supper time. And nothing would do but we must stay to supper, too. We was pinted toward a place on the railroad called Smithtown, but when we found we couldn't get a train from there till ten o'clock that night anyhow, and it was only three miles away, we said we'd stay.

After supper we calculated we'd better move. But the old man wouldn't hear of us walking that three miles. So about eight o'clock he hitched up a mule to a one-hoss wagon, and we jogged along.

They was a yaller moon sneaking up over the edge of the world when we started. It was so low down in the sky yet that it threw long shadders on the road, and they was thick and black ones, too. Because they was a lot of trees alongside the road, and the road was narrow, we went ahead mostly through the darkness, with here and there patches of moonlight splashed onto the ground. Doctor Kirby and Old Man Withers was setting on the seat, still gassing away about books and things, and I was setting on the suit case in the wagon box right behind 'em. Sam, he was sometimes in the back of the wagon. He had been more'n half asleep all afternoon, but now it was night he was waked up, the way niggers and cats will do, and every once in a while he would get out behind and cut a few capers in a moonlight patch, jest fur the enjoyment of it, and then run and ketch up with the wagon and crawl in agin, fur it was going purty slow.

The ground was sandy in spots, and I guess we made a purty good load fur Beck, the old mule. She stopped, going up a little slope, after we had went about a mile from the Witherses'. Sam says he'll get out and walk, fur the wheels was in purty deep, and it was hard going.

"Giddap, Beck!" says the old man.

But Beck, she won't. She don't stand like she is stuck, neither, but like she senses danger somewheres about. A hoss might go ahead into danger, but a mule is more careful of itself and never goes butting in unless it feels sure they is a way out.

"Giddap," says the old man agin.

But jest then the shadders on both sides of the road comes to life. They wakes up, and moves all about us. It was done so sudden and quiet it was half a minute before I seen it wasn't shadders but about thirty men had gathered all about us on every side. They had guns.

"Who are you? What d'ye want?" asts the old man, startled, as three or four took care of the mule's head very quick and quiet.

"Don't be skeered, Daddy Withers," says a drawly voice out of the dark; "we ain't goin' to hurt *you*. We got a little matter o' business to tend to with them two fellers yo' totin' to town."

———————————————————

CHAPTER XIX

THIRTY men with guns would be considerable of a proposition to buck against, so we didn't try it. They took us out of the wagon, and they pinted us down the road, steering us fur a country schoolhouse which was, I judged from their talk, about a quarter of a mile away. They took us silent, fur after we found they didn't answer no questions we quit asking any. We jest walked along, and guessed what we was up against, and why. Daddy Withers, he trailed along behind. They had tried to send him along home, but he wouldn't go. So they let him foller and paid no more heed to him.

Sam, he kept a-talking and a-begging, and several men a-telling of him to shut up. And him not a-doing it. Till finally one feller says very disgusted-like:

"Boys, I'm going to turn this nigger loose."

"We'll want his evidence," says another one.

"Evidence!" says the first one. "What's the evidence of a scared nigger worth?"

"I reckon that one this afternoon was considerable scared, when he give us that evidence against himself—that is, if you call it evidence."

"A nigger can give evidence against a nigger, and it's all right," says another voice—which it come from a feller that had a-holt of my wrist on the left-hand side of me—"but these are white men we are going to try to-night. The case is too serious to take nigger evidence. Besides, I reckon we got all the evidence any one could need. This nigger ain't charged with any crime himself, and my idea is that he ain't to be allowed to figure one way or the other in this thing."

So they turned Sam loose. I never seen nor hearn tell of Sam since then. They fired a couple of guns into the air as he started down the road, jest fur fun, and mebby he is running yet.

The feller had been talking like he was a lawyer, so I asts him what crime we was charged with. But he didn't answer me. And jest then we gets in sight of that schoolhouse.

It set on top of a little hill, partially in the moonlight, with a few sad-looking pine trees scattered around it, and the fence in front broke down. Even after night you could see it was a shabby-looking little place.

Old Daddy Withers tied his mule to the broken down fence. Somebody busted the front door down. Somebody else lighted matches. The first thing I knowed, we was all inside, and four or five dirty little coal oil lamps, with tin reflectors to 'em, which I s'pose was used ordinary fur school exhibitions, was being lighted.

We was waltzed up onto the teacher's platform, Doctor Kirby and me, and set down in chairs there, with two men to each of us, and then a tall, rawboned feller stalks up to the teacher's desk, and raps on it with the butt end of a pistol, and says:

"Gentlemen, this meeting will come to order."

Which they was orderly enough before that, but they all took off their hats when he rapped, like in a court room or a church, and most of 'em set down.

They set down in the school kids' seats, or on top of the desks, and their legs stuck out into the aisles, and they looked uncomfortable and awkward. But they looked earnest and they looked sollum, too, and they wasn't no joking nor skylarking going on, nor no kind of rowdyness, neither. These here men wasn't toughs, by any manner of means, but the most part of 'em respectable farmers. They had a look of meaning business.

"Gentlemen," says the feller who had rapped, "who will you have for your chairman?"

"I reckon you'll do, Will," says another feller to the raw-boned man, which seemed to satisfy him. But he made 'em vote on it before he took office.

"Now then," says Will, "the accused must have counsel."

"Will," says another feller, very hasty, "what's the use of all this fuss an' feathers? You know as well as I do there's nothing legal about this. It's only necessary. For my part—"

"Buck Hightower," says Will, pounding on the desk, "you will please come to order." Which Buck done it.

"Now," says the chairman, turning toward Doctor Kirby, who had been setting there looking thoughtful from one man to another, like he was sizing each one up, "now I must explain to the chief defendant that we don't intend to lynch him."

He stopped a second on that word_lynch_ as if to let it soak in. The doctor, he bowed toward him very cool and ceremonious, and says, mocking of him:

"You reassure me, Mister—Mister—What is your name?" He said it in a way that would of made a saint mad.

"My name ain't any difference," says Will, trying not to show he was nettled.

"You are quite right," says the doctor, looking Will up and down from head to foot, very slow and insulting, "it's of no consequence in the world."

Will, he flushed up, but he makes himself steady and cool, and he goes on with his little speech: "There is to be no lynching here to-night. There is to be a trial, and, if necessary, an execution."

"Would it be asking too much," says the doctor very polite, "if I were to inquire who is to be tried, and before what court, and upon what charge?"

There was a clearing of throats and a shuffling of feet fur a minute. One old deaf feller, with a red nose, who had his hand behind his ear and was leaning forward so as not to miss a breath of what any one said, ast his neighbour in a loud whisper, "How?" Then an undersized little feller, who wasn't a farmer by his clothes, got up and moved toward the platform. He had a bulging-out forehead, and thin lips, and a quick, nervous way about him:

"You are to be tried," he says to the doctor, speaking in a kind of shrill sing-song that cut your nerves in that room full of bottled-up excitement like a locust on a hot day. "You are to be tried before this self-constituted court of Caucasian citizens—Anglo-Saxons, sir, every man of them, whose forbears were at Runnymede! The charge against you is stirring up the negroes of this community to the point of revolt. You are accused, sir, of representing yourself to them as some kind of a Moses. You are arraigned here for endangering the peace of the county and the supremacy of the Caucasian race by inspiring in the negroes the hope of equality."

Old Daddy Withers had been setting back by the door. I seen him get up and slip out. It didn't look to me to be any place fur a gentle old poet. While that little feller was making that charge you could feel the air getting tingly, like it does before a rain storm.

"Billy Harden was in the state legislature, and quite a speaker, and knowed it"

Some fellers started to clap their hands like at a political rally and to say, "Go it, Billy!" "That's right, Harden!" Which I found out later Billy Harden was in the state legislature, and quite a speaker, and knowed it. Will, the chairman, he pounded down the applause, and then he says to the doctor, pointing to Billy Harden:

"No man shall say of us that we did not give you a fair trial and a square deal. I'm goin' to appoint this gentleman as your counsel, and I'm goin' to give you a reasonable time to talk with him in private and prepare your case. He is the ablest lawyer in southwest Georgia and the brightest son of Watson County."

The doctor looks kind of lazy and Bill Harden, and back agin at Will, the chairman, and smiles out of the corner of his mouth. Then he says, sort of taking in the rest of the crowd with his remark, like them two standing there paying each other compliments wasn't nothing but a joke:

"I hope neither of you will take it too much to heart if I'm not impressed by your sense of justice—or your friend's ability."

"Then," said Will, "I take it that you intend to act as your own counsel?"

"You may take it," says the doctor, rousing of himself up, "you may take it —from me—that I refuse to recognize you and your crowd as a court of any kind; that I know nothing of the silly accusations against me; that I find no reason at all why I should take the trouble of making a defence before an armed mob that can only mean one of two things."

"One of two things?" says Will.

"Yes," says the doctor, very quiet, but raising his voice a little and looking him hard in the eyes. "You and your gang can mean only one of two things. Either a bad joke, or else—"

And he stopped a second, leaning forward in his chair, with the look of half raising out of it, so as to bring out the word very decided—

"MURDER!"

The way he done it left that there word hanging in the room, so you could almost see it and almost feel it there, like it was a thing that had to be faced and looked at and took into account. They all felt it that-a-way, too; fur they wasn't a sound fur a minute. Then Will says:

"We don't plan murder, and you'll find this ain't a joke. And since you refuse to accept counsel—"

Jest then Buck Hightower interrupts him by yelling out, "I make a motion Billy Harden be prosecuting attorney, then. Let's hurry this thing along!" And several started to applaud, and call fur Billy Harden to prosecute. But Will, he pounded down the applause agin, and says:

"I was about to suggest that Mr. Harden might be prevailed upon to accept that task."

"Yes," says the doctor, very gentle and easy. "Quite so! I fancied myself that Mr. Harden came along with the idea of making a speech either for or against." And he grinned at Billy Harden in a way that seemed to make him wild, though he tried not to show it. Somehow the doctor seemed to be all keyed up, instead of scared, like a feller that's had jest enough to drink to give him a fighting edge.

"Mr. Chairman," says Billy Harden, flushing up and stuttering jest a little, "I b-beg leave to d-d-decline."

"What," says the doctor, sort of playing with Billy with his eyes and grin, and turning like to let the whole crowd in on the joke, "*decline*? The eminent gentleman declines! And he is going to sit down, too, with all that speech bottled up in him! O Demosthenes!" he says, "you have lost your pebble in front of all Greece."

Several grinned at Billy Harden as he set down, and three or four laughed outright. I guess about half of them there knowed him fur a wind bag, and some wasn't sorry to see him joshed. But I seen what the doctor was trying to do. He knowed he was in an awful tight place, and he was feeling that crowd's pulse, so to speak. He had been talking to crowds fur twenty years, and he knowed the kind of sudden turns they will take, and how to take advantage of 'em. He was planning and figgering in his mind all the time jest what side to ketch 'em on, and how to split up the one, solid crowd-mind into different minds. But the little bit of a laugh he turned against Billy Harden was only on the surface, like a straw floating on a whirlpool. These men was here fur business.

Buck Hightower jumps up and says:

"Will, I'm getting tired of this court foolishness. The question is, Does this man come into this county and do what he has done and get out again? We know all about him. He sneaked in here and gave out he was here to turn the niggers white—that he was some kind of a new-fangled Jesus sent especially to niggers, which is blasphemy in itself—and he's got 'em stirred up. They're boilin' and festerin' with notions of equality till we're lucky if we don't have to lynch a dozen of 'em, like they did in Atlanta last summer, to get 'em back into their places again. Do we save ourselves more trouble by stringing him up as a warning to the negroes? Or do we invite trouble by turning him loose? Which? All it needs is a vote."

And he set down agin. You could see he had made a hit with the boys. They was a kind of a growl rolled around the room. The feelings in that place was getting stronger and stronger. I was scared, but trying not to show it. My fingers kept feeling around in my pocket fur something that wasn't there. But my brain couldn't remember what my fingers was feeling fur. Then it come on me sudden it was a buckeye I picked up in the woods in Indiany one day, and I had lost it. I ain't superstitious about buckeyes or horse-shoes, but remembering I had lost it somehow made me feel worse. But Doctor Kirby had a good holt on himself; his face was a bit redder'n usual, and his eyes was sparkling, and he was both eager and watchful. When Buck Hightower sets down the chairman clears his throat like he is going to speak. But—

"Just a moment," says Doctor Kirby, getting on his feet, and taking a step toward the chairman. And the way he stopped and stood made everybody look at him. Then he went on:

146

"Once more," he says, "I call the attention of every man present to the fact that what the last speaker proposes is—"

And then he let 'em have that word agin, full in their faces, to think about

—

"*Murder!* Merely murder."

He was bound they shouldn't get away from that word and what it stood fur. And every man there *did* think, too, fur they was another little pause. And not one of 'em looked at another one fur a minute. Doctor Kirby leaned forward from the platform, running his eyes over the crowd, and jest natcherally shoved that word into the room so hard with his mind that every mind there had to take it in.

But as he held 'em to it they come a bang from one of the windows. It broke the charm. Fur everybody jumped. I jumped myself. When the end of the world comes and the earth busts in the middle, it won't sound no louder than that bang did. It was a wooden shutter. The wind was rising outside, and it flew open and whacked agin' the building.

Then a big, heavy-set man that hadn't spoke before riz up from one of the hind seats, like he had heard a dare to fight, and walked slowly down toward the front. He had a red face, which was considerable pock-marked, and very deep-set eyes, and a deep voice.

"Since when," he says, taking up his stand a dozen feet or so in front of the doctor, "since when has any civilization refused to commit murder when murder was necessary for its protection?"

One of the top glasses of that window was out, and with the shutter open they come a breeze through that fluttered some strips of dirty-coloured papers, fly-specked and dusty and spider-webbed, that hung on strings acrost the room, jest below the ceiling. I guess they had been left over from some Christmas doings.

"My friend," said the pock-marked man to the doctor—and the funny thing about it was he didn't talk unfriendly when he said it—"the word you insist on is just a *word*, like any other word."

They was a spider rousted out of his web by that disturbance among the strings and papers. He started down from above on jest one string of web, seemingly spinning part of it out of himself as he come, the way they do. I couldn't keep my eyes off'n him.

"Murder," says the doctor, "is a thing."

"It is a *word*," says the other man, "*For* a thing. For a thing which

147

sometimes seems necessary. Lynching, war, execution, murder—they are all words for different ways of wiping out human life. Killing sometimes seems wrong, and sometimes right. But right or wrong, and with one word or another tacked to it, it is *done* when a community wants to get rid of something dangerous to it."

That there spider was a squat, ugly-looking devil, hunched up on his string amongst all his crooked legs. The wind would come in little puffs, and swing him a little way toward the doctor's head, and then toward the pock-marked man's head, back and forth and back and forth, between them two as they spoke. It looked to me like he was listening to what they said and waiting fur something.

"Murder," says the doctor, "is murder—illegal killing—and you can't make anything else out of it, or talk anything else into it."

It come to me all to oncet that that ugly spider was swinging back and forth like the pendulum on a clock, and marking time. I wondered how much time they was left in the world.

"It would be none the less a murder," said the pock-marked man, "if you were to be hanged after a trial in some county court. Society had been obliged to deny the privilege of committing murder to the individual and reserve it for the community. If our communal sense says you should die, the thing is neither better nor worse than if a sheriff hanged you."

"I am not to be hanged by a sheriff," says the doctor, very cool and steady, "because I have committed no crime. I am not to be killed by you because you dare not, in spite of all you say, outrage the law to that extent."

And they looked each other in the eyes so long and hard that every one else in the schoolhouse held their breath.

"*Dare* not?" says the pock-marked man. And he reached forward slow and took that spider in his hand, and crushed it there, and wiped his hand along his pants leg. "Dare not? *Yes, but we dare.* The only question for us men here is whether we dare to let you go free."

"Your defence of lynching," says Doctor Kirby, "shows that you, at least, are a man who can think. Tell me what I am accused of?"

And then the trial begun in earnest.

CHAPTER XX

The doctor acted as his own lawyer, and the pock-marked man, whose name was Grimes, as the lawyer agin us. You could see that crowd had made up its mind before-hand, and was only giving us what they called a trial to satisfy their own conscience. But the fight was betwixt Grimes and Doctor Kirby the hull way through.

One witness was a feller that had been in the hotel at Cottonville the night we struck that place. We had drunk some of his licker.

"This man admitted himself that he was here to turn the niggers white," said the witness.

Doctor Kirby had told 'em what kind of medicine he was selling. We both remembered it. We both had to admit it.

The next witness was the feller that run the tavern at Bairdstown. He had with him, fur proof, a bottle of the stuff we had brought with us. He told how we had went away and left it there that very morning.

Another witness told of seeing the doctor talking in the road to that there nigger bishop. Which any one could of seen it easy enough, fur they wasn't nothing secret about it. We had met him by accident. But you could see it made agin us.

Another witness says he lives not fur from that Big Bethel church. He says he has noticed the niggers was worked up about something fur several days. They are keeping the cause of it secret. He went over to Big Bethel church the night before, he said, and he listened outside one of the windows to find out what kind of doctrine that crazy bishop was preaching to them. They was all so worked up, and the power was with 'em so strong, and they was so excited they wouldn't of hearn an army marching by. He had hearn the bishop deliver a message to his flock from the Messiah. He had seen him go wild, afterward, and preach an equality sermon. That was the lying message the old bishop had took to 'em, and that Sam had told us about. But how was this feller to know it was a lie? He believed in it, and he told it in a straight-ahead way that would make any one see he was telling the truth as he thought it to be.

Then they was six other witnesses. All had been in the gang that lynched the nigger that day. That nigger had confessed his crime before he was lynched. He had told how the niggers had been expecting of a Messiah fur several days, and how the doctor was him. He had died a-preaching and a-prophesying and thinking to the last minute maybe he was going to get took up in a chariot of fire.

Things kept looking worse and worse fur us. They had the story as the niggers thought it to be. They thought the doctor had deliberately represented himself as such, instead of which the doctor had refused to be represented as that there Messiah. More than that, he had never sold a bottle of that medicine. He had flung the idea of selling it way behind him jest as soon as he seen what the situation really was in the black counties. He had even despised himself fur going into it. But the looks of things was all the other way.

Then the doctor give his own testimony.

"Gentlemen," he says, "it is true that I came down here to try out that stuff in the bottle there, and see if a market could be worked up for it. It is also true that, after I came here and discovered what conditions were, I decided not to sell the stuff. I didn't sell any. About this Messiah business I know very little more than you do. The situation was created, and I blundered into it. I sent the negroes word that I was not the person they expected. The bishop lied to them. That is my whole story."

But they didn't believe him. Fur it was jest what he would of said if he had been guilty, as they thought him. And then Grimes gets up and says:

"Gentlemen, I demand for this prisoner the penalty of death.

"He has lent himself to a situation calculated to disturb in this county the peaceful domination of the black race by the white.

"He is a Northern man. But that is not against him. If this were a case where leniency were possible, it should count for him, as indicating an ignorance of the gravity of conditions which confront us here, every day and all the time. If he were my own brother, I would still demand his death.

"Lest he should think my attitude dictated by any lingering sectional prejudice, I may tell him what you all know—you people among whom I have lived for thirty years—that I am a Northern man myself.

"The negro who was lynched to-day might never have committed the crime he did had not the wild, disturbing dream of equality been stirring in his brain. Every speech, every look, every action which encourages that idea is a crime. In this county, where the blacks outnumber us, we must either rule as masters or be submerged.

"This man is still believed by the negroes to possess some miraculous power. He is therefore doubly dangerous. As a sharp warning to them he must die. His death will do more toward ending the trouble he has prepared than the death of a dozen negroes.

"And as God is my witness, I speak and act not through passion, but from the dictates of conscience."

He meant it, Grimes did. And when he set down they was a hush. And then Will, the chairman, begun to call the roll.

I never been much of a person to have bad dreams or nightmares or things like that. But ever since that night in that schoolhouse, if I do have a nightmare, it takes the shape of that roll being called. Every word was like a spade grating and gritting in damp gravel when a grave is dug. It sounded so to me.

"Samuel Palmour, how do you vote?" that chairman would say.

Samuel Palmour, or whoever it was, would hist himself to his feet, and he would say something like this:

"Death."

He wouldn't say it joyous. He wouldn't say it mad. He would be pale when he said it, mebby—and mebby trembling. But he would say it like it was a duty he had to do, that couldn't be got out of. That there trial had lasted so long they wasn't hot blood left in nobody jest then—only cold blood, and determination and duty and principle.

"Buck Hightower," says the chairman, "how do you vote?"

"Death," says Buck; "death for the man. But say, can't we jest *lick* the kid and turn him loose?"

And so it went, up one side the room and down the other. Grimes had showed 'em all their duty. Not but what they had intended to do it before Grimes spoke. But he had put it in such a way they seen it was something with even *more* principle to it than they had thought it was before.

"Billy Harden," says the chairman, "how do you vote?" Billy was the last of the bunch. And most had voted fur death. Billy, he opened his mouth and he squared himself away to orate some. But jest as he done so, the door opened and Old Daddy Withers stepped in. He had been gone so long I had plumb forgot him. Right behind him was a tall, spare feller, with black eyes and straight iron-gray hair.

"I vote," says Billy Harden, beginning of his speech, "I vote for death. The reason upon which I base—"

But Doctor Kirby riz up and interrupted him.

"You are going to kill me," he said. He was pale but he was quiet, and he spoke as calm and steady as he ever done in his life. "You are going to kill me like the crowd of sneaking cowards that you are. And you *are* such cowards that you've talked two hours about it, instead of doing it. And I'll tell you why you've talked so much: because no *one* of you alone would dare to do it, and every man of you in the end wants to go away thinking that the other fellow had the biggest share in it. And no *one* of you will fire the gun or pull the rope—you'll do it *all together*, in a crowd, because each one will want to tell himself he only touched the rope, or that *his gun* missed.

"I know you, by God!" he shouted, flushing up into a passion—and it brought blood into their faces, too—"I know you right down to your roots, better than you know yourselves."

He was losing hold of himself, and roaring like a bull and flinging out taunts that made 'em squirm. If he wanted the thing over quick, he was taking jest the way to warm 'em up to it. But I don't think he was figgering on anything then, or had any plan up his sleeve. He had made up his mind he was going to die, and he was so mad because he couldn't get in one good lick first that he was nigh crazy. I looked to see him lose all sense in a minute, and rush amongst them guns and end it in a whirl.

But jest as I figgered he was on his tiptoes fur that, and was getting up my own sand, he throwed a look my way. And something sobered him. He stood there digging his finger nails into the palms of his hands fur a minute, to get himself back. And when he spoke he was sort of husky.

"That boy there," he says. And then he stops and kind of chokes up. And in a minute he was begging fur me. He tells 'em I wasn't mixed up in nothing. He wouldn't of done it fur himself, but he begged fur me. Nobody had paid much attention to me from the first, except Buck Hightower had put in a good word fur me. But somehow the doctor had got the crowd listening to him agin, and they all looked at me. It got next to me. I seen by the way they was looking, and I felt it in the air, that they was going to let me off.

But Doctor Kirby, he had always been my friend. It made me sore fur to see him thinking I wasn't with him. So I says:

"You better can that line of talk. They don't get you without they get me, too. You orter know I ain't a quitter. You give me a pain."

And the doctor and me stood and looked at each other fur a minute. He grinned at me, and all of a sudden we was neither one of us much giving a whoop, fur it had come to us both at oncet what awful good friends we was with each other.

But jest then they come a slow, easy-going sort of a voice from the back part of the room. That feller that had come in along with Old Daddy Withers come sauntering down the middle aisle, fumbling in his coat pocket, and speaking as he come.

"I've been hearing a great deal of talk about killing people in the last few minutes," he says.

Everybody rubbered at him.

CHAPTER XXI

There was something sort of careless in his voice, like he had jest dropped in to see a show, and it had come to him sudden that he would enjoy himself fur a minute or two taking part in it. But he wasn't going to get *too* worked up about it, either, fur the show might end by making him tired, after all.

As he come down the aisle fumbling in his coat, he stopped and begun to slap all his pockets. Then his face cleared, and he dived into a vest pocket. Everybody looked like they thought he was going to pull something important out of it. But he didn't. All he pulled out was jest one of these here little ordinary red books of cigarette papers. Then he dived fur some loose tobacco, and begun to roll one. I noticed his fingers was long and white and slim and quick. But not excited fingers; only the kind that seems to say as much as talking says.

He licked his cigarette, and then he sauntered ahead, looking up. As he looked up the light fell full on his face fur the first time. He had high cheek bones and iron-gray hair which he wore rather long, and very black eyes. As he lifted his head and looked close at Doctor Kirby, a change went over both their faces. Doctor Kirby's mouth opened like he was going to speak. So did the other feller's. One side of his mouth twitched into something that was too surprised to be a grin, and one of his black eyebrows lifted itself up at the same time. But neither him nor Doctor Kirby spoke.

He stuck his cigarette into his mouth and turned sideways from Doctor Kirby, like he hadn't noticed him pertic'ler. And he turns to the chairman.

"Will," he says. And everybody listens. You could see they all knowed him, and that they all respected him too, by the way they was waiting to hear what he would say to Will. But they was all impatient and eager, too, and they wouldn't wait very long, although now they was hushing each other and leaning forward.

"Will," he says, very polite and quiet, "can I trouble you for a match?"

And everybody let go their breath. Some with a snort, like they knowed they was being trifled with, and it made 'em sore. His eyebrows goes up agin, like it was awful impolite in folks to snort that-away, and he is surprised to hear it. And Will, he digs fur a match and finds her and passes her over. He lights his cigarette, and he draws a good inhale, and he blows the smoke out like it done him a heap of good. He sees something so interesting in that little cloud of smoke that everybody else looks at it, too.

"Do I understand," he says, "that some one is going to lynch some one, or something of that sort?"

"That's about the size of it, colonel," says Will.

"Um!" he says, "What for?"

Then everybody starts to talk all at once, half of them jumping to their feet, and making a perfect hullabaloo of explanations you couldn't get no sense out of. In the midst of which the colonel takes a chair and sets down and crosses one leg over the other, swinging the loose foot and smiling very patient. Which Will remembers he is chairman of that meeting and pounds fur order.

"Thank you, Will," says the colonel, like getting order was a personal favour to him. Then Billy Harden gets the floor, and squares away fur a longwinded speech telling why. But Buck Hightower jumps up impatient and says:

"We've been through all that, Billy. That man there has been tried and found guilty, colonel, and there's only one thing to do—string him up."

"Buck, *I* wouldn't," says the colonel, very mild.

But that there man Grimes gets up very sober and steady and says:

"Colonel, you don't understand." And he tells him the hull thing as he believed it to be—why they has voted the doctor must die, the room warming up agin as he talks, and the colonel listening very interested. But you could see by the looks of him that colonel wouldn't never be interested so much in anything but himself, and his own way of doing things. In a way he was like a feller that enjoys having one part of himself stand aside and watch the play-actor game another part of himself is acting out.

"Grimes," he says, when the pock-marked man finishes, "I wouldn't. I really wouldn't."

"Colonel," says Grimes, showing his knowledge that they are all standing solid behind him, "*we will!*"

"Ah," says the colonel, his eyebrows going up, and his face lighting up like he is really beginning to enjoy himself and is glad he come, "indeed!"

"Yes," says Grimes, "*we will!*"

"But not," says the colonel, "before we have talked the thing over a bit, I hope?"

"There's been too much talk here now," yells Buck Hightower, "talk, talk, till, by God, I'm sick of it! Where's that *rope*?"

155

"But, listen to him—listen to the colonel!" some one else sings out. And then they was another hullabaloo, some yelling "no!" And the colonel, very patient, rolls himself another smoke and lights it from the butt of the first one. But finally they quiets down enough so Will can put it to a vote. Which vote goes fur the colonel to speak.

"Boys," he begins very quiet, "I wouldn't lynch this man. In the first place it will look bad in the newspapers, and—"

"The newspapers be d—-d!" says some one.

"And in the second place," goes on the colonel, "it would be against the law, and—"

"The law be d——d!" says Buck Hightower.

"There's a higher law!" says Grimes.

"Against the law," says the colonel, rising up and throwing away his cigarette, and getting interested.

"I know how you feel about all this negro business. And I feel the same way. We all know that we must be the negros' masters. Grimes there found that out when he came South, and the idea pleased him so he hasn't been able to talk about anything else since. Grimes has turned into what the Northern newspapers think a typical Southerner is.

"Boys, this thing of lynching gets to be a habit. There's been a negro lynched to-day. He's the third in this county in five years. They all needed killing. If the thing stopped there I wouldn't care so much. But the habit of illegal killing grows when it gets started.

"It's grown on you. You're fixing to lynch your first white man now. If you do, you'll lynch another easier. You'll lynch one for murder and the next for stealing hogs and the next because he's unpopular and the next because he happens to dun you for a debt. And in five years life will be as cheap in Watson County as it is in a New York slum where they feed immigrants to the factories. You'll all be toting guns and grudges and trying to lynch each other.

"The place to stop the thing is where it starts. You can't have it both ways —you've got to stand pat on the law, or else see the law spit on right and left, in the end, and *nobody* safe. It's either law or—"

"But," says Grimes, "there's a higher law than that on the statute books. There's—"

"There's a lot of flub-dub," says the colonel, "about higher laws and unwritten laws. But we've got high enough law written if we live up to it. There's—"

"Colonel Tom Buckner," says Buck Hightower, "what kind of law was it when you shot Ed Howard fifteen years ago? What—"

"You're out of order," says the chairman, "Colonel Buckner has the floor. And I'll remind you, Buck Hightower, that, on the occasion you drag in, Colonel Buckner didn't do any talking about higher laws or unwritten laws. He sent word to the sheriff to come and get him if he dared."

"Boys," says the colonel, "I'm preaching you higher doctrine than I've lived by, and I've made no claim to be better or more moral than any of you. I'm not. I'm in the same boat with all of you, and I tell you it's up to *all* of us to stop lynchings in this county—to set our faces against it. I tell you—"

"Is that all you've got to say to us, colonel?"

The question come out of a group that had drawed nearer together whilst the colonel was talking. They was tired of listening to talk and arguments, and showed it.

The colonel stopped speaking short when they flung that question at him. His face changed. He turned serious all over. And he let loose jest one word:

"*No!*"

Not very loud, but with a ring in it that sounded like danger. And he got 'em waiting agin, and hanging on his words.

"No!" he repeats, louder, "not all. I have this to say to you—"

And he paused agin, pointing one long white finger at the crowd—

"*If you lynch this man you must kill me first!*"

I couldn't get away from thinking, as he stood there making them take that in, that they was something like a play-actor about him. But he was in earnest, and he would play it to the end, fur he liked the feelings it made circulate through his frame. And they saw he was in earnest.

"You'll lynch him, will you?" he says, a kind of passion getting into his voice fur the first time, and his eyes glittering. "You think you will? Well, you *won't!*

"You won't because *I* say *not*. Do you hear? I came here to-night to save him.

"You might string *him* up and not be called to account for it. But how about *me?*"

He took a step forward, and, looking from face to face with a dare in his eyes, he went on:

"Is there a man among you fool enough to think you could kill Tom Buckner and not pay for it?"

He let 'em all think of that for jest another minute before he spoke agin. His face was as white as a piece of paper, and his nostrils was working, but everything else about him was quiet. He looked the master of them all as he stood there, Colonel Tom Buckner did—straight and splendid and keen. And they felt the danger in him, and they felt jest how fur he would go, now he was started.

"You didn't want to listen to me a bit ago," he said. "Now you must. Listen and choose. You can't kill that man unless you kill me too.

"Try it, if you think you can!"

He reached over and took from the teacher's desk the sheet of paper Will had used to check off the name of each man and how he voted. He held it up in front of him and every man looked at it.

"You know me," he says. "You know I do not break my word. And I promise you that unless you do kill me here tonight—yes, as God is my witness, I *threaten* you—I will spend every dollar I own and every atom of influence I possess to bring each one of you to justice for that man's murder."

They knowed, that crowd did, that killing a man like Colonel Buckner—a leader and a big man in that part of the state—was a different proposition from killing a stranger like Doctor Kirby. The sense of what it would mean to kill Colonel Buckner was sinking into 'em, and showing on their faces. And no one could look at him standing there, with his determination blazing out of him, and not understand that unless they did kill him as well as Doctor Kirby he'd do jest what he said.

"I told you," he said, not raising his voice, but dropping it, and making it somehow come creeping nearer to every one by doing that, "I told you the first white man you lynched would lead to other lynchings. Let me show you what you're up against to-night.

"Kill the man and the boy here, and you must kill me. Kill me, and you must kill Old Man Withers, too."

Every one turned toward the door as he mentioned Old Man Withers. He had never been very far into the room.

"Oh, he's gone," said Colonel Tom, as they turned toward the door, and then looked at each other. "Gone home. Gone home with the name of every man present. Don't you see you'd have to kill Old Man Withers too, if you killed me? And then, *his wife*! And then—how many more?"

"Do you see it widen—that pool of blood? Do you see it spread and spread?"

He looked down at the floor, like he really seen it there. He had 'em going now. They showed it.

"If you shed one drop," he went on, "you must shed more. Can't you see it —widening and deepening, widening and deepening, till you're wading knee deep in it—till it climbs to your waists—till it climbs to your throats and chokes you?"

It was a horrible idea, the way he played that there pool of blood and he shuddered like he felt it climbing up himself. And they felt it. A few men can't kill a hull, dern county and get away with it. The way he put it that's what they was up against.

"Now," says Colonel Tom, "what man among you wants to start it?"

Nobody moved. He waited a minute. Still nobody moved. They all looked at him. It was awful plain jest where they would have to begin. It was awful plain jest what it would all end up in. And I guess when they looked at him standing there, so fine and straight and splendid, it jest seemed plumb unpossible to make a move. There was a spirit in him that couldn't be killed. Doctor Kirby said afterward that was what come of being real "quality," which was what Colonel Tom was—it was that in him that licked 'em. It was the best part of their own selves, and the best part of their own country, speaking out of him to them, that done it. Mebby so. Anyhow, after a minute more of that strain, a feller by the door picks up his gun out of the corner with a scrape, and hists it to his shoulder and walks out. And then Colonel Tom says to Will, with his eyebrow going up, and that one-sided grin coming onto his face agin:

"Will, perhaps a motion to adjourn would be in order?"

CHAPTER XXII

So many different kinds of feeling had been chasing around inside of me that I had numb spots in my emotional ornaments and intellectual organs. The room cleared out of everybody but Doctor Kirby and Colonel Tom and me. But the sound of the crowd going into the road, and their footsteps dying away, and then after that their voices quitting, all made but very little sense to me. I could scarcely realize that the danger was over.

I hadn't been paying much attention to Doctor Kirby while the colonel was making that grandstand play of his'n, and getting away with it. Doctor Kirby was setting in his chair with his head sort of sunk on his chest. I guess he was having a hard time himself to realize that all the danger was past. But mebby it wasn't that—he looked like he might really of forgot where he was fur a minute, and might be thinking of something that had happened a long time ago.

The colonel was leaning up agin the teacher's desk, smoking and looking at Doctor Kirby. Doctor Kirby turns around toward the colonel.

"You have saved my life," he says, getting up out of his chair, like he had a notion to step over and thank him fur it, but was somehow not quite sure how that would be took.

The colonel looks at him silent fur a second, and then he says, without smiling:

"Do you flatter yourself it was because I think it worth anything?"

The doctor don't answer, and then the colonel says:

"Has it occurred to you that I may have saved it because I want it?"

"*Want* it?"

"Do you know of any one who has a better right to *take* it than I have? Perhaps I saved it because it *belongs* to me—do you suppose I want any one else to kill what I have the best right to kill?"

"Tom," says Doctor Kirby, really puzzled, to judge from his actions, "I don't understand what makes you say you have the right to take my life."

"Dave, where is my sister buried?" asts Colonel Tom.

"Buried?" says Doctor Kirby. "My God, Tom, is she *dead*?"

"I ask you," says Colonel Tom.

"And I ask you," says Doctor Kirby.

And they looked at each other, both wonderized, and trying to understand. And it busted on me all at oncet who them two men really was.

I orter knowed it sooner. When the colonel was first called Colonel Tom Buckner it struck me I knowed the name, and knowed something about it. But things which was my own consarns was attracting my attention so hard I couldn't remember what it was I orter know about that name. Then I seen him and Doctor Kirby knowed each other when they got that first square look. That orter of put me on the track, that and a lot of other things that had happened before. But I didn't piece things together like I orter done.

It wasn't until Colonel Tom Buckner called him "Dave" and ast him about his sister that I seen who Doctor Kirby must really be.

He was that there david armstrong!

And the brother of the girl he had run off with had jest saved his life. By the way he was talking, he had saved it simply because he thought he had the first call on what to do with it.

"Where is she?" asts Colonel Tom.

"I ask you," says Doctor Kirby—or David Armstrong—agin.

Well, I thinks to myself, here is where Daniel puts one acrost the plate. And I breaks in:

"You both got another guess coming," I says. "She ain't buried anywheres. She ain't even dead. She's living in a little town in Indiany called Athens—or she was about eighteen months ago."

They both looks at me like they thinks I am crazy.

"What do you know about it?" says Doctor Kirby.

"Are you David Armstrong?" says I.

"Yes," says he.

"Well," I says, "you spent four or five days within a stone's throw of her a year ago last summer, and she knowed it was you and hid herself away from you."

Then I tells them about how I first happened to hear of David Armstrong, and all I had hearn from Martha. And how I had stayed at the Davises in Tennessee and got some more of the same story from George, the old nigger there.

"But, Danny," says the doctor, "why didn't you tell me all this?"

161

I was jest going to say that not knowing he was that there David Armstrong I didn't think it any of his business, when Colonel Tom, he says to Doctor Kirby—I mean to David Armstrong:

"Why should you be concerned as to her whereabouts? You ruined her life and then deserted her."

Doctor Kirby—I mean David Armstrong—stands there with the blood going up his face into his forehead slow and red.

"Tom," he says, "you and I seem to be working at cross purposes. Maybe it would help some if you would tell me just how badly you think I treated Lucy."

"You ruined her life, and then deserted her," says Colonel Tom agin, looking at him hard.

"I *didn't* desert her," said Doctor Kirby. "She got disgusted and left *me*. Left me without a chance to explain myself. As far as ruining her life is concerned, I suppose that when I married her—"

"Married her!" cries out the colonel. And David Armstrong stares at him with his mouth open.

"My God! Tom," he says, "did you think—?"

And they both come to another standstill. And then they talked some more and only got more mixed up than ever. Fur the doctor thinks she has left him, and Colonel Tom thinks he has left her.

"Tom," says the doctor, "suppose you let me tell my story, and you'll see why Lucy left me."

Him and Colonel Tom had been chums together when they went through Princeton, it seems—I picked that up from the talk and some of his story I learned afterward. He had come from Ohio in the beginning, and his dad had had considerable money. Which he had enjoyed spending of it, and when he was a young feller never liked to work at nothing else. It suited him. Colonel Tom, he was considerable like him in that way. So they was good pals when they was to that school together. They both quit about the same time. A couple of years after that, when they was both about twenty-five or six years old, they run acrost each other accidental in New York one autumn.

The doctor, he was there figgering on going to work at something or other, but they was so many things to do he was finding it hard to make a choice. His father was dead by that time, and looking fur a job in New York, the way he had been doing it, was awful expensive, and he was running short of money. His father had let him spend so much whilst he was alive he was very disappointed to find out he couldn't keep on forever looking fur work that-a-way.

So Colonel Tom says why not come down home into Tennessee with him fur a while, and they will both try and figger out what he orter go to work at. It was the fall of the year, and they was purty good hunting around there where Colonel Tom lived, and Dave hadn't never been South any, and so he goes. He figgers he better take a good, long vacation, anyhow. Fur if he goes to work that winter or the next spring, and ties up with some job that keeps him in an office, there may be months and months pass by before he has another chance at a vacation. That is the worst part of a job—I found that out myself—you never can tell when you are going to get shut of it, once you are fool enough to start in.

In Tennessee he had met Miss Lucy. Which her wedding to Prent McMakin was billed fur to come off about the first of November, jest a month away.

"I don't know whether I ever told you or not," says the doctor, "but I was engaged to be married myself, Tom, when I went down to your place. That was what started all the trouble.

"You know engagements are like vaccination—sometimes they take, and sometimes they don't. Of course, I had thought at one time I was in love with this girl I was engaged to. When I found out I wasn't, I should have told her so right away. But I didn't. I thought that she would get tired of me after a while and turn me loose. I gave her plenty of chances to turn me loose. I wanted her to break the engagement instead of me. But she wouldn't take the hints. She hung on like an Ohio Grand Army veteran to a country post-office. About half the time I didn't read her letters, and about nineteen twentieths of the time I didn't answer them. They say hell hath no fury like a woman scorned. But it isn't so—it makes them all the fonder of you. I got into the habit of thinking that while Emma might be engaged to me, I wasn't engaged to Emma. Not but what Emma was a nice girl, you know, but—

"Well, I met Lucy. We fell in love with each other. It just happened. I kept intending to write to the other girl and tell her plainly that everything was off. But I kept postponing it. It seemed like a deuce of a hard job to tackle.

"But, finally, I did write her. That was the very day Lucy promised to throw Prent McMakin over and marry me. You know how determined all your people were that Lucy should marry McMakin, Tom. They had brought her up with the idea that she was going to, and, of course, she was bored with him for that reason.

"We decided the best plan would be to slip away quietly and get married. We knew it would raise a row. But there was bound to be a row anyhow when they found she intended to marry me instead of McMakin. So we figured we might just as well be away from there.

"We left your place early on the morning of October 31, 1888—do you remember the date, Tom? We took the train for Clarksville, Tennessee, and got there about two o'clock that afternoon. I suppose you have been in that interesting centre of the tobacco industry. If you have you may remember that the courthouse of Montgomery County is right across the street from the best hotel. I got a license and a preacher without any trouble, and we were married in the hotel parlour that afternoon. One of the hotel clerks and the county clerk himself were the witnesses.

"We went to Cincinnati and from there to Chicago. There we got rooms out on the South Side—Hyde Park, they called it. And I got me a job. I had some money left, but not enough to buy kohinoors and race-horses with. Beside, I really wanted to get to work—wanted it for the first time in my life. You remember young Clayton in our class? He and some other enterprising citizens had a building and loan association. Such things are no doubt immoral, but I went to work for him.

"We had been in Chicago a week when Lucy wrote home what she had done, and begged forgiveness for being so abrupt about it. At least, I suppose that is what she wrote. It was—"

"I remember exactly what she wrote," says Colonel Tom.

"I never knew exactly," says the doctor. "The same mail that brought word from you that your grandfather had had some sort of a stroke, as a consequence of our elopement, brought also two letters from Emma. They had been forwarded from New York to Tennessee, and you had forwarded them to Chicago.

"Those letters began the trouble. You see, I hadn't told Emma when I wrote breaking off the engagement that I was going to get married the next day. And Emma hadn't received my letter, or else had made up her mind to ignore it. Anyhow, those letters were regular love-letters.

"I hadn't really read one of Emma's letters for months. But somehow I couldn't help reading these. I had forgotten what a gift for the expression of sentiment Emma had. She fairly revelled in it, Tom. Those letters were simply writhing with clinging female adjectives. They *squirmed* with affection.

"You may remember that Lucy was a rather jealous sort of a person. Right in the midst of her alarm and grief and self-reproach over her grandfather, and in the midst of my efforts to comfort her, she spied the feminine handwriting on those two letters. I had glanced through them hurriedly, and laid them on the table.

"Tom, I was in bad. The dates on them, you know, were so *recent*. I didn't want Lucy to read them. But I didn't dare to *act* as if I didn't want her to. So I handed them over.

"I suppose—to a bride who had only been married a little more than a week —and who had hurt her grandfather nearly to death in the marrying, those letters must have sounded rather odd. I tried to explain. But all my explanations only seemed to make the case worse for me. Lucy was furiously jealous. We really had a devil of a row before we were through with it. I tried to tell her that I loved no one but her. She pointed out that I must have said much the same sort of thing to Emma. She said she was almost as sorry for Emma as she was for herself. When Lucy got through with me, Tom, I looked like thirty cents and felt like twenty-five of that was plugged.

"I didn't have sense enough to know that it was most of it grief over her grandfather, and nerves and hysteria, and the fact that she was only eighteen years old and lonely, and that being a bride had a certain amount to do with it. She had told me that I was a beast, and made me feel like one; and I took the whole thing hard and believed her. I made a fine, five-act tragedy out of a jealous fit I might have softened into comedy if I had had the wit.

"I wasn't so very old myself, and I hadn't ever been married before. I should have kept my mouth shut until it was all over, and then when she began to cry I should have coaxed her up and made her feel like I was the only solid thing to hang on to in the whole world.

"But the bottom had dropped out of the universe for me. She had said she hated me. I was fool enough to believe her. I went downtown and began to drink. I come home late that night. The poor girl had been waiting up for me —waiting for hours, and becoming more and more frightened when I didn't show up. She was over her jealous fit, I suppose. If I had come home in good shape, or in anything like it, we would have made up then and there. But my condition stopped all that. I wasn't so drunk but that I saw her face change when she let me in. She was disgusted.

"In the morning I was sick and feverish. I was more than disgusted with myself. I was in despair. If she had hated me before—and she had said she did —what must she do now? It seemed to me that I had sunk so far beneath her that it would take years to get back. It didn't seem worth while making any plea for myself. You see, I was young and had serious streaks all through me. So when she told me that she had written home again, and was going back— was going to leave me, I didn't see that it was only a bluff. I didn't see that she was really only waiting to forgive me, if I gave her a chance. I started downtown to the building and loan office, wondering when she would leave, and if there was anything I could do to make her change her mind. I must repeat again that I was a fool—that I needed only to speak one word, had I but known it.

"If I had gone straight to work, everything might have come around all right even then. But I didn't. I had that what's-the-use feeling. And I stopped in at the Palmer House bar to get something to sort of pull me together.

"While I was there, who should come up to the bar and order a drink but Prent McMakin."

"Yes!" says Colonel Tom, as near excited as he ever got.

"Yes," says Armstrong, "nobody else. We saw each other in the mirror behind the bar. I don't know whether you ever noticed it or not, Tom, but McMakin's eyes had a way of looking almost like cross-eyes when he was startled or excited. They were a good deal too near together at any time. He gave me such a look when our eyes met in the mirror that, for an instant, I thought that he intended to do me some mischief—shoot me, you know, for taking his bride-to-be away from him, or some fool thing like that. But as we turned toward each other I saw he had no intention of that sort."

"Hadn't he?" says Colonel Tom, mighty interested.

"No," says the doctor, looking at Colonel Tom very puzzled, "did you think he had?"

"Yes, I did," says the colonel, right thoughtful.

"On the contrary," says Armstrong, "we had a drink together. And he congratulated me. Made me quite a little speech, in fact; one of the flowery kind, you know, Tom, and said that he bore me no rancour, and all that."

"The deuce he did!" says Colonel Tom, very low, like he was talking to himself. "And then what?"

"Then," says the doctor, "then—let me see—it's all a long time ago, you know, and McMakin's part in the whole thing isn't really important."

"I'm not so sure it isn't important," says the colonel, "but go on."

"Then," says Armstrong, "we had another drink together. In fact, a lot of them. We got awfully friendly. And like a fool I told him of my quarrel with Lucy."

"*Like* a fool," says Colonel Tom, nodding his head. "Go on."

"There isn't much more to tell," says the doctor, "except that I made a worse idiot of myself yet, and left McMakin about two o'clock in the afternoon, as near as I can recollect. Somewhere about ten o'clock that night I went home. Lucy was gone. I haven't seen her since."

"Dave," says Colonel Tom, "did McMakin happen to mention to you, that day, just why he was in Chicago?"

"I suppose so," says the doctor. "I don't know. Maybe not. That was twenty years ago. Why?"

"Because," says Colonel Tom, very grim and quiet, "because your first thought as to his intention when he met you in the bar was *my* idea also. I thought he went to Chicago to settle with you. You see, I got to Chicago that same afternoon."

"The same day?"

"Yes. We were to have come together. But I missed the train, and he got there a day ahead of me. He was waiting at the hotel for me to join him, and then we were going to look you up together. He found you first and I never did find you."

"But I don't exactly understand," says the doctor. "You say he had the idea of shooting me."

"I don't understand everything myself," says Colonel Tom. "But I do understand that Prent McMakin must have played some sort of a two-faced game. He never said a word to me about having seen you.

"Listen," he goes on. "When you and Lucy ran away it nearly killed our grandfather. In fact, it finally did kill him. When we got Lucy's letter that told you were in Chicago I went up to bring her back home. We didn't know what we were going to do, McMakin and I, but we were both agreed that you needed killing. And he swore that he would marry Lucy anyhow, even—"

"*Marry her!*" sings out the doctor, "but we *were* married."

"Dave," Colonel Tom says very slow and steady, "you keep *saying* you were married. But it's strange—it's right *strange* about that marriage."

And he looked at the doctor hard and close, like he would drag the truth out of him, and the doctor met his look free and open. You would of thought Colonel Tom was saying with his look: "You *must* tell me the truth." And the doctor with his was answering: "I *have* told you the truth."

"But, Tom," says the doctor, "that letter she wrote you from Chicago must —"

"Do you know what Lucy wrote?" interrupts Colonel Tom. "I remember exactly. It was simply: '*Forgive me. I loved him so. I am happy. I know it is wrong, but I love him so you must forgive me.*'"

"But couldn't you tell from *that* we were married?" cries out the doctor.

"She didn't mention it," says Colonel Tom.

"She supposed that her own family had enough faith in her to take it for granted," says the doctor, very scornful, his face getting red.

"But wait, Dave," says Colonel Tom, quiet and cool. "Don't bluster with me. There are still a lot of things to be explained. And that marriage is one of them.

"To go back a bit. You say you got to the house somewhere around ten o'clock that evening and found Lucy gone. Do you remember the day of the month?"

"It was November 14, 1888."

"Exactly," says Colonel Tom. "I got to Chicago at six o'clock of that very day. And I went at once to the address in Lucy's letter. I got there between seven and eight o'clock. She was gone. My thought was that you must have got wind of my coming and persuaded her to leave with you in order to avoid me—although I didn't see how you could know when I would get there, either, when I thought it over."

"And you have never seen her since," says Armstrong, pondering.

"I *have* seen her since," says Colonel Tom, "and that is one thing that makes me say your story needs further explanation."

"But where—when—did you see her?" asts the doctor, mighty excited.

"I am coming to that. I went back home again. And in July of the next year I heard from her."

"Heard from her?"

"By letter. She was in Galesburg, Illinois, if you know where that is. She was living there alone. And she was almost destitute. I wrote her to come home. She would not. But she had to live. I got rid of some of our property in Tennessee, and took enough cash up there with me to fix her, in a decent sort of way, for the rest of her life, and put it in the bank. I was with her there for ten days; then I went back home to get Aunt Lucy Davis to help me in another effort to persuade her to return. But when I got back North with Aunt Lucy she had gone."

"Gone?"

"Yes, and when we returned without her to Tennessee there was a letter telling us not to try to find her. We thought—I thought—that she might have taken up with you once again."

"But, my God! Tom," the doctor busts out, "you were with her ten days there in Galesburg! Didn't she tell you then—couldn't you tell from the way she acted—that she had married me?"

"That's the odd thing, Dave," says the colonel, very slow and thoughtful. "That's what is so very strange about it all. I merely assumed by my attitude that you were not married, and she let me assume it without a protest."

"But did you ask her?"

"Ask her? No. Can't you see that there was no reason why I should ask her? I was sure. And being sure of it, naturally I didn't talk about it to her. You can understand that I wouldn't, can't you? In fact, I never mentioned you to her. She never mentioned you to me."

"You must have mistaken her, Tom."

"I don't think it's possible, Dave," said the colonel. "You can mistake words and explanations a good deal easier than you can mistake an atmosphere. No, Dave, I tell you that there's something odd about it—married or not, Lucy didn't *believe* herself married the last time I saw her."

"But she *must* have known," says the doctor, as much to himself as to the colonel. "She *must* have known." Any one could of told by the way he said it that he wasn't lying. I could see that Colonel Tom believed in him, too. They was both sicking their intellects onto the job of figgering out how it was Lucy didn't know. Finally the doctor says very thoughtful:

"Whatever became of Prentiss McMakin, Tom?"

"Dead," says Colonel Tom, "quite a while ago."

"H-m," says the doctor, still thinking hard. And then looks at Colonel Tom like they was an idea in his head. Which he don't speak her out. But Colonel Tom seems to understand.

"Yes," he says, nodding his head. "I think you are on the right track now. Yes—I shouldn't wonder."

Well, they puts this and that together, and they agrees that whatever happened to make things hard to explain must of happened on that day that Prentiss McMakin met the doctor in the bar-room, and didn't shoot him, as he had made his brags he would. Must of happened between the time that afternoon when Prentiss McMakin left the doctor and the time Colonel Tom went out to see his sister and found she had went. Must of happened somehow through Prent McMakin.

We goes home with Colonel Tom that night. And the next day all three of us is on our way to Athens, Indiany, where I had seen Miss Lucy at.

———————————————

CHAPTER XXIII

Fur my part, as the train kept getting further and further north, my feelings kept getting more and more mixed. It come to me that I might be steering straight fur a bunch of trouble. The feeling that sadness and melancholy and seriousness was laying ahead of me kept me from really enjoying them dollar-apiece meals on the train. It was Martha that done it. All this past and gone love story I had been hearing about reminded me of Martha. And I was steering straight toward her, and no way out of it. How did I know but what that there girl might be expecting fur to marry me, or something like that? Not but what I was awful in love with her whilst we was together. But it hadn't really set in on me very deep. I hadn't forgot about her right away. But purty soon I had got to forgetting her oftener than I remembered her. And now it wasn't no use talking—I jest wasn't in love with Martha no more, and didn't have no ambition to be. I had went around the country a good bit, and got intrusted in other things, and saw several other girls I liked purty well. Keeping steady in love with jest one girl is mighty hard if you are moving around a good bit.

But I was considerable worried about Martha. She was an awful romanceful kind of girl. And even the most sensible kind is said to be fools about getting their hearts broke and pining away and dying over a feller. I would hate to think Martha had pined herself sick.

I couldn't shut my eyes to the fact we was engaged to each other legal, all right. And if she wanted to act mean about it and take it to a court it would likely be binding on me. Then I says to myself is she is mean enough to do that I'll be derned if I don't go to jail before I marry her, and stay there.

And then my conscience got to working inside of me agin. And a picture of her getting thin and not eating her vittles regular and waiting and waiting fur me to show up, and me never doing it, come to me. And I felt sorry fur poor Martha, and thought mebby I would marry her jest to keep her from dying. Fur you would feel purty tough if a girl was to get so stuck on you it killed her. Not that I ever seen that really happen, either; but first and last there has been considerable talk about it.

It wasn't but what I liked Martha well enough. It was the idea of getting married, and staying married, made me feel so anxious. Being married may work out all right fur some folks. But I knowed it never would work any with me. Or not fur long. Because why should I want to be tied down to one place, or have a steady job? That would be a mean way to live.

Of course, with a person that was the doctor's age it would be different. He had done his running around and would be willing to settle down now, I guessed. That is, if he could get his differences with this here Buckner family patched up satisfactory. I wondered whether he would be able to or not. Him and Colonel Tom were talking constant on the train all the way up. From the little stretches of their talk I couldn't help hearing, I guessed each one was telling the other all that had happened to him in the time that had passed by. Colonel Tom what kind of a life he had lived, and how he had married and his wife had died and left him a widower without any kids. And the doctor—it was always hard fur me to get to calling him anything but Doctor Kirby—how he had happened to start out with a good chancet in life and turn into jest a travelling fakir.

Well, I thinks to myself now that he has got to be that, mebby her and him won't suit so well now, even if they does get their differences patched up. Fur all the forgiving in the world ain't going to change things, or make them no different. But, so long as the doctor appeared to want to find her so derned bad, I was awful glad I had been the means of getting him and Miss Lucy together. He had done a lot fur me, first and last, the doctor had, and I felt like it helped pay him a little. Though if they was to settle down like married folks I would feel like a good old sport was spoiled in the doctor, too.

We had to change cars at Indianapolis to get to that there little town. We was due to reach it about two o'clock in the afternoon. And the nearer we got to the place the nervouser and nervouser all three of us become. And not owning we was. The last hour before we hit the place, I took a drink of water every three minutes, I was so nervous. And when we come into the town I was already standing out onto the platform. I wouldn't of been surprised to find Martha and Miss Lucy down there to the station. But, of course, they wasn't. Fur some reason I felt glad they wasn't.

"Now," I says to them two, as we got off the train, "foller me and I will show you the house."

Everybody rubbers at strangers in a country town, and wonders why they have come, and what they is selling, and if they are mebby going to start a new grain elevator, or buy land, or what. The usual ones around the depot rubbered at us, and I hearn one geezer say to another:

"See that big feller there? He was through here a year or two ago selling patent medicine."

"The usual ones around the depot rubbered at us"

"You don't say so!" says the other one, like it was something important, like a president or a circus had come, and his eyes a-bugging out. And the doctor hearn them, too. Fur some reason or other he flushed up and cut a look out of the corner of his eye at Colonel Tom.

We went right through the main street and out toward the edge of town, by the crick, where Miss Lucy's house was. And, if anything, all of us feeling nervouser yet. And saying nothing and not looking at each other. And Colonel Tom rolling cigarettes and fumbling fur matches and lighting them and slinging them away. Fur how does anybody know how women is going to take even the most ordinary little things?

I knowed the way well enough, and where the house was, but as we went around the turn in the road I run acrost a surprised feeling. I come onto the place where our campfire had been them nights we was there. Looey had drug an old fence post onto the fire one night, and the post had only burned half up. The butt end of it, all charred and flaked, was still laying in the grass and weeds there. It hit me with a queer feeling—like it was only yesterday that fire had been lit there. And yet I knowed it had been a year and a half ago.

173

Well, it has always been my luck to run into things without the right kind of a lie fixed up ahead of time. They was three or four purty good stories I had been trying over in my head to tell Martha when I seen her. Any one of them stories might of done all right; but I hadn't decided *which* one to use. And, of course, I run plumb into Martha. She was standing by the gate, which was about twenty yards from the veranda. And all four lies popped into my head at oncet, and got so mixed up with one another there, I seen right off it was useless to try to tell anything that sounded straight. Besides, when you are in the fix I was in, what can you tell a girl anyhow?

So I jest says to her:

"Hullo!"

Martha, she had been fussing around some flower bushes with a pair of shears and gloves on. She looks up when I says that, and she sizes us all up standing by the gate, and her eyes pops open, and so does her mouth, and she is so surprised to see me she drops her shears.

And she looks scared, too.

"Is Miss Buckner at home?" asts Colonel Tom, lifting his hat very polite.

"Miss B-B-Buckner?" Martha stutters, very scared-like, and not taking her eyes off of me to answer him.

"Miss Hampton, Martha," I says.

"Y-y-y-es, s-sh-she is," says Martha. I wondered what was the matter with her.

It is always my luck to get left all alone with my troubles. The doctor and the colonel, they walked right past us when she said yes, and up toward the house, and left her and me standing there. I could of went along and butted in, mebby. But I says to myself I will have the derned thing out here and now, and know the worst. And I was so interested in my trouble and Martha that I didn't even notice if Miss Lucy met 'em at the door, and if so, how she acted. When I next looked up they was all in the house.

"Martha—" I begins. But she breaks in.

"Danny," she says, looking like she is going to cry, "don't l-l-look at me l-l-like that. If you knew *all* you wouldn't blame me. You—"

"Wouldn't blame you fur what?" I asts her.

"I know it's wrong of me," she says, begging-like.

"Mebby it is and mebby it ain't," I says. "But what is it?"

"But you never wrote to me," she says.

"You never wrote to me," I says, not wanting her to get the best of me, whatever it was she might be talking about.

"And then *he* came to town!—"

"Who?" I asts her.

"Don't you know?" she says. "The man I am going to marry."

When she said that I felt, all of a sudden, like when you are broke and hungry and run acrost a half dollar you had forgot about in your other pants. I was so glad I jumped.

"Great guns!" I says.

I had never really knowed what being glad was before.

"Oh, Danny, Danny," she says, putting her hands in front of her face, "and here you have come to claim me for your bride!"

Which showed me why she had looked so scared. That there girl had went and got engaged to another feller. And had been laying awake nights suffering fur fear I would turn up agin. And now I had. Looey, he always said never to trust a woman!

"Martha," I says, "you ain't acted right with me."

"Oh, Danny, Danny," she says, "I know it! I know it!"

"Some fellers in my place," I says, "would raise a dickens of a row."

"I *did* love you once," she says, looking at me from between her fingers.

"Yes," says I, acting real melancholy, "you did. And now you've quit it, they don't seem to me to be nothing left to live fur." Martha, she was an awful romanceful girl. I got the notion that mebby she was enjoying her own remorsefulness a little bit. I fetched a deep sigh and I says:

"Some fellers would kill theirselves on the spot!" "Oh!—Oh!—

Oh!—" says Martha.

"But, Martha," says I, "I ain't that mean. I ain't going to do that."

That dern girl ackshellay give me a disappointed look! If anything, she was jest a bit *too* romanceful, Martha was.

"No," says I, cheering up a little, "I am going to do something they ain't many fellers would do, Martha. I'm going to forgive you. Free and fair and open. And give you back my half of that ring, and—"

Dern it! I had forgot I had lost that half of that there ring! I remembered so quick it stopped me.

"You always kept it, Danny?" she asts me, very soft-spoken, so as not to give pain to one so faithful and so noble as what I was. "Let me see it, Danny."

I made like I was feeling through all my pockets fur it. But that couldn't last forever. I run out of pockets purty soon. And her face begun to show she was smelling a rat. Finally I says:

"These ain't my other clothes—it must be in them."

"Danny," she says, "I believe you *lost* it."

"Martha," I says, taking a chancet, "you know you lost *your* half!"

She owns up she has lost it a long while ago. And when she lost it, she says, she knowed that was fate and that our love was omened in under an evil star. And who was she, she says, to struggle agin fate?

"Martha," I says, "I'll be honest with you. Fate got away with my half too one day when I didn't know they was crooks like her sticking around."

Well, I seen that girl seen through me then. Martha was awful smart sometimes. And each one was so derned tickled the other one wasn't going to do any pining away we like to of fell into love all over agin. But not quite. Fur neither one would ever trust the other one agin. So we felt more comfortable with each other. You ain't never comfortable with a person you know is more honest than you be.

"But," says Martha, after a minute, "if you didn't come back to make me marry you, what does Doctor Kirby want to see Miss Hampton about? And who was that with him?"

I had been nigh to forgetting the main thing we had all come here fur, in my gladness at getting rid of any danger of marrying Martha. But it come to me all to oncet I had been missing a lot that must be taking place inside that house. I had even missed the way they first looked when she met 'em at the door, and I wouldn't of missed that fur a lot. And I seen all to oncet what a big piece of news it will be to Martha.

"Martha," I says, "they ain't no Dr. Hartley L. Kirby. The man known as such is David Armstrong!"

I never seen any one so peetrified as Martha was fur a minute.

"Yes," says I, "and the other one is Miss Lucy's brother. And they are all three in there straightening themselves out and finding where everybody gets off at, and why. One of these here serious times you read about. And you and me are missing it all, like a couple of gumps. How can we hear?"

Martha says she don't know.

"You *think*," I told her. "We've wasted five good minutes already. I've *got* to hear the rest of it. Where would they be?"

Martha guesses they will all be in the sitting room, which has got the best chairs in it.

"What is next to it? A back parlour, or a bedroom, or what?" I was thinking of how I happened to overhear Perfessor Booth and his fambly that-a-way.

Martha says they is nothing like that to be tried.

"Martha," I says, "this is serious. This here story they are thrashing out in there is the only derned sure-enough romanceful story either you or me is ever lible to run up against personal in all our lives. It would of been a good deal nicer if they had ast us in to see the wind-up of it. Fur, if it hadn't of been fur me, they never would of been reunited and rejuvenated the way they be. But some people get stingy streaks with their concerns. You think!"

Martha, she says: "Danny, it wouldn't be honourable to listen."

"Martha," I tells her, "after the way you and me went and jilted each other, what kind of senses of honour have *we* got to brag about?"

She remembers that the spare bedroom is right over the sitting room. The house is heated with stoves in the winter time. There is a register right through the floor of the spare bedroom and the ceiling of the sitting room. Not the kind of a register that comes from a twisted-around shaft in a house that uses furnace heat. But jest really a hole in the floor, with a cast-iron grating, to let the heat from the room below into the one above. She says she guesses two people that wasn't so very honourable might sneak into the house the back way, and up the back stairs, and into the spare bedroom, and lay down on their stummicks on the floor, being careful to make no noise, and both see and hear through that register. Which we done it.

CHAPTER XXIV

I could hear well enough, but at first I couldn't see any of them. But I gathered that Miss Lucy was standing up whilst she was talking, and moving around a bit now and then. I seen one of her sleeves, and then a wisp of her hair. Which was aggervating, fur I wanted to know what she was like. But her voice was so soft and quiet that you kind of knowed before you seen her how she orter look.

"Prentiss McMakin came to me that day," she was saying, "with an appeal —I hardly know how to tell you." She broke off.

"Go ahead, Lucy," says Colonel Tom's voice.

"He was insulting," she said. "He had been drinking. He wanted me to—to —he appealed to me to run off with him.

"I was furious—*naturally*." Her voice changed as she said it enough so you could feel how furious Miss Lucy could get. She was like her brother Tom in some ways.

"I ordered him out of the house. His answer to that was an offer to marry me. You can imagine that I was surprised as well as angry—I was perplexed.

"'But I *am* married!' I cried. The idea that any of my own people, or any one whom I had known at home, would think I wasn't married was too much for me to take in all at once.

"'You *think* you are,' said Prentiss McMakin, with a smile.

"In spite of myself my breath stopped. It was as if a chilly hand had taken hold of my heart. I mean, physically, I felt like that.

"'I *am* married,' I repeated, simply.

"I suppose that McMakin had got the story of our wedding from *you*." She stopped a minute. The doctor's voice answered:

"I suppose so," like he was a very tired man.

"Anyhow," she went on, "he knew that we went first to Clarksville. He said:

"'You think you are married, Lucy, but you are not.'

"I wish you to understand that Prentiss McMakin did it all very, very well. That is my excuse. He acted well. There was something about him—I

178

scarcely know how to put it. It sounds odd, but the truth is that Prentiss McMakin was always a more convincing sort of a person when he had been drinking a little than when he was sober. He lacked warmth—he lacked temperament. I suppose just the right amount put it into him. It put the devil into him, too, I reckon.

"He told me that you and he, Tom, had been to Clarksville, and had made investigations, and that the wedding was a fraud. And he told it with a wealth of convincing detail. In the midst of it he broke off to ask to see my wedding certificate. As he talked, he laughed at it, and tore it up, saying that the thing was not worth the paper it was on, and he threw the pieces of paper into the grate. I listened, and I let him do it—not that the paper itself mattered particularly. But the very fact that I let him tear it showed me, myself, that I was believing him.

"He ended with an impassioned appeal to me to go with him.

"I showed him the door. I pretended to the last that I thought he was lying to me. But I did not think so. I believed him. He had done it all very cleverly. You can understand how I might—in view of what had happened?"

I wanted to see Miss Lucy—how she looked when she said different things, so I could make up my mind whether she was forgiving the doctor or not. Not that I had much doubt but what they would get their personal troubles fixed up in the end. The iron grating in the floor was held down by four good-sized screws, one at each corner. They wasn't no filling at all betwixt it and the iron grating that was in the ceiling of the room below. The space was hollow. I got an idea and took out my jack-knife.

"What are you going to do?" whispers Martha.

"S-sh-sh," I says, "shut up, and you'll see."

One of the screws was loose, and I picked her out easy enough. The second one I broke the point off of my knife blade on. Like you nearly always do on a screw. When it snapped Colonel Tom he says:

"What's that?" He was powerful quick of hearing, Colonel Tom was. I laid low till they went on talking agin. Then Martha slides out on tiptoe and comes back in three seconds with one of these here little screw-drivers they use around sewing-machines and the little oil can that goes with it. I oils them screws and has them out in a holy minute, and lifts the grating from the floor careful and lays it careful on the rug.

By doing all of which I could get my head and shoulders down into that there hole. And by twisting my neck a good deal, see a little ways to each side into the room, instead of jest underneath the grating. The doctor I couldn't see

179

yet, and only a little of Colonel Tom, but Miss Lucy quite plain.

"You mean thing," Martha whispers, "you are blocking it up so I can't hear."

"Keep still," I whispers, pulling my head out of the hole so the sound wouldn't float downward into the room below. "You are jest like all other women—you got too much curiosity."

"How about yourself?" says she.

"Who was it thought of taking the grating off?" I whispers back to her. Which settles her temporary, but she says if I don't give her a chancet at it purty soon she will tickle my ribs.

When I listens agin they are burying that there Prent McMakin. But without any flowers.

Miss Lucy, she was half setting on, half leaning against, the arm of a chair. Which her head was jest a bit bowed down so that I couldn't see her eyes. But they was the beginnings of a smile onto her face. It was both soft and sad.

"Well," says Colonel Tom, "you two have wasted almost twenty years of life."

"There is one good thing," says the doctor. "It is a good thing that there was no child to suffer by our mistakes."

She raised her face when he said that, Miss Lucy did, and looked in his direction.

"You call that a good thing?" she says, in a kind of wonder. And after a minute she sighs. "Perhaps," she says, "you are right. Heaven only knows. Perhaps it *was* better that he died."

"*Died!*" sings out the doctor.

And I hearn his chair scrape back, like he had riz to his feet sudden. I nearly busted my neck trying fur to see him, but I couldn't. I was all twisted up, head down, and the blood getting into my head from it so I had to pull it out every little while.

"Yes," she says, with her eyes wide, "didn't you know he died?" And then she turns quick toward Colonel Tom. "Didn't you tell him—" she begins. But the doctor cuts in.

"Lucy," he says, his voice shaking and croaking in his throat, "I never knew there was a child!"

I hears Colonel Tom hawk in *his* throat like a man who is either going to

180

spit or else say something. But he don't do either one. No one says anything fur a minute. And then Miss Lucy says agin:

"Yes—he died."

And then she fell into a kind of a muse. I have been myself in the fix she looked to be in then—so you forget fur a while where you are, or who is there, whilst you think about something that has been in the back part of your mind fur a long, long time.

What she was musing about was that child that hadn't lived. I could tell that by her face. I could tell how she must have thought of it, often and often, fur years and years, and longed fur it, so that it seemed to her at times she could almost touch it. And how good a mother she would of been to it. Some women has jest natcherally *got* to mother something or other. Miss Lucy was one of that kind. I knowed all in a flash, whilst I looked at her there, why she had adopted Martha fur her child.

It was a wonderful look that was onto her face. And it was a wonderful face that look was onto. I felt like I had knowed her forever when I seen her there. Like the thoughts of her the doctor had been carrying around with him fur years and years, and that I had caught him thinking oncet or twicet, had been my thoughts too, all my life.

Miss Lucy, she was one of the kind there's no use trying to describe. The feller that could see her that-a-way and not feel made good by it orter have a whaling. Not the kind of sticky, good feeling that makes you uncomfortable, like being pestered by your conscience to jine a church or quit cussing. But the kind of good that makes you forget they is anything on earth but jest braveness of heart and being willing to bear things you can't help. You knowed the world had hurt her a lot when you seen her standing there; but you didn't have the nerve to pity her none, either. Fur you could see she had got over pitying herself. Even when she was in that muse, longing with all her soul fur that child she had never knowed, you didn't have the nerve to pity her none.

"He died," she says agin, purty soon, with that gentle kind of smile.

Colonel Tom, he clears his throat agin. Like when you are awful dry.

"The truth is—" he begins.

And then he breaks off agin. Miss Lucy turns toward him when he speaks. By the strange look that come onto her face there must of been something right curious in *his* manner too. I was jest simply laying onto my forehead mashing one of my dern eyeballs through a little hole in the grating. But I couldn't, even that way, see fur enough to one side to see how *he* looked.

"The truth is," says Colonel Tom, trying it agin, "that I—well, Lucy, the child may be dead, but he didn't die when you thought he did."

There was a flash of hope flared into her face that I hated to see come there. Because when it died out in a minute, as I expected it would have to, it looked to me like it might take all her life out with it. Her lips parted like she was going to say something with them. But she didn't. She jest looked it.

"Why did you never tell me this—that there was a child?" says the doctor, very eager.

"Wait," says Colonel Tom, "let me tell the story in my own way."

Which he done it. It seems when he had went to Galesburg this here child had only been born a few days. And Miss Lucy was still sick. And the kid itself was sick, and liable to die any minute, by the looks of things.

Which Colonel Tom wishes that it would die, in his heart. He thinks that it is an illegitimate child, and he hates the idea of it and he hates the sight of it. The second night he is there he is setting in his sister's room, and the woman that has been nursing the kid and Miss Lucy too is in the next room with the kid.

She comes to the door and beckons to him, the nurse does. He tiptoes toward her, and she says to him, very low-voiced, that "it is all over." Meaning the kid has quit struggling fur to live, and jest natcherally floated away. The nurse had thought Miss Lucy asleep, but as both her and Colonel Tom turn quick toward her bed they see that she has heard and seen, and she turns her face toward the wall. Which he tries fur to comfort her, Colonel Tom does, telling her as how it is an illegitimate child, and fur its own sake it was better it was dead before it ever lived any. Which she don't answer of him back, but only stares in a wild-eyed way at him, and lays there and looks desperate, and says nothing.

In his heart Colonel Tom is awful glad that it is dead. He can't help feeling that way. And he quits trying to talk to his sister, fur he suspicions that she will ketch onto the fact that he is glad that it is dead. He goes on into the next room.

He finds the nurse looking awful funny, and bending over the dead kid. She is putting a looking-glass to its lips. He asts her why.

She says she thought she might be mistaken after all. She couldn't say jest *when* it died. It was alive and feeble, and then purty soon it showed no signs of life. It was like it hadn't had enough strength to stay and had jest went. I didn't show any pulse, and it didn't appear to be breathing. And she had watched it and done everything before she beckoned to Colonel Tom and told

182

him that it was dead. But as she come back into the room where it was she thought she noticed something that was too light to be called a real flutter move its eyelids, which she had closed down over its eyes. It was the ghost of a move, like it had tried to raise the lids, or they had tried to raise theirselves, and had been too weak. So she has got busy and wrapped a hot cloth around it, and got a drop of brandy or two between its lips, and was fighting to bring it back to life. And thought she was doing it. Thought she had felt a little flutter in its chest, and was trying if it had breath at all.

Colonel Tom thinks of what big folks the Buckner fambly has always been at home. And how high they had always held their heads. And how none of the women has ever been like this before. Nor no disgrace of any kind. And that there kid, if it is alive, is a sign of disgrace. And he hoped to God, he said, it wasn't alive.

But he don't say so. He stands there and watches that nurse fight fur to hold onto the little mist of life she thinks now is still into it. She unbuttons her dress and lays the kid against the heat of her own breast. And wills fur it to live, and fights fur it to, and determines that it must, and jest natcherally tries fur to bullyrag death into going away. And Colonel Tom watching, and wishing that it wouldn't. But he gets interested in that there fight, and so purty soon he is hoping both ways by spells. And the fight all going on without a word spoken.

But finally the nurse begins fur to cry. Not because she is sure it is dead. But because she is sure it is coming back. Which it does, slow.

"'But I have told *her* that it is dead,'" says Colonel Tom, jerking his head toward the other room where Miss Lucy is lying. He speaks in a low voice and closes the door when he speaks. Fur it looks now like it was getting strong enough so it might even squall a little.

"I don't know what kind of a look there was on my face," says Colonel Tom, telling of the story to his sister and the doctor, "but she must have seen that I was—and heaven help me, but I *was!*—sorry that the baby was alive. It would have been such an easy way out of it had it been really dead!

"'She mustn't know that it is living,' I said to the nurse, finally," says Colonel Tom, going on with his story. I had been watching Miss Lucy's face as Colonel Tom talked and she was so worked up by that fight fur the kid's life she was breathless. But her eyes was cast down, I guess so her brother couldn't see them. Colonel Tom goes on with his story:

"'You don't mean—' said the nurse, startled.

"'No! No!' I said, 'of course—not that! But—why should she ever know that it didn't die?'"

"'It is illegitimate?' asked the nurse.

"'Yes,' I said." The long and short of it was, Colonel Tom went on to tell, that the nurse went out and got her mother. Which the two of them lived alone, only around the corner. And give the child into the keeping of her mother, who took it away then and there.

Colonel Tom had made up his mind there wasn't going to be no bastards in the Buckner fambly. And now that Miss Lucy thought it was dead he would let her keep on thinking so. And that would be settled for good and all. He figgered that it wouldn't ever hurt her none if she never knowed it.

The nurse's mother kept it all that week, and it throve. Colonel Tom was coaxing of his sister to go back to Tennessee. But she wouldn't go. So he had made up his mind to go back and get his Aunt Lucy Davis to come and help him coax. He was only waiting fur his sister to get well enough so he could leave her. She got better, and she never ast fur the kid, nor said nothing about it. Which was probable because she seen he hated it so. He had made up his mind, before he went back after their Aunt Lucy Davis, to take the baby himself and put it into some kind of an institution.

"I thought," he says to Miss Lucy, telling of the story, "that you yourself were almost reconciled to the thought that it hadn't lived."

Miss Lucy interrupted him with a little sound. She was breathing hard, and shaking from head to foot. No one would have thought to look at her then she was reconciled to the idea that it hadn't lived. It was cruel hard on her to tear her to pieces with the news that it really had lived, but had lived away from her all these years she had been longing fur it. And no chancet fur her ever to mother it. And no way to tell what had ever become of it. I felt awful sorry fur Miss Lucy then.

"But when I got ready to leave Galesburg," Colonel Tom goes on, "it suddenly occurred to me that there would be difficulties in the way of putting it in a home of any sort. I didn't know what to do with it—"

"What *did* you? What *did* you? *What did you?*" cries out Miss Lucy, pressing her hand to her chest, like she was smothering.

"The first thing I did," says Colonel Tom, "was to get you to another house —you remember, Lucy?"

"Yes, yes!" she says, excited, "and what then?"

"Perhaps I did a very foolish thing," says Colonel Tom.

"After I had seen you installed in the new place and had bidden you good-bye, I got a carriage and drove by the place where the nurse and her mother lived. I told the woman that I had changed my mind—that you were going to raise the baby—that I was going to permit it. I don't think she quite believed me, but she gave me the baby. What else could she do? Besides, I had paid her well, when I discharged her, to say nothing to you, and to keep the baby until I should come for it. They needed money; they were poor.

"I was determined that it should never be heard of again. It was about noon when I left Galesburg. I drove all that afternoon, with the baby in a basket on the seat of the carriage beside me. Everybody has read in books, since books were first written—and seen in newspapers, too—about children being left on door steps. Given an infant to dispose of, that is perhaps the first thing that occurs to a person. There was a thick plaid shawl wrapped about the child. In the basket, beside the baby, was a nursing bottle. About dusk I had it refilled with warm milk at a farmhouse near—"

My head was beginning fur to swim. I pulled my head out of that there hole, and rammed my foot into it. It banged against that grating and loosened it. It busted loose some plaster, which showered down into the room underneath. Miss Lucy, she screamed. And the doctor and Colonel Tom both yelled out to oncet:

"Who's that?"

"It's me," I yells, banging that grating agin. "Watch out below there!" And the third lick I give her she broke loose and clattered down right onto a centre table and spilled over some photographs and a vase full of flowers, and bounced off onto the floor.

"Look out below," I yells, "I'm coming down!"

I let my legs through first, and swung them so I would land to one side of the table, and held by my hands, and dropped. But struck the table a sideways swipe and turned it over, and fell onto the floor. The doctor, he grabbed me by the collar and straightened me up, and give me a shake and stood me onto my feet.

"What do you mean—" he begins. But I breaks in.

"Now then," I says to Colonel Tom, "did you leave that there child sucking that there bottle on the doorstep of a blacksmith's house next to his shop at the edge of a little country town about twenty miles northeast of Galesburg wrapped up in that there plaid shawl?"

"I did," says Colonel Tom.

"Then," says I, turning to Miss Lucy, "I can understand why I have been feeling drawed to *you* fur quite a spell. I'm him."